IVY'S TREE

IVY'S TREE

WENDY BURTON

thistledown press

Thistledown Press Ltd.
410 2nd Avenue North
Saskatoon, Saskatchewan, S7K 2C3
www.thistledownpress.com

Library and Archives Canada Cataloguing in Publication

Title: Ivy's tree / Wendy Burton.
Names: Burton, Wendy, 1949- author.
Identifiers: Canadiana (print) 20200280309 | Canadiana (ebook) 20200280317 | ISBN 9781771871990 (softcover) | ISBN 9781771872003 (HTML) | ISBN 9781771872010 (PDF)
Classification: LCC PS8603.U779 I99 2020 | DDC C813/.6—dc23

Cover painting, *Old Growth*, by Robin de Lavis
Cover and book design by Jackie Forrie
Printed and bound in Canada

sk arts

Canada Council   Conseil des Arts
for the Arts   du Canada

Canada

Thistledown Press gratefully acknowledges the financial assistance of the Canada Council for the Arts, SK Arts, and the Government of Canada for its publishing program.

IVY'S TREE

For Roger Peter Tro, beloved comrade

Sakura is on its way. The wind carries promise of blossoms so sweet they will make us forgive everything the winter has brought us. It is the equinox. Small glass globes have been placed on gravestones. Miniature temples are festooned with garlands of those flowers already in bloom. The cherry trees bend over the graves. For much of every day, these are the only company for the dead.

Two young men walk around the stones, pausing to notice and comment to each other. One holds a small crocheted doll and the other a taper. Dappled by sunlight, they appear as the boys they were ten years before and the men they will be many years from now. Their beautiful faces bend toward the stones before them. One kneels. The other remains standing, a willowy creature with his grandmother's eyes.

ONE

Ivy sits on a hard plastic chair at the Yew Street Clinic. Holding a *Chatelaine* magazine closed in her lap, she peers through plastic-framed reading glasses at the clipboard-supported patient information sheet. Still reluctant to check widow, still considering herself married, she tries to remember the names of the drugs she takes every day, before every meal, at waking and going to bed. Synthyroid, an unpronounceable one for cholesterol, Periot for acid reflux, high blood pressure medication, a diuretic, iron, calcium, vitamins — little blue pills, big beige horse pills, two white pills that are identical except for a faint *h* on one of them, an *h* she can barely see and sometimes imagines she sees. As she imagines the thread through the needle's eye when she's replacing a button or mending.

The length of this list alarms her. At fifty-six she took no pills, and her new family doctor expressed surprise. Now, twenty-one years later, orphaned in the medical system, she worries she has forgotten something in her long list. A pill could probably be prescribed to combat forgetfulness. Even if she isn't. Yet. Not really.

She writes she is five foot three and wonders if there will be an embarrassing revelation of how tall she really is. Maybe she's shrunk and is no longer five foot three. Because of a lack of calcium or the inexorable bone

9

loss that runs in her family. When her mother died (she learned from her aunt), she was barely four foot eleven, with a stoop that began with a dowager's hump. Another sign of age she vowed in vain she would not get, like liver spots on her hands. Wrinkles on her elbows. Deep furrows to bracket her lips. Whiskers on her chin.

Ivy stares around the waiting room, bewildered. She is a grey-haired, stooped, over-weight woman. She asks herself, almost out loud, "How did I get here?" Because if she could answer this question, she could return to her earlier self.

"How *did* I get here?"

She took the bus because she has given up driving. Jack always drove, and a few months after he died, she took the car out to discover she couldn't parallel park, turn left against traffic or remember where she had left the car in Royal Oak Mall. Her biggest mistake, however, was to blurt this out over the phone to Cynthia when pressed to explain why she'd given up driving.

She looks down at the sheet, and writes 170 pounds instead of the corresponding kilograms notation. A diligent and dutiful citizen, she tries to multiply 170 by 2.2 until she realizes she has to divide instead. These lapses frighten her; she looks around the room as if the answer to the lapses — and the division question — might be found on one of the posters on the walls. Five people were sitting in the room when she arrived, and no one has been called during the many minutes she has been wrestling with the patient information sheet.

All of this, she acknowledges with a wry upturn of one side of her mouth, is to cover the failure she feels at the figure 170. She weighs nearly sixty pounds more than she did when she met Jack in 1946 in the post-war want of southern England.

Aldershot. Springtime. A white cotton skirt with delicate embroidered flowers. A plum-coloured wool sweater over her blouse. Light wind on her cheek. Bare legs. Her mother's Oxford pumps. Oh, she could walk forever, and when she wasn't walking she was riding the family's bicycle. Aldershot. The ocean. The cliffs. Jack in his Canadian army uniform.

One hundred and seventy pounds. Sixty pounds in sixty years. If she loses weight the way she gained it, she'll be dead forty years before she loses it all. It is also probably too late to grow the several inches she would need to make her weight match her height, according to the old Metropolitan Life Insurance tables. Is she getting shorter as she ages, as Jack used to tease her? Because in their day, at six foot two if he stood up very straight, he was a foot taller than she was. Or so he claimed. If she is shrinking, she is therefore getting fatter while not gaining an ounce.

This clinic doctor will be hurried, will read her chart while greeting her, and will tell her she has to lose weight. How this doctor will tell her will depend, but he will tell her. Or *she* will. "Oh," she imagines herself exclaiming, "I had no idea!" as they put her on the scale and discover the lie on her form. What else, they might then wonder, is she lying about? Her use of alcohol? Funny these forms did not ask how much chocolate a person consumed in a week, the way they asked about how much alcohol. Would anyone tell the truth about that?

She can put her finger on the spot where the stitch resides in her lower abdomen on the left. A pinching pain, barely there, right beside her hip. She tells the doctor who is, to her surprise, East Indian, with a bright blue turban high on his head. He speaks English with an English accent, and his brown skin is stark against his bright white shirt collar and less white, even dingy, lab coat. She is surprised, and then embarrassed because she is surprised. Her effort to remember drug names is stymied by her confusion, his accent, and the long unfamiliar name on his tag. He listens to her heart, thumps her back, looks in her mouth, her ear, her eye. He takes her blood pressure and expresses faint distaste at her inability to recite the name and dosage of her blood pressure medication. When she asks what her reading is, he clicks his pen shut and puts it in his lab coat pocket. "Slightly above normal."

What does that mean? Slightly above normal for someone with high blood pressure on blood pressure pills? Or slightly above normal for anyone?

The doctor neither knows nor cares she is a widow. He does not offer sleeping pills, or sedatives, or anti-depressants, because he does not know she is newly widowed. He knows her lungs are sound, her throat is healthy, her heart is steady, and her eyes are not yet clouded by cataracts. He does not know her heart is broken. He doesn't know her right knee aches sometimes, and when she moves in a certain way her left hip gives her a shooting pain that leaves her breathless, and sometimes when she needs to sleep her shoulders ache. He knows she needs to lose weight, and he gives her a prescription for an increased dosage of thyroid medication. He hears her complaint about the stitch in her belly but he doesn't know what it is. Faced with a woman in old age, this usually caring doctor does not plan to recommend a fleet of tests to clog the already clogged system. It is, after all, a minor complaint. He doesn't know what this minor pain is. Everyone has to die of something. This stitch may be Ivy's something.

Her six minutes are up. She leaves.

Ivy rides the bus, listening to the stitch in her side and looking for the trees that flank Beach Avenue. Fall is upon Vancouver, and the trees are changing their leaves only to lose them. The old wide-hipped homes of Beach Avenue were the ones she wanted to live in when she arrived in Vancouver in 1947. To walk out onto the verandah, to be embraced by the thick sprawling limbs of what she thought were elm trees, but turned out to be horse chestnuts. To see the ocean. To feel the rain. To see crocuses return year after year. Daffodils and cherry blossoms.

These homes are mostly gone now. She travels down Burrard to the old train station, and makes her way to the Sea Bus. The bustle of the corridor, the music of the licensed buskers, the quality of light, the anticipation of Lonsdale Quay, lifts her. The large clock advises her she has thirteen minutes to the next departure, and she knows she can make the walk in time. Downhill all the way, she reflects wryly. Buying a ticket, hearing the music, walking downhill with plenty of time, she registers, as if ticking a box, a small satisfaction she might have called happiness BJD. Before Jack died, which happened several months before he died in this world.

The sea bus journey always pleases her, and today the water is grey and glittering, and Vancouver looks splendid, with the sails of Canada Place, and North Vancouver with its woolly green sleeves and zipper-like roads running up the mountain sides. The sky is also grey, shot with light; ah, the elegance of greys.

At the Quay, she spends her supper money on fresh buns, imported new potatoes and a salmon steak. She no longer witlessly orders two steaks, two buns, two cakes and then cries all the way up the hill. She occasionally whimpers, or has a spurt of tears, but no longer cries as if she will never stop.

She tucks her to-be-splendid dinner into her bag, and walks to the bus stop. Rain begins to fall, a half-hearted drizzle, and she dons a pleated rain hat. Like most long-time residents of Vancouver, she does not own, and therefore does not carry, an umbrella.

TWO

"I have my new shoes on. Do you like them?" Ivy asks, turning her foot outward toward Norma.

"Those are nice. How much were they?"

"I'm not ever going to tell. They were so expensive. But Dr. Gillespie, he said I had to get fresh runners every six months or I'd get that plantar thing again and . . . "

"You don't want to get that again. That was awful. I felt so sorry for you."

Ivy and Norma are standing at London Drugs, "pushing down the wall" as they call it, doing their stretching exercises. It's seven thirty in the morning, and she still experiences the thrill of trespass she feels every time she does her mall walk at such an hour. No one is around except the mall walkers. And you have to be at least sixty-five to be a mall walker, so most of the shadowy figures are hardly elusive, very senior citizens. Some of them are in their eighties, although she knows she shouldn't feel smug since at least two of them are also members of the Senior Olympics swim team. She hates to even think about what she'd look like in a bathing suit these days. Still, in her new runners, and her rustling fabric track pants and T-shirt, she feels quite — sprightly. What a word.

Norma is already talking about the coffee break they will have after they finish their walk. Consulting their sport watches, they stride off, Ivy stepping out with the confidence a brand new pair of really expensive shoes can give a person. Norma is taller and leaner, apparently hinged at the hips so her stride is even and long. However the hip replacement has left Norma with ever-present pain, and she still has the vertigo from her ear infection, so that effortless stride will only last until they reach the corner and head toward Sears.

The hushed empty mall corridor always fills her with enthusiasm. Maybe it's because everything is shut so she can't buy anything. The shops are all closed and she can't be tempted to stop and consider a scarf or chocolates or a remaindered book.

In the silence of the mall, she can hear Norma beginning to puff. She really is out of shape, no matter how much time she spends at Curves. She can't do the cardio. Ivy has always been a great walker. She and Jack walked for miles along the lanes back home when they were courting. Their favourite time of day was early morning, and she can, if she closes her eyes, almost hear the birds in those hawthorn hedges flanking the lanes, the whoosh of Jack's uniformed pant legs, and the blood of first love pounding in her ears. As she and Norma turn the treacherous corner to behold the nearly half mile stretching away from them toward Sears, she recalls her private pride that she was able to keep up with the lanky Canadian soldier who would become her husband. How he would laugh now, if he could see her looking longingly down that fine stretch of smooth floor in dawn mall light, toward the food court that is out of bounds until they've done their 4000 steps.

Can he see her?

At the food fair, while Norma "sources the tea" as she likes to express it, Ivy selects their table. Once again the two quartet tables hold five men and a woman. These people seem to have taken root in the food fair. All are older than Ivy by at least five years. The men holding forth in the way men hold forth and the woman sitting quietly, occasionally glancing at people walking by, her face soft and curious. Indifferent to the conversation. Has she heard it all before? Which one is she married to? Ivy often fancies herself an amateur anthropologist. At times, she supplies a plummy voice-over for Norma, the kind favoured in BBC documentaries. Her commentary isn't very nice; she adopts a judgmental tone she has not heard since she left her mother's home nearly sixty years ago. She can adopt that tone effortlessly, whenever she wishes, and indeed it gives her private glee. Who is this woman married to? For certainly she is married to one of these men. Beside this group on the banquette, five women sit, all separately, facing the empty chairs in front of them at their tables for two.

The solitary women all wear bright colours, burgundy, fuchsia, turquoise, hot pink, and jewellery, make up, with dandelion puff hair, short and doubtless permed. Ivy straightens her rustling mall-walking outfit, grey with a navy stripe, proud her hair is unpermed, unblued, and in a bob that sweeps her shoulders. A woman walks by with a man presumably her husband; he carries a bag from SportChek and her hand is tucked into the crook of his arm. She remembers with a pang walking just like this with Jack. When was the last time they walked so? This woman is wearing stylish dark brown and grey clothes, with beautiful brown-leather walking shoes, and an immaculate scarf tied just so. Ivy suddenly feels dowdy. Her bobbed grey hair no longer passes for brown in certain lights, and she wears no makeup, not even her lipstick. Her mother would be horrified she has gone "to town" without lipstick. Norma approaches, looking tired and a bit confused. Or perhaps Ivy is just superstitious about those around her, those she loves, who evidence confusion for whatever reason.

Jack, her stalwart companion, her soldier, the man of the house who took care of everything from the hydro bill and the new meter, to the storm windows, to the depth of tread on her car's tires, suddenly "became confused" and then went downhill so fast she did not even have time to be frightened. From the first appointment to admission to a long-term care facility was less than two years, with her trundling behind the professionals like a small boat tied to a yacht.

THREE

"Mother? You sound tired."

Ivy tries to sound not tired. "I'm not tired. I was out on the porch, and — "

"I hope you remembered to lock the front door when you did that. Remember that time."

"I know. Yes, dear, I did lock the front door. It's locked all the time when I'm home. And how are you? And the boys, ah — " She pauses, realizing she has yet again lost the names of Cynthia's sons.

"Well, how was the doctor? Did you get something for sleeping?"

"No, I didn't. I seem to be sleeping quite well."

"Did you ask about your knee? I still think it's time to consider a replacement. Lots of people have a knee replacement in their mid-seventies and then do very well into their eighties. Are you still able to walk well enough?"

While Ivy listens to her daughter, she extends her right leg. Covered in bright pink cotton, her knee looks fine. She touches the kneecap and then looks at the photograph of Jack on the kitchen window ledge. She has been dozing in the sun on the porch. She's tired these days; maybe Cynthia is right. About what, she does not know.

"Mother, Mikio and I have been talking, and we wondered, well, if you would come to stay with us."

"In Tokyo?"

"Well, of course in Tokyo. That's where we live. Mother, are you sure you're all right?"

"Yes, of course. Tokyo. Are you inviting me for a visit for . . . " Ivy tries to think when the next holiday is in Japan. Remembrance Day? She smiles at her extended right leg. Do Japanese people celebrate American Thanksgiving? Seems even more unlikely. She does not know if her grandsons celebrate Christmas, although she has sent them a parcel every year since the older boy was born. In the early days, the parcel was acknowledged by cute notes written by Cynthia. Now, she receives formal letters of thanks from her grandsons, formal notes telling her little but that they both have untidy printing.

"Mother, what do you think? You could sell the house and come to live with us. Mikio and I think you would find Tokyo interesting, and the boys would be happy to see you. They could practise their English with you." Cynthia laughs the breathy laugh she began to use when she was a teenager. Ivy has still not figured out what the breathy laugh means, but she has retrieved "sell the house" from the words churning down the line toward her.

"Mother? Mom? I have contacted Bill, and he has a realtor all set to help you. Bill said the house would sell quickly, you always kept it so beautifully, and the land itself would be worth a fortune. Probably a tear-down, but you never know. Anyway, he will be in touch. What do you think?"

Ivy slowly lowers her foot to the floor, acknowledging it hurts more going down then it did going up. She rubs the knee carefully, as if consoling it. Sell her house? Sell?

Live with Cynthia and Mikio and the boys in Tokyo? What would that be like? She stands at the kitchen sink and looks out the window into her garden. Cynthia is right about the garden; it is well kept. It looks like a larger version of the gardens favoured by gardeners in terraced homes in England. The garden is probably ten times bigger than anything her mother had in her gardening heyday. Mum was so proud of her garden. She would send blurry, dramatically coloured "snaps" of the latest triumphs. Ivy never had the heart to tell her the pictures looked fake. In Ivy's garden, the bird feeders are catching the light of the evening sun, and the finches are about. The grey squirrel sits in the neighbour's tree, chattering his indignation because Ivy has finally purchased a squirrel-proof feeder that is, indeed, squirrel proof. Perhaps, though, the squirrel is yelling at the cat, sitting as he does often directly under the bird feeder, hoping, apparently, a bird will just fall into his mouth. Cats are supposed to be responsible for millions of songbird deaths every minute, but her cat has, as far as she knows, not once contributed to this declining population, in spite of many hours of patient vigilance.

Would Bill, or this friend of Bill — for a moment she cannot remember who Bill is anyway — be able to organize a sale of this house with this lovely garden and make a covenant so that the squirrel, the birds, and the cat can all remain, just as they are, on this sunny late-winter evening in North Vancouver?

Covenants. What an odd word to use for protecting that which we have to leave but still want to keep. Ivy stares out the window and remembers the last time Cynthia saw this garden, pretty much exactly this time of year, or was it later, in July? She left so angry with them, but called a few weeks later, taking up her habit of calling, "Just to see how things are."

That was a disastrous visit, the trip to the Queen Charlottes. She remembers Jack's patient endurance as she and Cynthia struggled over everything. She gazes at the wooden shed Jack built for her oh so long ago, and remembers with a clarity that brings tears to her eyes his hands, his well-worn and well-loved hands on the steering wheel of the rented car on a nameless street in Queen Charlotte City. They renamed the islands, but they did not or could not rename the city bearing the name of the old Queen, an homage meaningless now to nearly everyone.

The car door slammed, enclosing them in the warm cocoon of the car. Cynthia's footsteps clicked away from them, from the silence of children sleeping in the back seat, the motor ticking briefly. Ivy stared straight ahead, her husband in similar fixity beside her. His hands were in the ten o'clock-two o'clock position he learned in the military so many years before. She grimaced and peered at the guidebook in her lap. If she turned, she would see the boys, their bare legs, their entwined bodies, their black heads, their light-brown skin. Their grandsons. If she looked out the window, she would see her daughter's head bent over her embossed leather cheque book. Cynthia was buying yet another reference book, to add to her pile of books about the islands. Her forty-five-year-old chin was disguised by the careful swing of expensively cut hair. When had Cynthia's towhead been turned by intricate dye into this lovely silver-blond? Ivy didn't know. She hadn't seen that happen. Cynthia lived so far away. Japan was so far away.

22

She cleared her throat, and her husband looked beyond her, out the side window of their rental car. "Tired?" Jack inquired unnecessarily.

Muttering, the younger boy flung out a leg, kicking the window and leaving the mark of his wee foot. Ivy turned to look at these beautiful boys who were her grandsons. At the airport, after accepting her very best attempt at a grandmotherly hug, they had addressed her in a form of English only they and their mother could understand. When that failed, they spoke to her in Japanese. She hadn't even understood when they called her Obaasan until Cynthia translated, with an arch of her expertly drawn eye-brow. It's true. That the boys wouldn't speak or understand English hadn't occurred to her. These grandsons lived in Japan; they were born in Tokyo; they spoke Japanese. If she had thought about it, she would have gone to the library for some audio tapes. If she had thought about it.

Ivy and Jack were stunned when Cynthia swept them up at the Vancouver airport and announced she had a surprise for them. The surprise was the trip to Haida Gwaii, an expensive, tiring trip. They had planned the visit of their only daughter and their only grandchildren for weeks. The boys would spend time in her garden with her, and time with Jack and his soldiers. The soldiers were a disaster. Jack started to set them up, and the boys seemed to be interested, in spite of their jet lag. When her husband was about to identify the Japanese soldiers as "the enemy," she diverted the boys' attention by turning on the baseball game.

She looks down at her hands. Her hands seem to belong to a stranger.

At the airport, greeting her grandchildren for the first time in their lives, she raised her peachy hands to their faces and was astonished and somehow appalled at the difference in colour. How had this happened? How had the peach of her skin become the brown of these boys? Their black eyes. Their black hair. Nowhere on their faces was any sign of Jack, the man who was their grandfather. Nowhere on their bodies was any sign of the man who had spent two years in the camps, waiting to drive the jeeps home. Nowhere. How had this happened?

"Mother?" says Cynthia. "What do you think? Come to Tokyo and live with us. We could plan for some excursions. You know, like the trip to Skedans. That was fun, remember?"

The excursion to Skedans in Haida Gwaii. Looking back, Ivy feels like one of those mortuary poles with huckleberry growing out of the space where the cedar burial box had been. That, indeed, was where her sore knee originated. She banged her knee getting from the *Black Duck* into the zodiac. She cracked it on the piece of wood holding the motor. All she heard from her Cynthia was, "Look out, Mother," and then the first child was lowered into the zodiac.

At the Skedans beach, they all scrambled out onto the knee-deep beach pebbles. By the time she'd hobbled over to sit on a log, pretending to admire the view, black dots of pain were dancing in her eyes. She was too old for this kind of trip, just as it seemed the boys were too young. They didn't understand about the poles, now old logs half-buried in the grass, and they didn't understand the guide who was, of course, not speaking Japanese.

Just before they'd clambered back into the unstable zodiac, the older boy cut himself with his knife, the beautiful Swiss Army knife Cynthia had bought for him on the ferry through the Inside Passage. Nearly eighty dollars for a knife for a child, and how dangerous the knife was — with its many blades and gadgets. Just opening the knife seemed impossibly dangerous, and, unlike the six-year-old Canadian boy on the tour, who had obviously been born with a knife in his hand, her grandson did not know the first thing about his new treasure. After the tears over the wound and the discovery none of them had bandages and had to borrow them from the Canadian boy's competent mother, who negotiated the zodiac with aplomb, asked the tour guide all the right questions, and had a well-equipped first-aid kit, they all realized this injury-induced delay had made the long-way-around return trip, past special bird-nesting rocks, impossible. The other members of the trip had been very gracious, in spite of the lack of apology from Cynthia.

After another nasty encounter with the zodiac, Cynthia pushed her way aboard the *Black Duck* and then claimed one of two cushioned seats for her mother. Ivy wanted the stool behind the swivel chair of the captain, because the bench seat was too high for her, particularly with her aching knee. Cynthia rebuked her for not accepting the claimed seat and would not listen as Ivy tried, without offending anyone, to explain that the seat was uncomfortable. Cynthia whispered a clear, "Oh, Mother, please." She had not been called Mother in that way for years, not since the wedding, when it seemed she was constantly violating some protocol she could not begin to understand. Even the gifts they had been warned to bring had been wrapped in the wrong colour and kind of paper.

Their travelling companions on this expensive trip to Skedans pretended to be very interested in the last glimpses of the beach — the solemn German tourist, two women from Switzerland, the couple from Chilliwack with the little boy, the man from Leeds.

In an effort to distract them all, Ivy heard herself brightly inform everyone Leeds was her hometown, too.

Can she still claim Leeds as her hometown when she has not been there since before the war? Is this what her mother had gone through when Ivy moved to Canada to be with her Canadian soldier husband? Mum was left behind in the row house in Aldershot by her only daughter who heard her mother grow old through the monthly phone calls and newsy letters that never once broke the surface of "I'm fines" and photographs of smiling faces over Christmas dinners. Mum never held Cynthia in her arms. She wrote cheerful letters for nearly forty years and then subsided into dementia and died in the arms of her only sister, who wrote a short note into which Ivy read criticism and curt rejection. Neither of them deserved it; there had been no breach. It was only that at seventeen Ivy fell in love with a Canadian soldier who drove the jeeps.

With the warmth of the sun on her face, listening to her daughter's voice discussing selling houses in North Vancouver, she remembered the intimacy of the car filled with the breath of those she loved. She also remembered the other quarrel, the one over the milk. Milk was hard to find on those islands, and Cynthia became so angry, her voice rising in exasperation as she confronted her mother, who held the litre package of milk, three-quarters full but not full enough, apparently.

"What are you doing, Mother?"

The boys had not looked up from the television as the women faced each other in the tiny kitchen of this extraordinarily expensive, cramped motel room.

"I'm — your father wants a cup of tea, and I'm — " Ivy gestured with the milk carton.

Cynthia took it away from her, her voice rising in reprimand. "Mother, the boys need the milk! They need a glass each with dinner, and then they always have milk with their cereal for a snack." Cynthia also gestured with the carton. How alike they seemed in that moment. "Of course they need a glass each for breakfast."

Ivy recited this list in her head a dozen times. Their cereal and a glass each with dinner and a glass each with breakfast.

That greedy tone in her daughter's voice still irritates her. Between them, she and Jack needed less than a quarter-cup of milk for their tea; why was it so hard to accommodate that? These boys didn't know how lucky they were. During the war, no one had a glass of milk each for their dinner and bowls of cereal with more milk and a glass of milk each for breakfast. No one. Not even the babies failing to thrive.

Cynthia is talking about an upcoming celebration in Tokyo, and her encouraging voice begins to sound perilously close to whining.

Those boys were so demanding, so weepy when they were sea-sick, so indifferent to her and Jack. They had lots of relatives in Japan. They didn't need two old people in a tiny house high on the North Shore mountains in a country across the ocean from their home. They were Japanese.

Ivy realizes she is fuming about the milk quarrel all over again, clutching the cordless phone Cynthia insisted she buy and carry into the bathroom whenever she was having a bath. Oh, Jack. She invokes Jack's silence. Jack never complained. He was a mild go-along man. He never said anything about the brisk take-charge stranger who was their daughter, who sat in the back seat like the queen — flanked by her two boys — reading tediously from guidebooks.

"So, Mom, what do you think? Do you want to come to Tokyo to spend some time with us?" Cynthia's tone is so close to the one she used when she was cajoling her mother to let her go to a party that would be past her curfew.

All Ivy can think about is that trip. They travelled for six days, covered a thousand miles and then Cynthia and her boys were gone. On the launch coming back from Skedans, the older boy was sea-sick and the younger fell asleep, both half lying in their grandfather's lap. Jack ran his old fingers through the hair of his sleeping grandsons, and the expression on his face cut her to the bone. He had such a well of love to give those children. It was all such a waste.

The silence on the line begins to hum. She considers "accidentally" clicking the disconnect button, as she has done so many times when they first got the phone. She suddenly wants to slap her daughter's face — hard — as she has done only once before, when Cynthia was fifteen. She had just learned her mother had died, and Cynthia had shrugged in that annoying fifteen-year-old manner. She slapped Cynthia then, and she wants to slap her now.

Cynthia flew away from them, leaving them to the sudden, unexpected end of their lives together. Ivy turned away from watching the airplanes. Jack was over by the departures screen, looking up through the reading part of his glasses, his head tipped so far back she was afraid he'd fall over.

"Well, they're gone. Plane's left," he said. "Hey, old girl, may I buy you a cup of tea?"

"Why, I hardly know you, sir!"

"We can take a table here, in the square, where everyone can see I mean you no harm."

"Where everyone can see us," Ivy dutifully finished her side of their first conversation; the one they repeated for fun every so often.

"Let's go see what that Bill Reid has put up in the international departure lounge."

"We — we already saw it, Jack. We saw it before they left. Remember?"

He narrowed his eyes, as if the lights had suddenly become too bright.

"We didn't already get a cup of tea, did we?" he teased.

"No." she poked him in the ribs with her elbow. "You still owe me a cup of tea. In the square where everyone can see us."

"Do you think the car will be all right?"

"We've only been here for two hours. I think we have three, don't we?"

"I'd know that if you were allowed to keep the ticket, but you aren't. We have to leave it in the car. Do you remember?"

"We have another hour. I'm sure of it."

Ivy sat at the table and watched Jack buy the tea. He was wearing green shorts, green paisley suspenders, green striped short-sleeve shirt, black socks and black dress shoes. In his early 80s, his legs were as fine and strong as they had been when she looked shyly at them the first time, when he was waiting in line for tea at the outdoor shop in Aldershot. No veins or warts or mysterious brown splotches, just fine, thickly muscled legs, and his belly rising proudly over his waist band, the suspenders like brackets.

She watched as he hesitated, not knowing, she feared, whether he was coming or going. She watched him, protective. Trays, cups, metal teapots, stir sticks, tiny containers of cream, packets of sugar, all waiting to hurl themselves onto the floor with an immense and humiliating clatter. Not this time, though. Not this time.

"The Charlottes were something."

"You mean Haida Gwaii, Jack," she mocked him with Cynthia's refrain.

"Haida Gwaii. They were something too. Weren't they?"

"Totems."

"Fish and chips."

"Sea-sick boys on ferries."

"The most expensive Chinese food in the world."

"Wee deer."

"Cynthia looked well."

"Yes."

"She's starting to look like you."

"Oh, don't let her hear that!" Ivy laughed and then closed her eyes against the knowledge Cynthia was in a

30

plane 100 kilometres into the 7500 kilometre flight away from them.

His death was not a kind one, but it was mercifully swift. He forgot, it seemed, how to swallow.

Ivy has not forgotten how to swallow. She speaks into the vast distance between herself and her daughter and hears herself agreeing yes, it is time to sell, and yes, it would be lovely to get to know the boys and Cynthia's husband, and — she mumbles over the name of the festival — sounds like a good place to start.

She puts the phone down carefully. Out the window, the evening sun is gone, and the shadows are stretching like fingers toward the bird feeder and the pink dogwood tree Jack gave her for their twenty-fifth wedding anniversary.

FOUR

Bill's friend the realtor is a glamorous man in his mid-forties, with a firm handshake, a smile revealing bright white, perfect teeth, and a sympathetic gaze. When he speaks, he always pats her gently on her upper arm, as if to assure her. The sign goes up, balloons are attached to signal the open house, and Ivy goes to the mall to browse the shops and have a cup of tea. When she returns, three offers are sitting on the kitchen table before the gleeful realtor. Just like that, the house is sold.

Packing, now that's another matter. She recently helped Norma move from her home into a suite in a retirement home, but what she mostly remembers about that move is how much they laughed. Packing dishes, sorting through underwear and knick-knacks, they laughed about the amassed trivial belongings of a life. Norma kept an immaculate house and had not accumulated much that she intended to take with her. Ivy did discover Norma's engagement ring in a teacup on the top shelf of the kitchen cupboard, a discovery that had them both in stitches before Norma placed it with difficulty over her swollen arthritic finger. Norma's move seemed effortless, at least from the outside.

Ivy's house is a different matter. Jack had been a great haunter of garage sales, and she had often abandoned him to his treasure seeking while she went to buy groceries.

The basement, comprised of two unfinished rooms, four work benches, and the furnace, hot water heater and garden tools, is crammed with Jack's paraphernalia collected over many years and is beyond her to sort.

"Call one of those places. You know, those junk places," advises Marilyn, one of her mall friends. They are sitting in formation at a table for four: four women, four mugs of tea, four cinnamon buns and twenty reasons why eating a cinnamon bun is a bad idea. Why is it the slender women, unkindly called skinny as they grow older, are the ones most likely to bemoan what would happen if they were to yield to temptation and eat a cinnamon bun? Ivy always feels self-conscious, worried her friends must assume she eats cinnamon buns and similar evils all the time, considering her weight.

"Yes, that's what my son did when I moved," Audrey agrees. "It's called Got Junk, I think." Audrey seems to have forgotten she bitterly complained when her son took over the removal of her and all her belongings to the apartment at Sunrise.

This unlikely and perfectly apt name causes a fit of giggles. Norma starts riffing on Got Junk. "Junk Dump, Junk Junk, Junk Your Junk, Dunk Your Junk . . . "

Ivy finds the company, it's called Junkology, but it turns out they don't come to North Vancouver. She settles instead for the more sedately named Lions Gate Moving.

Imagining Jack's voice loud and alarmed, she greets the two young men with the huge truck parked in her lane. She shows them the basement, and then goes back to her kitchen, certain they are probably hauling away a fortune in tools and the accoutrements of a true handyman. While they are carrying boxes filled with stuff out the basement door, straight down the path and out the gate, she considers the dimensions of the trunk she has purchased at Cynthia's direction. This trunk is to hold everything bound for Tokyo.

The task of packing the trunk seems impossible and therefore it becomes easy. She goes from room to room, taking only what attracts her, and when the trunk is full she stops looking through all that remains. After the second-hand dealer comes, all that does remain are her clothes, which fit quite nicely into two suitcases. She even finds room for wool she bought years and years ago at a sale at Woodward's, and she's humming, "Dollar Forty-Nine Day! Tuesday!" as she puts the yarn and pattern into a precious spot in her suitcase. And crochet hooks. These are easy to squirrel away, and as she roams about collecting them, Ivy looks out the window of every room, trying to figure a way to put the view into her suitcase. Because that is all she really wants to take. She even uses her digital camera, the one Cynthia sent her the year Jack was "in decline" to somehow document this and email the pictures to Japan. That Ivy had no idea how to get photographs into the laptop sitting on the dining room sideboard was lost on her daughter. She still has her efforts on the camera, and sometimes when she is fumbling with it a picture of Jack will pop up at her, scaring her and making her cry.

No one wants Ivy's old cat. He is sixteen, and she has been treating him for thyroid problems for nearly six years. He is well trained; at or near dinner time he gets onto the dining room table, and watches attentively as she finishes cooking her dinner. Before she serves herself, he gets his pill mashed in liver treats, a wet paste that he

34

would eat with ground glass if necessary. She can't afford to feed him solely liver treats, so he gets just enough to get the pill down and then she gives him the cheap dry food that is probably slowly killing him. Not fast enough, though, because he is sixteen and skinny and cranky and no one wants a "mature cat needing a good home without children."

Ivy begins to wish to find him dead in the morning or dead in his sleep in the sunlight on the window sill. This does not happen, and she finds herself carrying him to the bus in his case, with his whining the whole way. The bus driver looks as if she is going to tell Ivy she cannot bring the cat on, but decides against it, perhaps because of the bewildered pain on this old lady's face. Ivy sits with her old cat beside her, him complaining every lurching stop, reaching through the case to catch at her sleeve, yowling in panic, until they reach the vet's office.

They are very kind to her, knowing she's there to put an end to this life entrusted to her sixteen years ago when she bought him at the market on Lonsdale Avenue from two little kids who had four kittens in a box. Jack was as happy as she was at the arrival of this kitten in their lives, and his antics amused them for years. As he grew older, as they grew older, she would find Jack watching TV, or rather looking vacantly at the TV, and stroking the cat's ears. Hypnotized, they both seemed to her, the cat purring in fits and starts, in ecstasy to be so loved.

She holds her cat on her lap for the last time, and then they take him away for a few minutes. When they return, he has a bandage on his front paw covering an intravenous device. The vet injects something into his veins. Her cat is purring. Ivy bends to kiss his old head, and the vet listens to his heart. She does not need to be told he is gone; she can feel it in the slackening of his limbs, and the absence at last of his breathing.

And that's that. She leaves the case with them, pays the extraordinarily high fee, and is presented with the even more expensive option of having his body cremated "separately" and the ashes preserved, an option she has to refuse. Refusing this option gives her more information than she wants to know about how they will dispose of the body of her old cat. She then retraces her steps, fearing irrationally she will be confronted by the same bus driver, demanding to know what she has done with her cat.

Put him to sleep, she would say. They put him to sleep. No one wanted him, she laments as if explaining her actions to an invisible critic. He was too old. No one wanted him. When she gets home, she makes tea, believing tea can cure most wounds. And it might have worked, if she hadn't looked upon the cat's food dish and water bowl sitting beside the back door.

FIVE

Ivy's food fair friends know she is leaving Vancouver in two days, and they have "clubbed in," as Rolf cheerfully says, to buy her a guidebook for Tokyo. Second hand, it features a garish photograph on the front cover that captures all any of them might wish to know of Tokyo. A chorus of goodbyes and hugs sends Ivy away from the tables, the cups of coffee and tea, the conversation paused long enough for her to be bid farewell, and then, as she turns to glances back one last time, the two fellows sit down, her best friend Norma adjusts her polyester zip jacket and considers the rings on her fingers.

In some ways, Ivy feels relief. She started to "hang out" at the mall with Jack when he discovered the phenomenon of "retired old men eating out" by joining a group of old geezers at the local A&W. He acknowledged he felt vaguely guilty sneaking a second, high-calorie, breakfast with his buddies while she stayed at home tidying the kitchen. He took her along to meet some of his friends and their wives, and she was surprised by how many people their age met and hung about the food court in the mall.

After Jack died, she lost almost all her friends, who came in couples with the man dominating. She had heard about this reaction to widows, on the radio and in the newspaper, but she was still puzzled when it began to happen to her. Some of the women, who had been friendly toward her for several years, began to demonstrate what she could only explain as jealousy. As if she would be at all tempted to steal one of these pompous old guys whose only effort to be attractive was to make quite horrid sex jokes, always half-heartedly apologizing if one of the women expressed displeasure. The awkwardness did not dissipate, awkwardness often emphasized by Jack's best friend Rolf — who kept referring to Jack as if he had just left them to get milk for the tea.

The day before her flight, Ivy leaves her home for the last time. The house is empty, the garden devoid of any of her gardening gear, and the bird feeders gone. The crocuses and daffodils are in full display, and the snowdrops have just finished. She thinks she can detect the blossoms on the dwarf apple tree, but that's simply wishful thinking. Last March she did not know it was her last March. If she had, what would she have done differently?

Expecting the taxi, the extravagance she had been persuaded into by common sense and Norma, wary about her making a trip by taxi all the way across Vancouver during morning rush hour, Ivy stands at the kitchen sink looking out the window. Thinking of not much in particular, not allowing grief to creep in, she looks at the spring garden she has tended for most of her adult life. She would live nowhere as long as she has lived in this place. No matter what lies before her, she will live nowhere for another fifty-seven years. When the doorbell sounds, she comes out of a reverie about details to do with the trip across Vancouver, its cost, and the unfamiliar hotel at the end. She is annoyed with herself for this mindless fretting, which has blotted out her last minutes with her home, her garden, and her memories.

The fare is an astonishing forty-five dollars, which automatically includes a tip, much to her surprise. She stands uncertainly beside the cab, and then the driver gets out and puts her large black suitcase before her, the small black suitcase on top of it, and hands her the carry-all. He pops back into the cab and drives away before she can ask him to help her. No one appears either. Feeling as if the suitcase pile is probably taller than she is, and grateful that the big one has wheels, she steers it through the automatic doors, which hesitate just enough to make her wonder what Caution Automatic Doors means.

The doors jettison her into a cool, airy space, with a fire burning in the fireplace, easy chairs set around low tables and masses of crystal vases holding flowers. She has not seen so many flowers outside a funeral in her life. The vases and flowers seem to tower above her. Maybe like Alice she's shrinking to the size of a minute. Oddly, the smile of the Chinese girl at the desk does remind her of the Cheshire Cat and she cannot stifle a gasp of laughter.

Paperwork is presented, signatures acquired, declarations about shuttles and breakfast fly past her, and then she is handed keys and told, "The elevators are behind you."

Ivy turns, and they are not behind her. She knocks over her tower of luggage, making a clatter in this elegant, hushed lobby, and it feels as if she is causing a scene in someone's living room. A young man appears beside her and asks if she needs assistance carrying her bags, and swiftly steers her into an elevator that is certainly not behind her but rather to the left and down the hallway. The young man is not wearing a name tag or any sort of hotel uniform, but rather a pair of high-tech running shoes, a black T-shirt and black name-branded sweat-pants. Is he even a hotel employee? Has she fallen for the common tricks people warn each other about when travelling in . . . Asia? South Asia? China? Will she never be seen again?

The young man brings her to the door of her room, holds out his hand for her electronic card, opens the door, and deposits her carry-all and her small suitcase on the floor, muttering something about storing her suitcase in the lock-up for the shuttle in the morning.

A tip. She has to give him a tip. She feels herself blinking rapidly, a sure sign she is about to be flustered, and she opens her purse, an unfamiliar large, soft hand-bag designed, the label assures her, for travel. Because unfamiliar, because stuffed with travel documents, accoutrements for the trip, lozenges, tissues, hair brush, lipstick and two wallets, one of which is to be strapped to her waist under her blouse when the time comes, she cannot find her change purse. For surely the tip for carrying one small, alarmingly small, black suitcase on wheels should only be a toonie.

When she travels in Vancouver on the bus and streetcar, as she still persists to call it, her change purse is exactly where it is meant to be — in her old-fashioned leather purse with the gold clasp Jack gave her for Mother's Day the first year Cynthia was gone. When it seemed she was no longer officially a mother. She used to pride herself that she could reach into her elegant bag, retrieve the change purse, select the exact change and board the bus all at the same time.

Here, instead, she is fumbling and almost talking to herself, and she believes she has caught on this young

40

man's face — what is he? Filipino? — the expression she catches often these days. She finds her wallet and as her internal voice expresses dismay, she extracts a five-dollar bill and hands it to him. Tips in these circumstances are supposed to be delivered discreetly; Jack had been the master of the disappearing coin, but this bill flutters in the air between them, the young man expressing professional and somehow meaningless gratitude, and then leaving. Ivy closes the door and reads the room description with the fire escapes marked in red, and the figure $569 leaps out.

Could it be? Could she have misheard the heavily accented voice when she made this reservation? Could it be not $169, which is bad enough, but really over $500 a night? Ivy turns toward the room, with its two queen-sized beds, two tub chairs, the cabinet that conceals the television set and the mini-fridge, and the view of an arm of the Fraser River. A river view? Maybe a river view costs that much more. Someone has made a mistake. $569 is more than her OAP for a month.

She stands uncertainly before the telephone and then looks up to find a complete stranger staring at her. She is frowning, as this stranger frowns at her. She looks small and wrinkled in her travel clothes. Wrinkled already. So much for the advertising that persuaded her to buy this expensive skirt, blouse and topper. It all looks sad and faded, when in the store the colour seemed so vibrant and contemporary. She looks into her own eyes. "Well, my friend. What *are* you going to do about this?"

"Hello, this is Ivy Birch in Room 419." She pauses, waiting for the foreign English speaker to catch up with her.

"Yes Ma'am, how can I assist you?"

"I noticed the price for this room seems different from the price I was quoted when I made my reservation. I have a reserv — "

"Your room rate is $169 plus appropriate taxes and any additional charges such as parking or dinner. If you select an item from the mini-bar that will also be added."

"Well, yes, but on the door it says — "

"Your room rate is $169 plus appropriate taxes and any additional charges," repeats the voice.

She begins to feel ridiculous. She is also mildly pleased that this woman can pronounce *plus* and *appropriate* without the common misplaced *r*'s and *l*'s. Amazing, she hears herself exclaim to Norma. If Norma were here, she would be laughing.

Her life is now reduced to a small suitcase open on the rack where the fellow placed it, zipper side toward the wall, and a larger one intact at the front desk awaiting the shuttle tomorrow morning. The trunk has been shipped. Cynthia arranged it and a man appeared to take it away, but Ivy doesn't know what any of it means.

She surveys the room. The carpet matches the curtains, which creates an oddly confined impression. She cannot easily detect where the floor ends and the wall begins. That could be dangerous for walking. She could acciden-tally walk into a wall, surely, and emerge from her night in this airport hotel with a bruise on her forehead. Her encounter, then, with Cynthia and her husband would begin with an explanation about the bump on her head. Probably, explaining the Canadian tendency to match floors and walls would be lost on anyone used to the design expectations of Japan. She has no idea, not a clue, what her daughter's home looks like. She does not even know where .in Tokyo their home is, because her brief effort with the guidebook explaining the prefectures of Tokyo left her more confused than illuminated. It must be like living in Vancouver but actually living in Port Moody, she has decided.

Ivy contemplates the unkempt appearance of the four pillows and bolster on the bed, and the duvet not tucked in neatly. The bed looks unmade. It is also alarmingly high, the top of the mattress level with her hip bone. How will she get into this bed? Is there a step-stool somewhere, perhaps tucked next to the ironing board? Which she will be using before she puts these clothes back on again. What will happen if she falls out of this bed? Another set of bruises to demonstrate once again that she is — as Jack used to observe fondly and frequently — a hazard to navigation. Jack would have observed this large, high, unmade bed with a quizzical expression and then turn to her with the mischievous "old letch" look on his face that signalled his desire. Ivy looks at the bed, imagining for a flicker the two of them, in their advanced age, making love, laughing at the unfamiliar contours of the bed, and probably, at some point or another, throwing one or more of the pillows onto the floor. Unlike many of her friends, detected through small comments made occasionally, she and Jack had a sex life, as the modern ones styled it, until almost the end. Until Jack wanted her but didn't know who she was. She shakes herself, glancing again at the stranger in the mirror, and concludes it's time for tea. And cookies.

She inspects the list of ingredients for the mini-fridge — and their prices — and decides to go down to the little gift shop she spotted as her bag was whisked away from her when she checked in.

Peek Frean cream cookies — birds' nest cookies her mother called them. Would she find Peek Frean cookies in Tokyo? Is this something she will find in the travel book? She has not had the nerve to open that book again. Lonely planet, indeed. What a name for a travel book. Shouldn't it be "Lively Planet" or "Crowded Planet" or "Tourist Planet" or something? Travel books, it appears, assume travel and return. Is there a "Staying put once I get there" travel book?

Ivy confronts the East Indian fellow with her purchases. She always feels guilty when purchases clearly indicate a descent into decadence, such as two chocolate bars and a can of pop. Or in this case two packages of Peek Frean cookies, four cookies apiece. No single person should eat eight such cookies all at once. She tries to appear as if she is buying cookies for at least two, if not four.

"I'm guessing you have tea in your room," the clerk asks her.

She tries to slip in "we" but fails. "Yes, I do."

She makes tea in the coffee maker, and sits with the TV on for company, eating her cookies — at least two too many — and drinks her tea, and looks out the window at the moon over the river.

This wildly expensive room, even if it is "only" $169, has a soaker tub. She does not know what a soaker tub is, and the tub looks normal except it is quite long and wider than her own. The one she used to own, she corrects herself. The bright overhead light is relentless, revealing her in the mirror over the sink as a little old lady with a heavily wrinkled face, faded blue eyes set in streaky red, and a bob that looks thin and dishevelled. Accustomed to the wattles that used to be her slight double chin, she is not used to the sagging skin around her cheeks. She puffs air into her cheeks, noting with interest that she still has a few spots on her face, spots her last doctor told her cheerfully was aging acne.

Staring at herself, she removes her bra and her underpants and considers her body in the evil lights of the hotel bathroom. She lifts her arms to inspect the wobbly skin hanging like sleeves on her underarms. Smiling slightly, she moves her shoulders to make the flesh sway back and forth. Why is it none of those elegantly aging actresses have this? Does Judi Dench have flappy underarms? Does she wear an arm girdle to control this effect? She tries to recall the last time she has seen this favourite actress — oh, sorry, actor — without sleeves. As she turns, she catches the curve from her rib cage to the top of her bottom. This was Jack's favourite view of her, a view that had not, he assured her, changed in all the years he had been privileged to see it. She notes with a tiny flicker of pride the curve still looks okay.

Will this be her last bath? It will certainly be her last bath in Canada, because her flight leaves at 7:00 AM. She steps into the tub, wary of slippery surfaces, and bends awkwardly to put the plug into place. It will not move or turn. She tries again, and still it will not move at all. Maybe it is already in, she considers, and turns on the water to test her theory. She cannot turn on the water. The handle is one of those dramatic new ones advertised on television, and so she finds herself naked, half-kneeling, protective of her bad knee, waving one and then both hands over the top of the gleaming brass and silver set of

45

knobs. Surely not really brass and silver, she observes to herself, considering whether she has the gumption to get out of the tub and call the inscrutable voice at the Front Desk. Although she suspects the Front Desk is actually somewhere in India. They would probably send someone up to help her, and the tap would be easily turned on, and she would be the butt of jokes for a generation. Or maybe they would think this was a ploy to lure the remote young man who had put her suitcase on the rack with the zippers facing the wall, so it was inaccessible. Fuming, Ivy taps the fixture and suddenly ice-cold water pours onto her head from the shower fixture. Rain water shower-head, she guesses, since she is soaked but not pummelled. Fiddling again, she manages to stop the flow from the shower-head and start the flow from the bottom tap. Merrily, it runs straight out the drain. Almost laughing, with the tinge of hysteria that tells her she's only a few breaths away from weeping, she stands up and doing so tips the plug so it settles quite nicely into its closed position. Triumph!

The hotel provides bath salts, and she pours in the whole wee bottle. Five grams. If it were poison, it would be enough to kill a horse. Her body is a mottled purple that turns to a rosy pink in the warm water. She has no scars, and of that she is proud. The last time Jack saw her naked body he kissed her belly button and rested his cheek on the soft skin there. If she had known it was the last time, she'd have added to the moment a glass globe filled with apple blossoms. She hadn't known, however, and at times she is not convinced it was the last time. The room fills with steam, obliterating her image in the mirror and she sinks into the tub, proud and not even willing to worry about what will happen when the bath is over and she cannot figure out how to drain the tub. Let someone else worry about that, she thinks a trifle rebelliously, sinking so that her nose is almost under water and her breasts begin to float.

SIX

The wake-up call comes at 4:30 AM. Ivy sits upright and nearly falls out of bed when she swings her sleepy legs off the side and finds her feet at least eighteen inches from the floor. At home, at this time in March, birds would be telling their "I'm awake" stories. She hears no birds. Would there be birds in Tokyo?

The moon, waning and half empty, hovers over the arm of the Fraser, the light glittering on the water, beating a path into her eyes. She stands at this unfamiliar window, looking at this unfamiliar view of the moon. In her home, at her kitchen window, the moon created a panoply of light and shadow, recalling the moonscapes of Aldershot.

Reminding herself she did not get up at this ungodly hour to reminisce with the moon, she dresses in her travel clothes, ironed so she will look presentable when she hands over her e-ticket and passport to the Cathay Pacific agent. The e-ticket reminds her again of the chilly tone in Cynthia's response when she admitted she did not have a printer attached to her laptop, although she did not admit she would not have known what to do if she had. The e-ticket arrived from Bill, via the helpful realtor, in one of his cheery envelopes.

The lobby is seized with the quiet of public spaces in the very early morning. This silence is different from the sense of abandon that fills the same space late at night. She has not been up this early for a very long time.

Jack died at 4:30 AM fourteen months ago. Four thirty in the morning, while she was dozing over their entwined hands. The machines had been turned off hours before, and she was startled awake when the carefully prepared, accented English voice said, "Mr. Birch has passed on, Mrs. Birch." Passed on to what, was on the edge of her mind as she registered that, technically, she was no longer Mrs. Birch and raised her hand from her husband's to wipe dried spittle off the corner of her mouth.

For weeks after that moment, no matter how deeply asleep, she would awaken with a start, to find the bright red numbers of the clock blinking at her. Her body seemed destined to be forever vigilant at 4:30 AM. She awoke day after day at the exact moment Jack had left her. Is it significant at all, she wonders, staring about the empty lobby, that 4:30 AM has come and gone without note, leaving her facing the five AM shuttle?

Now, she waits in the lobby, dressed, scarfed, hand-bagged, with two suitcases bracketing her body. She is wearing her sensible shoes, and she has her compression stockings at the ready in the pocket of her jacket.

Her fellow lobby inhabitants, a man and woman, or as Jack used to joke, a him-and-her, are husband and wife: she recognizes the signs. He has the tickets and has counted the luggage twice. She has checked the contents of her handbag at least twice too. They are both dressed in colourful polyester tracksuits, which, at this dark hour seems incongruous to say the least. Where are they going, with these clothes? Special Olympics for (very) old

49

athletes? For these two must be well into their seventies, and then Ivy looks away to hide her sudden smile. As I am, she thinks ruefully, staring at her reflection in the darkened window of the hotel. The woman wears teal-blue Capri pants and matching jacket. She has slender, tanned ankles and teal slip-on boating shoes. No socks.

On the shuttle the woman advises her husband to relax and stop counting the suitcases, but then they don't get off when the driver announces International Departures. They ask each other if Punta Cana is international. They don't ask Ivy, perhaps concluding she will be as ill-informed as they are. They ask each other if International includes Intercontinental. Ivy is so busy watching this little skit she almost forgets to alight herself, given that Tokyo *is* an international departure, much more international than Mexico.

The him-and-her head toward WestJet, and Ivy heads toward Cathay Pacific. The line is quite small, and a beautiful young Japanese woman asks her if she printed her boarding pass at the kiosk. Ivy doesn't even have time to look dismayed before the woman waves her toward a ticket agent who is also waving. The young woman bows at her. Her first bow of this journey, about which she has read some and experienced so often and inexplicably at Cynthia's wedding.

The ticket agent pronounces Ivy's name for the first time as she will probably hear it for the rest of her life: Ibee. Her pre-selected seat confirmed, her luggage is placed on the grey ramp and off it goes, dangling the teal luggage labels. The agent returns her passport and boarding pass, with the departure lounge number circled by a red sharpie. The agent also offers a gracious empty smile, to which Ivy responds by standing still and staring back for much longer than she should — at least five seconds. Terrific. This delay will persuade everyone she ought not to be allowed to travel unescorted, this English-speaking old lady. Wearing a label similar to the ones for Unescorted Minors, she will find herself in the custody of a Cathay Pacific attendant. Straightening, she throws her shoulders back, and marches off to find International Security and — God willing — a cup of tea somewhere in the unfamiliar land of International Departure.

At Security, a man waves her into a short line, away from those milling about hugging and exclaiming about safe journeys. She inspects others in the line and realizes she has been selected for the "old geezer" line, as she can hear Jack chortling. She takes a firm hold on her travelling purse strapped to her chest. No more confusion, she promises herself, and she almost manages this, except when the fellow in the turban asks her if she has turned off her computer and her cell phone and is her e-reader out of its sleeve. Conjuring immediately an image of a Kindle wearing a little knitted sweater, she answers crisply, "Don't have one," "Yes," and "Don't have one."

Considering Starbucks to be too pricey and fancy to provide a simple cup of English Breakfast tea, she turns to the Tim Hortons. Their Steeped Tea is a travesty of tea-making, but she orders one anyway. And yes, she wants a honey cruller, please. She carries her little tray, made precarious by her heavy travel purse dangling on her right arm, to a small table at the edge of the seating area with a view of the loading area. She can watch men stow luggage and food onto planes; she can watch a large animal crate and wonder what might be inside; she can watch brightly vested men — and the odd and occasional woman — doing tasks she does not understand. Many of the people she is watching are East Indian. Many of the people in the coffee bars are also foreigners. When she ordered her tea she could hardly understand the words the person was saying to her. Which explains how she got milk in her tea when she always took her tea plain. "Black?" Jack asked her that first time. "It looks brown to me." And she laughed. Not because she found his comment funny but because she found his way of delivering this tired quip funny.

The food fair is astonishingly untidy, with piles of detritus on every table but two. Coffee cups lie on their side, oozing the last vestiges of their double-double. Cookie bags and their crumbs are scattered on every flat surface, it seems. Considering that at 5:30 AM the airport has only been fully awake for thirty minutes, the mess is quite unsettling. Where is the ever-hovering clean-up artist, like the one at her mall in North Vancouver? She drinks her tea, refusing to concentrate on the mess. This is her last cup of tea in Canada, unless she is inclined to count the one they will serve her somewhere over the ocean thirty minutes into the flight.

When she finds the departure lounge at last, she settles and checks the contents of her carry-on again to be sure she has her passport and her boarding pass. A lot of Japanese people are sitting with her waiting to board, and she hears the wry teasing acknowledgment from her ever-present inner voice: Duh. Ivy as a visible minority.

Pre-boarding is announced, and she decides she does qualify as someone who needs extra time to board the plane. Walking alongside families pushing huge strollers, a man with a walker, and two old fellows with canes, she makes her way into the space that will be hers for the eight-hour flight to Tokyo. Over the Pacific Ocean. Farther than she has been on her own since she left Aldershot for Vancouver, a fact that causes her to instantly wonder if the distance to Tokyo is greater. Or, if she adds the two together, will she have flown around the world?

The wheels leave the ground and she lives no longer in Canada. Technically homeless the last night at the Airport Inn, she is now a woman without a country. If she decides not to stay, she will be homeless. The North Shore mountains are plain beneath her as the airplane veers away. This is her last glimpse, her last look at the guardian mountains she fell in love with when she arrived sixty years ago, and used to orient herself in her new home.

SEVEN

*Narita International Airport, Chiba prefect. Tuesday,
March 27, 2007*

"You don't need a visa if staying three months or less from
Canada," Cynthia said. "Get an open-ended ticket and
then we'll tell them at passport control that you will be
returning in a month or so. They won't care."

Do they know they won't care? Ivy worries. Trying
to hide from her mother the life she and Jack were
planning, she learned she was a terrible liar. Faced with
security personnel and border guards, she was an even
more terrible liar.

She approaches the desk in the queue for Other
Passport Holders, feeling sick. Her return ticket is folded
inside her passport, her daughter's address is written
in three places, including in her wallet, she has been
instructed to say nothing unless asked.

"The purpose of your visit?"

"Excuse me?"

"The purpose of your visit?"

"I'm coming to stay — to visit — my daughter. My
daughter and her family."

"And where do they live?"

"In Tokyo? Here. I mean. In Tokyo."

"Where in Tokyo?"

"Excuse me?"

"Where, what prefecture?"

"What? I'm sorry." Ivy shakes her head and feels it continue to shake of its own volition. She fears this wee tremor when she shakes her head; the ubiquitous shake she has used all her life to signal polite confusion or mild consternation, lately continues for a few more seconds, unless she deliberately stops the wobble. Great. They'll assume signs of Parkinson's or something and they'll quarantine her.

Her confusion, apparently, answers the question in the mind of the official. He waves her on to the next station, where she confronts a passport control agent wearing a health mask, and so she can't understand anything said to her. Is this agent even speaking English? The young woman points to two yellow footprints on the floor. She dutifully steps onto the footprints and looks about for the camera. She's directed to look at a little ball with a red light, like something from an old science fiction movie. While squinting at the little ball, the officer takes her passport and says something else. The photograph, then, will be of an old woman with an arch of dismay on her brow and lips decidedly parted. Why would any country let such a frail cranky being into their midst?

The comedy of call and response continues with another muffled command from the agent.

"I'm sorry, what?"

Eventually, feeling flustered and sick now with anxiety, she figures out she's to press her two index fingers onto the panel on the high counter, so her fingerprints can be recorded and presumably scanned for matches to international terrorists. She presses and a red light comes on. The officer directs her to try again. She does and is unsuccessful again. Of all the things she worried about on the eight-hour flight — deep-vein thrombosis, having an attack of impulse peeing, getting a headache so bad her teeth would ache, snoring loudly — she did not once consider she would not get into Japan because she can't press hard enough to register her fingerprints. If that's what they are trying to do. Maybe this is the first step of discovering she is an illegal alien.

She stands up on her toes, and presses down so hard with both hands she can feel the flesh of her underarms quivering. This trifle of old age, which has bothered her since her late sixties, is a sign of good luck. A green light goes on, several stamps are applied to her passport and . . . once again the officer waves her on. She is off to the tender mercies of second level passport control. She has watched the programs on Discovery Channel about Terminal Three security at Heathrow. The ever-present cameras are no doubt registering her discomfort and some Japanese psychologist specializing in anxiety in old English women is now directing the security team to apprehend her. She takes a step, two steps, and is brushed by the person behind her in line. Someone who is strong enough to make fingerprints in a few seconds rather than two minutes.

Has she landed? Is she there yet? At the baggage carousel, she registers the signs and directions in English. She did not expect signs in English. Behind her is a glass partition, and beyond, she hopes, is her daughter. Aware she might be scrutinized for signs of illness or wrong-doing, she pulls herself into a stalwart parade rest and consults the slip of paper in her hand as if it contains instructions of great import. What will happen if Cynthia is not here? If she does not recognize Cynthia's family? If they are delayed and she has to stand, as the crowd thins, alone?

This was exactly what she experienced when she took the ship to Canada, landed in Montreal, and then travelled by train across the unbelievably vast country into Jack's waiting arms in Vancouver. The beauty of the country was matched only by her fog of fear and her endless ability to worry herself into a sick frenzy. Every step of that journey could have been thwarted by missing a connection, asking for the wrong ticket, getting her directions mixed up and ending up in Halifax instead of Vancouver. When she successfully found the train station from the boat, she could not make herself understood to the ticket agent, who spoke French and did not understand her English dialect. She remembers retreating to a vast wooden bench in the echoing hall of the station and re-reading Jack's directions, writing down the ticket she wanted in English and then returning to a different ticket agent and presenting the piece of paper. Successful, she cried in the bathroom of the enormous palatial train station, sobbing onto her train ticket. Wherever would she find to cry here?

The girl who interviewed her for the book about war brides expressed her admiration for Ivy's courage, but she does not remember courage. She remembers fear. Uncertainty. Horror. She tried to tell this to the young girl with her laptop. How was it that Ivy did not meet Jack until 1946, and yet he was a soldier and she was a war bride? The girl waited expectantly for Ivy to explain and, as always, she was not able to explain. All she ever knew was the phrase "the camps."

The bags appear, festooned with the teal luggage tags, her neon green locks dangling unlocked on the zippers. She cannot remember one thing of value in these bags, but she's glad to see them nonetheless. Imagine having to buy underpants on her first day in her new country. In her new home. She approaches the customs person, holding out her Foreign Arrival declaration form. He says something and waves her on. She hesitates, wondering if the wave is to a secondary search or what. Apparently not, as the only person who seems interested in her is the young woman she had noticed on the plane, who mouths something in Japanese.

Ivy shoulders her alarmingly heavy carry-on, feels a warning twinge in her knee, and steps forward, wheeled bags gaining weight at her every step. Good up, bad down, she recites. Out of habit, she leads with her damaged right knee. She fixes what she hopes is a light smile on her face and begins the process of finding, in this mass of Japanese people who do, indeed, look all the same, her daughter. She walks down the rows of waiting people, many of whom are calling out greetings of delight, waving, hugging, laughing. She is afraid to look at anyone's face; she does not want to be embarrassed. A little boy is approaching this line of arrivals, holding a small bouquet of what look like freesias, lovely purple and white. How nice to be greeted that way, she thinks wistfully, as she steps around him and continues forward, nearing the end of the gauntlet, wondering what she will do now, does she have Cynthia's phone number, does she have any Japanese coins, will her credit card work in a call box?

"Mother! Mother, over here," she hears and she looks gratefully to her left. Indeed, a white woman is gesturing, but not at her. Momentarily seriously confused, she wonders if this is her daughter who has changed so much in the past four years she does not recognize her.

She feels a slight pressure on her handbag. She has been warned about this. She clasps her handbag to her stomach, pressing hard against the money belt around her waist and steps around a party stopped to be greeted. "Why don't people wait to hug until they get outside," she admonishes the gods, and then a small hand takes hers.

The little boy with the flowers is holding them out, his dark head bent; she focuses on the light brown of his hand, the vivid colour of the flowers wrapped in an intricate envelope. Oh, gracious, it's — and her mind goes blank. Her grandson, this must be, the younger one surely, but he seems so small for ten . . . her mind babbles onward as she looks at this little boy, whose face is obscured by his bow and by the flowers he is holding out to her.

"Mother!" And now it is her daughter's voice, irritated, impatient, signalling that once again — at the critical moment — Ivy has failed.

She has arrived.

EIGHT

Cynthia pulls both suitcases easily, her long, lean body striding forward so quickly Ivy worries she will have to break into a trot to keep up. The little boy walks on Cynthia's other side, still holding his flowers, peeking occasionally around his mother to look at this old woman everyone has probably been talking about for weeks. Wondering what he sees, she tries to catch and sustain his gaze, hoping to wink or smile. Cynthia is asking her all the questions travellers are asked: How was the flight? Are you tired? Did you eat? Did you watch any movies? Are you hungry? Was the plane crowded?

Each question is asked so quickly she has no time to respond before the next question lands. Cynthia walks like Jack. Ivy suddenly recognizes his loping gait in her daughter's long legs and strong shoulders. She looks like Jack. She has the planes and angles of her husband. For a moment, she feels the warning grimace signalling she is about to cry; terrified, she looks out one of the huge windows and blurts, "Oh, it is daytime."

They thread around people, noise, conversations, hubbub all in a language she cannot begin to understand. The airport loudspeaker blares in Japanese, then English, and then another language. Everywhere she looks, she sees dark hair, bright clothes, and faces she recognizes from the mixture of people in Vancouver. Some tall, for sure, but many her height. All much thinner, though, and all, it seems, dressed stylishly. The young men have exotic hair-dos and many of the young people have hair streaked bright candy colours. No longer frightened, although her stomach is still buzzing with anxiety, she begins to look about her for landmarks and signs that will tell her something about this gigantic airport leading into one of the largest cities in the world.

They enter the parkade, and Cynthia speaks quickly in Japanese into her slim cell phone. Moments later, a small car pulls up and Ivy recognizes Cynthia's husband seconds before she is about to identify him as the driver. She blanks on his name, however, and hopes that she will be able to catch it before she is embarrassed. The little boy says something to him, and she cannot catch any words that sound like a name. Although it is probably the Japanese equivalent of Dad. The three talk quickly in Japanese and then the man steps forward, bows, and extends his hand. She takes his warm strong hand, and he bows again. Moved to tears, holding the warm hand, looking down at this unfamiliar head, she catches her breath again.

"I am so grateful you have agreed to come to us," he says in precise English. He looks into her eyes, and she sees he is grateful. Kind, he is. "We will speak English when you are with us. This will be good for Benjiro," he puts an arm around the little boy. "We will call him Benji. And we will call me Mike." As he says this, she remembers he is Mikio. Benjiro and Mikio. At the sound of the word Mike, Benjiro starts to giggle, his hand in front of his mouth, his eyes dancing with glee at his father. He says "Mike," and his father smiles broadly. "You, young man,

61

will not call me Mike. You will call me sir," he teases, and she realizes the four of them are smiling and Cynthia is looking relaxed for the first time in — oh — the last thirty minutes.

"Please come into the car," Mikio invites. "We have hired this compact car for your pleasure and comfort. This means, of course, that Keiijiro, Number One Son, awaits you at home. He is unhappy he cannot meet you at the airport, but he is eager to greet you and show you your home."

The car is so compact she has difficulty folding herself into the front seat. Cynthia and Benjiro fold into the back seat, Mikio takes the wheel and off they go. Her first view of Tokyo is of Vancouver-like roads leading away from the airport times a thousand. Cars are streaming everywhere, the highway is six or eight lanes and they cross at least two bridges. Everything seems bright, gleaming in the late March sunlight. Cynthia is practising English with Benjiro, encouraging him to speak with Ivy, and he is floundering. His English is weak, and as if Cynthia has detected her mother's judgment, she tells them all he has only been studying English for two years at his public school. Everyone begins in Grade Two, and he is now in Grade Four. He is nearly at the top of his class in English, and at this boast Mikio makes a sound, too small for Cynthia to hear over the cacophony of the traffic, and she detects a tiny smile. It is a tender tiny smile. This man, her son-in-law, loves her daughter.

They travel for about half an hour or more, and the view seems to be of rows and rows of apartment buildings. Cynthia says something to Mikio in Japanese and he replies, quietly, "*Hai.*" Moments later, the car turns onto a narrow street with small bungalows that look like the pictures of 1940s homes from the picture book she borrowed from the library. The narrow street is lined with cars and the single lane of traffic is proceeding very slowly down the middle. Pink cherry blossoms blaze from the closely planted trees, creating an avenue of colour. Each tree looks like an artist's impression of a tree, the slender aubergine trunk and then the impossibly thick pink clusters of blooms. The sun is catching the colour and splashing it up into the sky. Ivy looks at Mikio and sees the pink has tinged his skin. His eyes are bright with joy; they are all silent in appreciation.

"Is this not gorgeous, Mother?" inquires Cynthia unnecessarily. "Have you ever seen anything like it?"

And she almost blows it, almost says, "Well, of course I have. Vancouver is filled with these streets." Which is true, but not necessary to report at this moment. Vancouver is filled with blossoms from Japanese cherry trees given to the city by Japan — after the war — as a token of peace. They all crane to look out the windows, following the steady procession down this street apparently frozen in time. This sight is easy to transpose onto the many years of admiring cherry blossoms in her own city, and she feels a shard of loss so deep and hard she gasps. Mikio notices, and she starts to babble again about how beautiful it all is and how lovely the weather and isn't it all just so much like Vancouver and . . .

She wonders why they don't just set her out on the street and drive away. She is so annoying.

They arrive at a building about five storeys high among several other buildings of the same height. For a moment she thinks they have arrived at a strip mall where they will surrender the rental car. The area seems very industrial, although with few businesses evident. Mikio pulls into a small parking lot and everyone gets out.

"Mikio will take the car back, Mother, and then he will join us by metro. The station is there," Cynthia gestures toward a clutch of small buildings and a large intersection. The streets are busy, with cars parked and people on foot. Ivy takes an unsteady step from the car and stumbles on the uneven pavement. Cynthia catches her arm and laughs in the breathless way she had when she was a teenager embarrassed by her parents. Ivy rights herself, the suitcases are set down, and the car pulls away. She squints and wants to shade her eyes to see Cynthia. This light sensitivity is new, and she wonders what is happening as they walk toward the entrance, which somehow appears at the back of the parking lot.

Cynthia enters numbers on the keypad and both doors open automatically onto the lobby. It resembles the lobbies of apartments in North Vancouver. There is a lamp on a side table, a couch, a set of boxes that must be mailboxes, a stack of flyers in garish colours, and three steps leading into the first floor. Cynthia presses the button for the elevator and then says, "We are on the third floor," in a way that signals pride. Ivy is not sure why the third floor is a prideful location, and she tucks this information into the mental envelope of the things, the many things, she does not understand.

Benjiro is talking to his mother in Japanese and Cynthia is responding. This conversation is quiet, the tones soft and subtle, and Ivy looks sideways at her daughter as she speaks to the boy. Her gaze is soft, and the two of them seem to be sharing a small and delightful topic. The boy runs his fingers over the buttons for the five floors, and then presses the one that must be three. It does not have the number three on it; it has a series of small raised dots and a symbol.

They enter a quiet hallway lit from above. The floors are wood or wood laminate, and the walls and floor are light. Cynthia flourishes a key fob at a panel beside the door and the door opens.

This is home.

She follows Cynthia toward the living room, and takes in its small, indeed tiny, dimensions. A small wooden table separates a small couch and a large TV fixed to the opposite wall. The room opens onto a small balcony and beyond this are rows of buildings.

Benjiro stands in the corner of this room, looking around as if he has never seen it before. She concludes there has been a fair amount of furniture shifting to accommodate her. She doesn't know what to say, or how to respond to Cynthia's commentary.

"Here is the kitchen," she announces, turning to the small narrow galley kitchen with a high counter faced by four stools. The counters are completely empty of the usual bric-a-brac of family living. No kettle, no coffee maker, no toaster oven, no oven at all. The small refrigerator is capped by a piece of kitchen equipment whose purpose is anyone's guess. It looks like a kitchen from a science fiction movie. Or a romantic comedy where the bachelor invites the spinster over and then they discover he cannot cook and has no pots or frying pans. She believes if she were left alone with this kitchen she would starve to death.

"We have a Western bathroom," Cynthia says, heading down the hallway. The bathroom is small, in keeping with the rest of the apartment, and contains a high bright white toilet, a faucet and small hose, a sink with a small cupboard above, a shower in a gleaming white enclosure, a vanity with a mirror, and a shelf with several small grey plastic baskets. One contains toothbrushes, and one is empty, the one Cynthia pulls forward and says, looking at herself in the mirror, "This is for your personal things, Mother."

Benjiro slides by as they leave the bathroom, the three of them doing an awkward dance in the small space at the end of the hallway.

"Here is your room. I hope you will be comfortable here," Cynthia declares.

Ivy opens the door immediately in front of her — but it is the closet filled with towels, toilet paper, cleaning supplies, and many unfamiliar objects, including rattan slippers bundled on the floor.

Cynthia makes a tsk-ing sound and reaches around her to open the bedroom door, then says something to Benjiro, who disappears, then reappears struggling with the suitcases. They take up an alarming amount of space in this small room. Ivy smiles and nods, afraid to notice too much. If this were a hotel, she would hand over the tip and then they would leave. Scrutinising her accommodation with Cynthia standing in the doorway seems rude, and so she composes her face to show pleasure and anticipation of comfort. Her stomach is buzzing and she needs to use the bathroom, but does not know how to ask about doing so.

"The boys are across the hall," Cynthia says, absently, and they both look down the hallway. The remaining door must be the parents' bedroom.

As if detecting the impression Ivy is gathering about the apartment, Cynthia says, as if addressing the hallway, "The cost of living is high in Tokyo. We were lucky to find this one so close to the subway stop for Mikio. And for the boys when they were at the primary school. Keiijiro — " and at that moment they both register the older boy is not in the apartment. Cynthia speaks again to Benjiro in Japanese as she looks at her phone. She begins to text, and then walks back to the kitchen/dining/living room.

"Would you like some tea?" she asks, a brittle cheer in her voice. "I'll leave you to get sorted. If you need help, just call." Cynthia has used one of Jack's favourite expressions, stolen, he would cheerfully tell anyone, from the people of his wife.

This is indeed the beginning of the rest of their lives together, and perhaps Cynthia is as frightened as she is. For she does feel quite daunted.

NINE

Tokyo. Saitama Prefecture

Ivy gently closes her door and looks about her. The room is impossibly small, barely able to contain the single bed. The suitcases take up most of the space on one side of the bed. On the other side is a window set high in the wall. If she stands on her tiptoes she can look out the window. She can see the sky. She sits on the bed, that is, like the one last night, so high her feet barely touch the floor. The bed is covered with a nubbly beige spread that matches the fabric skirt wrapped around the small table just beyond the foot of the bed, a table that is now her dresser, although it has no drawers. The room has no closet. No dresser, no closet. What is she supposed to do with her clothes? Her "things"?

She opens her carry-on and places her cosmetic bag carefully on the small table. Her thyroid medication and blood pressure pills have safely made the journey across the world. Three months of one and six months of the other, to be taken daily. Her lipstick and lip balm have also arrived safely. Her hairbrush and comb. Her mirror. Her toothbrush, toothpaste, and dental floss. Her cuticle tool and hand cream. Her toenail and fingernail scissors. She picks up the small polished piece of rose quartz and holds it to her cheek. She has carried this stone in her

68

pocket off and on for years. She bought it at a craft show, when Jack left her to buy himself a hot dog. The stones had been displayed under a warm light, so they glowed. Rose quartz for remembrance. For love. She has lost it several times, but it would always magically reappear — in the bottom of the washing machine, in her sock drawer, in a winter purse. She mislaid it months ago, and here it is. Tears flood into her eyes and she searches for the handkerchief in her purse. Nothing there; she remembers packing the handkerchief because it would not fit in the small travel purse she still wears strapped to her body.

If she never takes off her purse, can she go home one day? Wiping her dripping nose and watery eyes on her sleeve, she slips the leather strap off her body and undoes the money belt around her waist. The belt is stuffed with Japanese money. In Vancouver, after she checked in and before she wrestled herself through security, she stopped at the money exchange booth and purchased $250 Canadian in Japanese money. Yen. Yen. Ivy hears Jack's chuckle and almost feels his surreptitious nudge. Yen, indeed.

She places the money belt and travel purse on the table too. That's it for real estate. She pulls aside the fabric skirting and discovers four wire baskets about six inches by eighteen inches, in two rows of two. Ingenious, really, as each basket slides out independent of the others and then slides back. She plays with the sliders, intrigued.

Cynthia calls tea is ready. Ivy stands up, and her suitcase, handle still extended, topples over, blocking her exit from the bedroom. She rights it and starts to pick up her purse and then shakes her head. Her unattended purse

69

will not be stolen while she has tea with her daughter in her own home.

Although . . .

Mikio is nowhere to be seen in the living room/dining room/kitchen. Neither is the older son. She is still desperate to remember his name. Kiyoshi? Kiko? K-K-K-something. Benjiro is standing at the small island separating the kitchen from the sitting room. He continues to inspect his grandmother, and when she catches his gaze he giggles and covers his mouth with his hand. She sits on the corner of the small couch, registering with dismay that unlike her bed this couch is very low and her right knee is bending and complaining. The surface of the couch is soft, and she wonders if she will be able to get up when the time comes. No helpful arm of sofa for her. By the time she stops sinking, she feels as if she is in a squat.

Cynthia brings a cup of tea to her. This will be the first time the two of them have sat together alone for nearly thirty years. Sat together without the buffer of Jack, who could cajole a smile from his daughter with his teasing, goofy comments. She feels the piercing recognition of loss, another example of her widowhood. Yet another example.

The tea is in a small cup with no handles. It is like the small, flowery tea-cups she is used to finding in Chinese restaurants in Vancouver. Cups with no handles. The cup is hot, almost too hot, and she pictures herself spilling tea everywhere. She will scald her legs and they will all end up in the emergency ward. Are there emergency wards in Japan? In Tokyo? She stifles a grin, looks down into her teacup, and practises exchanging one nearly burnt finger for another.

"Are you very tired, Mother?" Cynthia asks. Benjiro remains standing at the corner of the sofa, and his mother ignores him.

"Well, let's see." She looks at Benjiro, who rewards her this time with a small grin. "It's today in Vancouver. It's 4:00 PM today here and about 10:00 AM there. So, no, I'm not too tired." She is, actually, exhausted, and knows that her left eyelid is starting to droop. She could not only murder a brew of English Breakfast tea, as they say on *Coronation Street*, but also a snooze.

"You are supposed to stay awake until bedtime, to get over jet lag quicker," Cynthia suggests as if she has read her mind, although she's looking at Benjiro. They are both looking at the little boy, as if he is the topic of conversation. He probably does not understand what they are saying; she remembers his visit to North Vancouver how many years ago? Four? So he is ten. He spoke no English four years ago . . . Cynthia says, "Are you okay? Can I get you anything? Water?"

They are polite strangers to each other. Ivy can think of nothing to say, except to make an observation about the weather. They both look out the balcony window, causing Benjiro to look too.

Out the window is a cityscape, buildings and telephone poles and wires of all sorts crossing each other. Surely not telephone, since everyone she has seen in Japan is carrying a cell phone, as is Benjiro, although so far he has not looked at it. As if also reading her mind, Benjiro lifts the phone and points it at her. There's a click, and Cynthia says something sharp in Japanese.

71

"He has taken your picture, Mother," she says, glaring at her son. "He wants to send it to his friends. Is that all right by you?"

Ivy is surprised to hear "all right by you" coming from her daughter. Another Jack phrase.

She nods, smiling. Her smile feels stretched. She is probably showing too much teeth, a habit she has that gives her away. Jack could always tell when she was unhappy or uncomfortable in company, because she would, as he observed, flash some teeth. She is flashing teeth for sure, she can feel it. Cynthia continues to look out the sliding glass window, as Benjiro plays with his phone. Ivy sips her tea while her younger grandson sends her picture to the universe.

As if the universe cares.

TEN

Tokyo. Saitama Prefecture

Mikio and the older boy arrive. This teenage son is slender, about five foot eight and thus tall for his culture, with a shock of hair dyed a tawny brown and sculpted or shaved over his left ear, which is pierced and festooned with several shiny objects. Not rings but rather figures of some sort. She wants to peer at his ear, as he bows deeply to her and then at a comment from his father, he extends his hand. His handshake is soft. She wonders if he needs to learn to shake hands more firmly or if Japanese boys shake hands this way; his fingers barely close over hers, slide away as soon as their skin touches. No hugs on offer here, certainly. What would he do if she grabbed him into an effusive cringe-worthy grandma hug, complete with a smacking kiss?

They'd probably all die of shock.

"Mother? Would you like to finish unpacking? Do you want some help getting your bedroom sorted out?"

Everyone looks expectantly at her. They are all standing in the small space between the end of the kitchen and the entry to the sitting room. The newly arrived teenager is looking down at his phone, one thumb moving rapidly. He is obviously nudged by someone, because he slides the phone out of sight into his impossibly tight jeans or

73

whatever they are and he bows slightly when he establishes eye contact. She smiles. Too many teeth again. What would be the correct answer here? If she says no, how will she fit her clothes and assorted things into those four small baskets? If she says yes, Cynthia will probably keel over when she discovers her mother did not bring enough socks.

She says yes. Moments later, the two women assemble in the bedroom, on either side of the bed. Cynthia has put on the fake cheerful attitude from her teenage years, always the airy response to "Get that look off your face." This effortless cheer, as if she doesn't have a sharp care in the world.

Her daughter sorts through her smalls, and tucks her underwear, bras and camisoles into one basket. She has rolled each item and then tucked them by colour into their slots. She makes no comment about the sad state of Ivy's favourite but very old cotton bras. It is true they probably do nothing for "her uplift" anymore, if they ever did; they are ragged around the bottom band, and the straps are dingy white from so many washings. But they are the only bras she ever found that did not turn into her enemy under her clothes, allowing a breast to escape, or pinch under the arm or droop woefully, revealing her sternum instead of her cleavage.

Cynthia is snapping the matching walking suits efficiently, and rolling them in the same way. "This is a nice colour, Mother," she observes about the fuchsia tracksuit rattling away under her quick fingers. The two pairs of black trousers are also rolled up, and then both women regard what remains. Another pair of grey sweatpants, three blouses, two nightgowns, six pairs of socks, two pairs of nylons, a pullover sweater and a cardigan, and a partridge in a pear tree.

Well, maybe not the bird.

Cynthia manages somehow to get all of these items into the wire baskets, and then hangs the cardigan on the back of the door. A towel and washcloth hang there too.

"We can put most of those things in your basket in the bathroom, Mother. That will give you more room. Where is your photograph of Dad?"

She gapes at her daughter. Stark loss flattens her. She does have a tiny one in her wallet, but where is the photograph from her kitchen window sill? What has she done with it? She has never been the sort of woman who has framed photographs on the walls of the people who live in the house, but where is the one she kept, had kept, on the window sill in her kitchen? Where did she put it? She sits down hard on the bed, reaching for the big bag she carried on, knowing she would find no photograph, just the three entertainment gossip magazines purchased at the airport in a spurt of extravagance, magazines she and Jack loved to read together, making comments about clothes, hairstyles, movies, and so on. Jack's voice drowns out everything as she takes out balled-up kleenex, her landing card, the documents the customs woman gave her, a copy of her landing photograph, lip balm, many — too many — balls of grey yarn, a single sheet of the pattern . . . the pile of useless things grows.

Cynthia stands. "I'll start on dinner. You are okay to finish up here?"

Ivy holds the half-empty carry-on in her lap. She has no photograph of her fellow. What has she done?

75

ELEVEN

Tokyo. Saitama Prefecture

Ivy sits on the bed, her hand absently stroking the nubbly texture of the bedspread. If she succumbs to her weariness and takes a nap, she will wake with red nubbles on her cheek, and a red mark on her nose where her glasses dug in. She sits, stroking, holding the carry-on, wondering erratically if her crochet hook is somewhere else. Beside her, half sat upon, is her elegant shoulder bag. Did Cynthia notice the money belt in the wire basket she efficiently filled with underwear? Does it matter if she spotted the fat belt or guessed it contained all the money she knew how to get hold of? Is that elegant inscrutable teenager a matter of concern? What if he is addicted to drugs, or video games, or candy? Inscrutable. Ivy recoils. If anyone heard her, they would think she was racist, or some kind of –ist. She can hear new voices in the apartment. One must be Mikio, a deep man's voice. Infrequently a sullen low voice contributes and amid all is the burble of what could only be an irrepressible ten-year-old. Not so unfamiliar after all, then.

She closes her eyes and remembers the moment when the train drew away from the platform and her mother's hand slowly dropped to her side. She lifted it again, because Ivy looked back, and then dropped it to clasp, for comfort perhaps, the ribbed edge of her cardigan. Her young face — she was only in her fifties — was shadowed by the sun crossing the railway station sign. Ivy had turned forward and then turned back, in her heedless eighteen-year-old fashion, to see her mother pull closed her sweater as if she had forgotten how to button it. This accidental glimpse into the rest of her mother's life revealed a life lived separate from her only child, a life of longing and grief. There in the distance the small figure, the woman twenty years younger than she is now, was trying to find the hole for the button she was gripping.

As Ivy has learned in the past fourteen months, she could not, in fact, die of grief. The news occasionally reported romantic tales of people dying one after the other, usually old folks in a home — death takes one and the other immediately follows. She would not die of grief. But this sudden memory would kill her if it could: her mother's hand, the hand she would never hold again, pulling the button toward the wrong button hole. Did she leave the train station with a mis-buttoned cardigan? Did she stop for tea? Did she find her way into a penny-stall and collapse on the splintery wooden seat as her daughter opened a magazine and read her way to the boat in Liverpool?

She reaches over all the things, causing many to fall onto the floor, and pulls aside the curtain concealing her clothes. She carried about this many clothes across the Atlantic then across Canada in 1947, including a new chambray cotton nightgown with hand appliqué, a nightgown she had worked while her mother and her aunt and several of her friends dropped in to advise the new bride.

77

She never had the heart to tell any of them she and Jack had been having sex since about three months after he returned to Aldershot. She did not tell any of her friends, even those she knew had "gone all the way" with their beaux. She'd kept that secret, even when for a few weeks she feared she might be pregnant. Coitus interruptus. What a concept. As it turned out, they took years to conceive a child, and she had not used contraception after Cynthia was born. They both thought another child or maybe two would just happen along. It was well into Cynthia's teen years before they realized she was their one and only.

She comes out of her awkward reach toward the baskets and sits upright. She can't even stay with one image for more than two minutes. Honestly.

The room has no mirror, so she can only imagine what she must look like. Cynthia has taken her cosmetic bag away, into the as-yet-untested bathroom. Her cheeks feel hot, her hair is probably standing on end; she no doubt looks exactly the way she feels.

The mirror in the small fastidious bathroom confirms her fears. She splashes cold water on her face, after mastering the handles and faucets. She remembers her search in the bathroom in the Montreal train station for the chain to pull, embarrassed to leave the toilet unflushed. No chain. A modern handle. Smiling, she washes her face again with her hands, then wipes the water off on her sleeve, which immediately shows the stains.

She takes a deep breath and walks down the short hallway into the main part of the apartment. Cynthia and her family are sitting in the small living room, the boys on the floor and the adults on the sofa. Mikio stands up and bows gracefully. He signals to the boys and they rise so Ivy can slide by them and sit down. Cynthia sits beside her, the boys return to their positions on the floor and Mikio brings a chair into the space, a chair that looks like a footstool, and he sits on it, folding his legs and then his hands.

"Mother," begins Cynthia, and then she hesitates.

For a wild moment, Ivy thinks maybe they have decided this is all a terrible mistake and they are going to send her home. Ah, what a tragedy. Ah, what a tragedy, she and Jack would chirp at each other when something trivial upset their day: the newsreader was not the one they liked; the last of the Marks and Spencer orange pekoe teabags was discovered on the counter languishing; their BC Lions lost in the semi-finals; the cat was protesting about something or other. Ah, what a tragedy, they would remind each other. Life, as they knew it, was now over.

"We want you to feel comfortable here, so please tell us if there is anything we can get for you. We are also hoping that you will not mind if we speak only English when you are present. This way, the boys will get so much practice with English. They take classes at their schools, of course, but they don't get much practice, because — well — as you can imagine — we speak Japanese. This means the boys won't have much to say for the first little while, if that's all right by you."

Is Cynthia aware that "all right by you" is an expression no one uses anymore in Canada? Ivy smiles, although she noticed husband and wife are both avoiding eye contact with her. She looks at the window, and then down at the bowed head of her older grandson, who is playing with his phone.

"That would be fine. Perhaps the boys can help me to learn some Japanese and — "

But Cynthia cuts her off with a gesture of impatience. She stands and says something in Japanese, and then says, "I'll make some tea."

The sitting room is so small moving out requires some shifting of people. When Cynthia moves by Mikio, he folds up for all the world like a paper fan, causing Benjiro to giggle, which causes Ivy to smile at him.

"*Ichi*," he says, holding up one finger. Unfortunately, the finger is his middle finger.

Ivy looks at him and says, "Ichi," hoping that this means one and not the word for "up yours".

"*Ichi*," the boys repeats, as if correcting her Japanese.

"Ichi," she repeats, wishing he would put his finger down.

Benjiro nods and holds up his index finger to join his middle finger.

"*Ni*," he says solemnly.

"Ni," Ivy repeats.

"*Ichi. Ni.*" He says, raising and lowering fingers.

"Ichi. Ni." Ivy echoes. "One," she raises her index finger. "Two" she raises her thumb.

"One." He repeats. "Two." He folds his thumb into his palm, says two and then lowers his index finger and says one.

Everyone smiles except the older boy, who is intent on his phone. She wonders if he is just allowed to do this or if his parents do not want to ruin the moment by hectoring him.

Her first meal in Japan is a medley of small bowls, saucer-like dishes, food she recognizes and food she does not.

"I suppose you are expecting sushi," Cynthia says from the kitchen as she and Mikio prepare dinner. Steam is rising from the cooking surface, the small refrigerator is opening and closing, Mikio is chopping with a large fierce-looking knife, unfamiliar odours are filling the spaces. Benjiro has taken up a position in the kitchen that can only be described as underfoot, whining and speaking to his parents in Japanese. When he is corrected by Cynthia in English, he lowers his voice and persists. Poor little bugger. Ten years old and suddenly he cannot speak his own language to his mom and dad, just because his grandmother has arrived.

"I don't know much about sushi," Ivy acknowledges. "There is a sushi place in the mall, but I don't eat there much. I get the chicken teriyaki sometimes. Your father liked the beef teriyaki. He didn't like sushi at all." She is about to embark on one of her favourite funny stories about Jack and sushi when she realizes telling it would be or could be construed as insensitive to the Japanese culture. Truth is, Jack did not like anything that reminded him of the starvation diet he endured for those years in the camp, and she could barely get him to eat rice when they ordered Chinese food. He didn't much like noodles either, or brothy soups with vegetables floating — like won ton chop suey.

When dinner is ready, the table is transformed into a sort of buffet space. She remains in her spot on the small sofa, Cynthia stands above her explaining the dishes, as small bowls and chopsticks are distributed. Benjiro darts among the legs of the adults and returns with a box containing a small fork, a knife, and a spoon. Ivy recognizes the Bunnykins set she and Jack sent when the older boy was born. He holds out the box, she takes the fork and he takes the spoon.

Cynthia fills her bowl with a few spoonfuls of rice and some broth and then she's on her own, leaning forward awkwardly to fetch bits of vegetables and what looks like fish and putting her bowl under her chin until she gets the food into her mouth. Benjiro is making a mighty mess with his spoon, and they are all stuck for conversation. This is a blessing because she gets a bite of fish into her mouth and it does not dissolve. It is quite tough — squid maybe — and if she tries to swallow it she'll probably choke to death. She chews, and chews, and pokes about in her bowl so they won't realize she's struggling. Magically, a glass of water arrives at her elbow. Mikio has provided everyone with a drink of water; she takes a big gulp and down it goes.

Whatever it is.

Although quite hungry, she is not able to get much into her mouth, and gives up after a few minutes when it becomes clear everyone has finished but her. The dish she thought was fish is probably squid but the dish that looked like vegetables is a tasty chicken-like dish and she could have cheerfully taken up the bowl and eaten all of it, plus all the rice. Somehow she doubts there is a stash of Peek Frean bird's nest cookies in the apartment, and she realizes with a pang of longing she has no idea how she would go about acquiring a stash of cookies.

Dinner is over. The table is cleared. Tea is brought. They all sit, not staring at each other. She feels hungry and full at the same time, and she needs to pee but can't imagine how to extricate herself from this space to get to the bathroom. The couch is so low, she wonders if she can get up anyway. Silence.

Cynthia makes a sound of suppressed impatience and goes into the kitchen. Both boys look up, as if they may have done something wrong. Mikio remains folded in his chair, looking patiently into the middle distance. She cannot think of one thing to say to this group, except for maybe the clichéd questions grandparents ask grandchildren they don't know very well: "What grade are you in? What's your favourite subject? Do you like to play hockey?"

Mikio makes a comment to the boys and they get up and disappear. A door closes and then there's a burst of Japanese and frantic giggling. They could only be laughing at her. She probably made a hundred cultural errors during the meal. Mikio rises effortlessly from cross legged and joins his wife in the kitchen. She is left alone, looking at the darkened television set dominating the wall. The evening has come on, and she can see nothing but her reflection and the hazy reflection of Mikio and Cynthia in the sliding glass doors.

What seems like hours later, she retires to her room. The mess from her carry-on is on her bed, so she scoops it heedlessly back into the bag. She goes to the bathroom, washes her face again with her hands, finds her toothbrush and brushes her teeth, pees, noting with mild concern that all she seems to be able to do is pee; will constipation be her next worry?

In her room, she realizes she has no bedside light, no bedside table, and nothing to read anyway. She lies on the bed for a few moments, looking up at the ceiling light fixture. She can hear the low voices of Cynthia's boys, and someone has turned on the television. Someone is using the shower. Life is returning to itself, with her removal. She has nothing to read. She turns off the light and goes under the covers. The blankets are stiff and smell funny. The pillow is narrow and thin. She folds it in half, and stares into the darkness.

If homesickness is something she could have, this would be it. Sorry for herself, missing the bedside light and her habit of reading herself to sleep, hungry, thirsty, the list could go on and on. Or she could simply tuck her hand between her thighs, turn her face partly into the pillow and fall dreamlessly asleep on this, her first night in Japan.

TWELVE

Tokyo, Saitama Prefecture. Sunday, April 1, 13°C, sunny with scattered clouds

The next day Cynthia informs her that this is Mikio's only day off in the week. They are going to take her to the Asakusa Kannon temple. She is advised to wear walking shoes. Ivy retreats to her room to consult her faithful guidebook and then dresses quickly. She laces up her trusty mall-walking shoes. Is Norma walking today, Saturday, in the wee hours before the mall truly opens? Is she missing her walking buddy? She pees again, even though she just went, because she cannot imagine where she will find a bathroom on this mysterious journey.

Assembled in the tiny hallway, there proceeds the dance of getting outdoor shoes on. It is clear from glances at her shoes that she has made an error by wearing her shoes from her bedroom to this shoe cache. She has left her slippers in her bedroom, and this is also an error.

"Where are your slippers, Mother?" Cynthia confirms the error in a tone that implies Ivy is wearing her underpants on her head. The protocol is to leave house slippers in the cupboard and step outside of the apartment to put on her walking shoes. Big gaff here, she realizes. As she stands shod watching everyone put their shoes on, crouching easily and tying and standing effortlessly, she wonders how she will put her shoes on in future, since standing on one foot to put a shoe on and stooping to tie laces are tasks she has not accomplished for many years. At home she ties her shoes sitting on her bed or on the little bench Jack made her for the back door. Will a little stool be provided so she can put her shoes on easily? Did she put that little bench into the trunk supposedly wending its way toward her?

The group heads out of the apartment building. The barrage of noise is deafening for a few moments and the glare of light is blinding. Everything is so unfamiliar that she sees nothing. The family leads her through the metro station with its cacophony of public address and crowds of people. Small plastic cards are brandished, and they enter the subway system. Cynthia has her hand lightly on her elbow, steering her.

Not many moments later, they emerge onto a very crowded intersection. Glimpses of a river, a walkway, and then they head up a steep sharp hill away from a bridge over what she does not know. Everyone is walking quickly, and she is soon out of breath and panting. Fortunately, no one is talking to her, so her panting is not noticed. She has a stitch in her side now and then they arrive at the back, it seems, of a very large crowd of people also heading into this public landmark, complete with ticket booths, a series of turnstiles, and young men wearing hundreds of maps. There are also rickshaw drivers, one of whom waves frantically when he spots her, then turns away to harass someone else when he realizes she is not alone.

Mikio arranges for two rickshaws, and Ivy sits with Cynthia in their traverse of the avenue. The huge red lantern, made of paper, Cynthia tells her, is a revelation. Then the mad throng of people makes it impossible to take in anything, and although Cynthia is talking to her she can hear nothing. It is all a blur, made more blurry by the sounds and smells and crush of people. The rickshaw halts beside a shrine, which Mikio identifies as a temple before they get down and walk the circumference. The temple of the god of mercy, it turns out, and by now she could really use some mercy, as her head is pounding and she is ready to keel over from exhaustion. After suitably admiring the shrine, they proceed down the avenue, flanked on both sides by kiosks jammed with every conceivable tourist-trap object of desire. This is free-admission day at the PNE, times 100. She even thinks she can smell candyfloss.

This array of stalls, the bright colours, the clusters of people, the unfamiliar food. The blatant commercialism of the stalls offends her. The goods are cheap and gaudy, reminding her of similar stalls at the Pacific National Exhibition. There, at least, selling gewgaws was part of the event. In a shrine, though? Or temple, as Mikio patiently corrects her twice. What keeps leaping into her mind is the common label to be found on so much claptrap when she first came to Canada. *Made in Japan* was synonymous with cheap, flimsy and unspeakably tacky. Much like *Made in Taiwan*, or, most recently, *Made in China*.

The older boy is oblivious to everything, as he is playing with his cell phone, either a game or some sort of music, using his thumbs, walking along staring at the screen. Cynthia and Mikio say nothing to him. Ivy remembers badgering Cynthia on their driving trip to Prince George when she was reading Archie comics. She had her head down, missing the wonderful scenery, including a black bear Jack spotted at the edge of the road. The ten-year-old is certainly paying attention, doing what kids do everywhere — bugging his parents to buy him something. He is fixed on the snacks, and by the end of the 300-metre gauntlet he has three huge suckers, a cone of some kind of rice, and a plush turtle about the size of his fist. He attaches it to his knapsack, where it joins three other dangling accoutrements. Happy, he barely glances at the point of the expedition: the gigantic red lantern. In size, the lantern is comparable to Lumberman's Arch in Stanley Park, where the huge log stands as a testament to the industry that gave Vancouver and BC their prosperity. Ivy recognizes the lantern from many cards and stickers she has seen over the years, thinking all the while it was the size one would find in a house or perhaps on a porch beside the door. This huge lantern looks more like a Goodyear blimp than a graceful, subtle signifier of Japan. She is somehow ashamed — at the crowds, the noise, the gauntlet of merchants, the cheapness of it all. Ancient Japan's eternal jewel, she thinks. At least in Stanley Park, you could sit with your back to the concession stand, and most commercialism is banned in Vancouver parks.

After a while, with Cynthia and Mikio apparently unsure what to do for Ivy, they head back down the hill toward the gates. Just before the entry to the subway swallows them, she spots a park nearby decorated with cherry blossoms, and masses of people wander there, many with cameras held aloft. Afraid if she evinces interest she will find herself plunged into the throng, she surreptitiously inspects the entrance of the park. She thinks she sees avenues of walking stones and expanses of green and gardens full of a flower blooming profusely in early spring. Not daffodils, or tulips, but something foreign to her. Registering the irony of "foreign", she looks again to find some shrub or flower she recognizes.

"That's Dembou-in," says Cynthia. "It is our most famous park."

What is this "our"? When did Cynthia begin to own this city? When did she stop referring to North Vancouver as home? These questions act like a small puncture in the balloon that is Ivy's energy. She suddenly cannot imagine taking another step. How far has she walked today? How much farther? And they walk so fast. She resorts to adjusting her purse, still looking up the avenue of cherry trees.

Everyone hesitates. She will die if they digress into this park. Her meagre reserves are seeping out the bottom of her mall-walking shoes.

"Mother?" asks Cynthia.

"Perhaps another day," she replies.

She trudges behind Cynthia and the boys, with Mikio nowhere to be seen. Have they lost the head of the family? Jack often joked about how easy it was to lose Ivy, given her size and "plain sparrow" plumage, as he explained it. So she knit herself a bright yellow sweater several years ago, and Jack appreciated how his plain sparrow became a goldfinch, thus easier to spot. If she had a magic wand, she would disperse them all and walk slowly through the avenue of sculpted greenery, holding Jack's hand.

When they reach the subway, Mikio appears, and they retrace their steps to the apartment building. Ivy is puffing, her feet hurt, her knee is throbbing and she is mortified that she is having so much trouble keeping up.

"Tea, Mother?" Cynthia asks, and they both hear Benjiro echoing "Tea, mother" in a whisper. Ivy says yes, hurries to the bathroom to pee, and avoids looking at herself in the mirror.

The household devolves into Sunday afternoon activity, leaving her to sit on the corner of the sofa, her sore legs crossed at the ankles, her view of the outside world obscured by the railing of the balcony. The tea is hot and not what she had yesterday. It smells like orange pekoe, and although weak even tastes like orange pekoe. Maybe she has conjured her tea from home, in an act of homesickness worthy of Heidi.

THIRTEEN

Tokyo, Saitama Prefecture. Monday, April 2, 2007. 16°C, clear

The door closes on Cynthia and Benjiro. Ivy will be alone in the apartment until they all return sometime later in the day, she has been informed. She does not know where everyone is going. Mikio and the older boy left almost an hour before Cynthia and Benji. The boys to school, presumably, and Mikio to work, whatever that was, but then Cynthia said she had to be "at school" by eight on Mondays. She delivered this information with a frosty expression, as if daring her mother to ask anything further. Cynthia also apologized for leaving her on her own and then told her the housekeeper would arrive by ten and she would therefore have company for part of the day.

"But, you know, we are all busy, so I leave you to take care of yourself, get used to things here. We'll see you for dinner. I'll take you for a walk after dinner. All right?" As if anticipating a negative response, Cynthia turned away, repeating "All right," as a statement and gathered up her younger son.

The door closing seems final. The resulting silence of the apartment alerts Ivy to the customary ringing in her ears. She goes to the bathroom and considers the wisdom of taking a shower. She then steps into her bedroom and looks at it carefully in the light of day. No one is standing at her elbow, waiting for her response. Her room is small. The bed is small. Uncomfortable. Her bedside gear is on the floor. Even if she had one, there is no room for a table lamp or something for it to sit on. Maybe she could get one of those futon mats and sleep on the floor. Although the idea of clambering to a standing position when she has to use the bathroom in the middle of the night is daunting. Could she even do it? She pictures herself crawling to the bathroom and using the toilet to haul herself to a sitting position, then suddenly feels her mouth quivering on its own; surely she is not about to disgrace herself by starting to cry? What would be the point? She is alone.

She goes to the window, which looks out at an apartment wall very close. If she stands right by the window and looks up, almost with her cheek pressed against the pane, she can see the sky. Feeling the cold against her cheek, she watches the grey clouds overtaking the blue sky. Eating the sun, perhaps, although this window does not face the sun. There will be no direct sunlight in this room — ever. The clouds, grey lined with white, puffy ones, are moving, pushed by wind. Clouds. Clouds are the same everywhere, and maybe this cloud was over North Vancouver not so long ago.

She pulls out the bins of her clothes and dumps them all onto the bed. Cynthia's careful rolling of two nights before is undone in a moment. Retreating from the mess, she peeks into the boys' room to discover two small desks on the floor. These are compact and tidy, with pens neatly arranged in racks at the back of the writing surface. Small cushions — bottom-shaped — sit in front of each. These are desks the boys use to do their homework. A small computer screen is set up on one. The boys must sleep on the mats that are rolled up. She cannot see any clothes, so she guesses they are stowed away in the small plastic bins beside the mats. This small room has no window. With the door closed, it is more like a storage closet. The boys have been moved together to give her a room of her own. It *is* a storage closet. She wonders what her hips and knees would be like if she had spent her life sitting cross legged on the floor and getting up and down from that position. There is none of the usual mess one associates with children. Partly visible, rolled up in one of the mats, is a comic or pages of a magazine. She touches it, but she cannot see enough to know what it is.

The next doorway is Cynthia and Mikio's bedroom. She lacks the nerve to open this door.

She tackles making herself a cup of tea. She spotted the device to boil water when they were preparing breakfast, so she takes it out of the cupboard, fills it with water, plugs it in and turns it on. These ordinary activities fill her with pride. Waiting for the water to boil, she inspects the living room. The sitting room. The front parlour?

The dominant feature is the large flat-screen TV, the largest she has ever been close to. Beneath the TV is a hardwood shelf holding three remotes. She and Jack often joked about the husband's right to hold and use the remote. As a result, she does not know how to use one remote, let alone three. She stands in front of the television, holding the remote that looks most like the one she has, she used to have, at home. She stands for a while running her fingers over the buttons, looking at the words, which are not English, and then replaces the device. After her experience with the discomfort of the sofa, she gingerly lowers herself to the floor, using the table as support. After a few seconds, less than a minute for sure, she discovers she cannot sit there any longer and doesn't think she can haul herself to her feet. Using her bottom as a tipping point, she rights herself, panting heavily.

The kitchen, with its long narrow counter and even narrower counter against the opposite wall, draws her away from the inscrutable television. She opens one cupboard after another, feeling vaguely sneaky. Cynthia has commanded her to make herself at home, but still, opening someone else's cupboards feels like an invasion just short of investigating the underwear drawer. The boxes, little bags, and bottles contain nothing she recognizes, except a jar of marmalade.

For years, she sent marmalade to Cynthia in her Christmas parcel, because Cynthia loved marmalade. This jar is unopened, and she holds it for a moment, remembering the shelf at Marks and Spencers in Metrotown where she had found it. How long did marmalade last? She turns the jar upside down and sees the expiry date: 27-11-2003. Slowly, she lifts the jar and places its side against her cheek. Gently, as if unwilling to disturb everything else in the cupboard, she replaces the jar. When had Cynthia stopped loving marmalade?

She is still mystified by the workings of the small stove, which appears to have no oven. She is afraid to look in the fridge, given the concoctions that emerged this morning as each person prepared his or her own breakfast meal. They all stood about in the kitchen, looking out in four directions, reaching over one another, taking in the sustenance that would get them through to — what? Elevenses? This remnant of her childhood and from the *Lord of the*

Rings movie Jack so loved drops down in front of her like one of those scary rubber spiders favoured by Halloween shops and Value Village. He loved his elevenses. Seeing the ten-year-old look into the fridge, hesitate, look at his parents and his brother, pause and then select items affected her oddly. She wonders in a flash what he would think if she made him porridge. Oatmeal porridge with raisins, brown sugar and milk. He is probably lactose intolerant. Is he?

Yesterday, she was offered a dish that contained cold noodles in a gelled broth festooned with what looked like white beans but were sour and so sharp that she didn't know if she could swallow them. No room for her in the crowded little kitchen, she stood in the archway, a mouth full of weird. She managed to swallow, experienced a flood of saliva, and she gagged. Cynthia quickly made her some noodles like the ramen noodles from the corner grocery store at home, and she gratefully ate them. At least they were familiar. This morning she ate noodles again; she would have cheerfully pushed someone out of the way if oatmeal had magically appeared on offer.

The noodle breakfast probably did not contain enough nutrition for a squirrel. She crosses the sitting room, opens the sliding balcony door. Ear open for the kettle, which seems to be taking a long time to boil, she steps out into the roar of the street below her. The balcony holds two small plastic chairs, but when she sits on one the railing obscures her view of anything. She stands up. According to the date, spring should be well underway in Tokyo; according to the lavish cherry blossom display she saw in that park, she knows trees are blossoming, leafing out. She cannot, however, see one single tree from this narrow balcony. Is that possible? She looks up and down the street, even lifting herself onto her tiptoes and balancing on her arms. Imagining plunging to her death, she subsides. No trees. Not one. The street is a landscape of signs, pavement, street lights, vehicles, and people. She does spot three little dogs, two being led by resigned-looking young men and one on its own, sniffing warily at every square of stone decorating the front of the building.

She hears the "beep beep" that signals the kettle, rushes back through the living space, catches her foot on the table leg, and flings her arms out to catch herself, just in time to fall almost directly into the arms of possibly the tiniest woman she has ever seen. This, then, is the housekeeper, who smiles peacefully, as if she started every morning being rushed at by a stumbling, agitated old white woman. She nods and bows. Ivy nods and bows. The tiny woman bows again and says something that is either her name or some invocation to the gods to keep her safe, because at that moment the smoke detector starts howling. It seems although the device to boil water appears space age, it does not contain the technology to switch off when the water boils.

In short order, all is restored, Ivy has a cup of tea, and she retreats to her room to clean up the mess she made with her things. The apartment is so neat, so uncluttered, so clean, she does not know what the housekeeper could find to do. Nevertheless, she sits on the edge of her bed, her legs dangling, for nearly two hours, waiting. At one point, there is a cautious tap on her door, but she does not respond and a while later she hears the apartment door open and then close.

It is noon.

She sleeps the afternoon away, waking twice to register the quiet of the apartment and falling to sleep again. She gets up when her watch tells her it is four o'clock. She is very hungry now, and thirsty.

She hears a click and a swoosh and the boy, the younger boy, Benjiro, stands in the entry taking off his shoes. When he bends down, his knapsack threatens to upend him. He hops about putting on his house slippers then rights himself. His school uniform is all sixes and sevens and his tie is dangling precariously. He bows when he sees her standing in the sitting room. She almost bows in response. He disappears. She stands for a moment, wondering if he will re-appear. He does not. She sits down. It's four thirty.

About twenty minutes later, Cynthia blows through the door, carrying her book bag and a string sack of groceries. She is talking as she comes through the doorway, and Ivy answers her, then realizes by her vacant gaze that Cynthia is on her phone. As she is finishing the call and changing her shoes and stowing her jacket, Benjiro somehow manages to slip by her and establishes himself in the sitting room on the floor beside the couch.

"How are you getting on," Cynthia asks, setting her bag on the counter.

"Fine," both Ivy and Benjiro reply, and in their unison lie exchange their first conspiratorial glance.

"Fine," Ivy repeats, embarrassed to be conspiring with her grandson against her own daughter.

Next to arrive is the older boy, silent, phone in hand, who disappears into the hallway. Is she the only one to notice smoke wafting about him like the dust clouds around Pigpen?

And Mikio? He does not arrive until nine or so, as the boys are heading for bed, and he eats his dinner standing in the kitchen, chopsticks and bowl in the same hand.

FOURTEEN

Tokyo, Saitama Prefecture. Thursday, April 5, 14°C, clear

The walk Cynthia promised did not materialize on Monday evening, Tuesday evening or Wednesday evening. Each day Ivy is left alone until Benjiro arrives at four thirty. He disappears into his room until Cynthia arrives home about six, with her string bag with unfamiliar vegetables poking out at various angles, to cook dinner swiftly and silently alone in the tiny space. Dinner is produced about ten minutes before Mikio enters the home.

Tonight, Benjiro sits on the floor, in his brother's way, playing a video game on his phone. Keiijiro, also sitting on the floor, every so often kicks his brother, quite hard. Benjiro flinches and looks toward Cynthia and then returns to his game. Ivy sits on the sofa, knowing the answer to "Can I help" will be a snort of derision. Cynthia seems annoyed by everything happening in the kitchen and everyone is just trying to keep out of her way. Or keep below her line of vision. The jangling noise from the two phones is the only sound, except for the sharp encounters with knives, cutting boards, and steaming pots in the kitchen.

Mikio arrives, disappears, and re-appears wearing a tracksuit and socks with spaces for his toes. Mittens for feet. How hard would it be to knit something like that? Her knitting days are long gone, and crocheting such an article is beyond even thinking about. Confined to English, no one has much to say. Cynthia begins by asking Ivy how her day was, but Ivy is not sure if she should answer. Describing her day would take about two minutes anyway and then what? She makes a mess, dropping broth and noodles on her top, and then dinner is done and dishes disappear. There's an eerie silence, while everyone looks at something else in this small room, then Benjiro says something to his father in Japanese, is rebuked by his mother but rewarded by the television screen sailing into life.

It's a game show. For more years than she cares to remember now, she and Jack would watch the news on the TV after dinner and then *Jeopardy* and *Wheel of Fortune.* Then they would tidy the kitchen and do the dishes. This game show is very loud. Even though Mikio turns it down, the noise is almost deafening. The host is shouting, the audience is shouting, the contestants are shouting, the colours are garish, the object of the game incomprehensible. This show is baffling, involving rapid-fire delivery of incomprehensible words, slap-stick comedy, and audience participation that seems too ferocious for the situation. Cream pies, sliding in mud, under-sized tricycles, over-sized boxing gloves, chicken costumes, conveyor belts, sticky substances. Cynthia is standing still in the kitchen, watching the television. Ivy is hoping for the promised and delayed Monday walk, registering this must be how dogs feel when trying to figure out how to get the master to take them out. If she knew where the leash was, she'd go get it and bring it to Cynthia.

The game show ends suddenly and inexplicably. A new program comes on, and Cynthia says something to Mikio in Japanese. The television goes off, the household ritual of bedtime is invoked, and in a few moments Ivy excuses herself and goes to her room. It is eight thirty.

She lies down on her bed, staring up at the ceiling, wondering what to do. She fetches the crocheting from the unruly contents of her carry-on. One day she will have to unpack that carry-on. Project in hand, hook, first skein, pattern, she surveys the room. Sitting on the edge of the bed with her legs dangling down is not going to work. Sitting against the wall on the bed causes the bed to shoot away from the wall, and she almost does a back flip onto the floor.

"Mother?" calls Cynthia, and Ivy rights herself, shoves the bed back, and calls out, "I'm fine, dear. Just picking up my crochet hook."

She lowers herself to the floor, puts her thin pillow under her butt, leans against the wall with her legs straight out in front of her and consults the pattern. Chain 128 stitches.

At chain 20, her legs and hips pained and her neck already sore, she laboriously hauls herself from the floor and stands for a few moments, holding her work, trying to decide what to do. Maybe she can go back out with her crochet and sit on the sofa? Imagining the consternation her re-appearance would cause, she puts her project back in her carry-on,. remembering with a pang the work basket Jack bought her years ago at a shop in Chinatown, a rattan basket with handles that began to fray about two weeks later. She used that basket for her handwork forever. Where is it now?

It is 9:10 PM. She dearly wants a cup of tea and a bath, in reverse order. She wants to watch the evening national news, with Jack commenting on the hair styles of all the reporters, while they drink their Sleepy Time tea. The cat would be let in, the lights turned off, the doors checked, curtains drawn, heat turned down, and then the two of them would toddle off to bed, Jack taking off all but his undershorts and socks and Ivy putting on one of her old flannel nighties. She would read for a bit, while Jack spooned against her body, his arm around her waist. Lights out, they would fall asleep. Except for those nights when they didn't — for a time.

Late in the night, Ivy wakes to the sound of crying. For an awful moment, she thinks it is her own sorrow that has awakened her. She lies still, listening to her breathing, and hears again someone crying.

She hears Cynthia's voice in the hallway, doors opening, and her daughter's soothing voice in Japanese. She hears the older boy speaking in angry tones, almost a shout, promptly shushed. Benjiro it was, crying in the deep night. Cynthia continues to soothe him, and Ivy imagines Cynthia gathering up that sweet boy, trying to heal his sorrow.

A fight with his brother? At this hour? A bad dream? What bad dreams do Japanese children have? Ivy has not had a nightmare since before Jack got sick. As if her waking life were bad dream enough. And mercifully she has had no dreams — so far — of her life "before".

Slowly, Benjiro's gulping sobs still and sounds tell her the boy is being led into his parents' room to finish the night. The last sound she hears is Mikio's deep and lovely voice, then silence.

Ivy lies on her back, staring up. Her mouth is dry, and she's hungry. Back home she would get up to make herself a cup of tea and read the obituaries in the day-old paper. She would sit in her dim kitchen peering at the death notices of no one she knew. She does not own that kitchen anymore, and there's no point in wishing for something she can't have.

She closes her eyes. She fancies the household is drifting onto clouds of sleep, the little boy cuddling his prickly mother, returning both to a time when all she had was love for him. Safe in those long-ago arms, he sleeps.

FIFTEEN

Tokyo, Saitama Prefecture. Saturday, April 7, 12°C, cloudy with rain in the evening

Two evenings later, Cynthia arrives with groceries as usual and says out loud to the room, "After dinner we'll go out and get ice cream. How does that sound?"

Benjiro does what Ivy wants to do. He shoots up from the floor without benefit of uncrossing his legs, or so it seems, and yelps. Cynthia frowns at him, so he turns to Ivy and bows his apology, his face suffused with anticipation. Ivy stands up and asks Cynthia if she needs any help.

Cynthia shakes her head dismissively, so Ivy takes herself down the hallway and finds her crochet. She carries it back to the sitting room, as she now calls it to herself, and sits on the corner of the sofa beside the window. Reading glasses perched on her nose, pattern balanced on her lap, she begins the lengthy starting chain for the work. Cynthia is making a great clatter in the kitchen, Benjiro is bent over his phone, and Ivy begins to chain, counting silently. Not silently enough, because she looks over her reading glasses to see Benjiro apparently repeating her numbers. She is up in the forties.

"Forty two, forty three, forty four," and at that word, Benjiro snorts with laughter, the sort of laughter a Canadian child would make only in response to a fart joke. Ivy wonders what forty-four means in Japanese, as she carries on counting, with Benjiro echoing her words. She gets to 120 and says it triumphantly, to hear him conclude with an equal flourish. He's standing at the other end of the table, his phone dangling from one hand, waiting for her to continue. She smiles, he smiles, and then Cynthia asks him to put the dishes on the table for dinner.

Mikio does not appear for dinner, and no one comments on this. Cynthia sits beside her older son on the floor, her long legs folded under her. She's sitting on her heels, looking comfortable. How long has it taken for her to learn to sit like that without giving up in ten minutes? Ivy knows she couldn't sit like that at all, let alone for one minute. They eat dinner in silence, the older boy occasionally sneaking peeks at his phone on the floor between his brother and himself. Ivy doesn't care, she's too excited to be going out for a walk. She recognizes how ridiculous this is, but she still finds herself scurrying through the last bits of rice, broth, vegetables and some sort of meat that might have been chicken.

There. Done. Time to go out.

Everyone seems to have forgotten the promise of ice cream. Mikio arrives, serves himself dinner and comes to sit beside his children on the floor. He's still in his work clothes: a spotless white shirt, a grey suit, a grey tie, and ear buds peeking out of the inside pocket of his jacket. He says nothing, although he smiles at Ivy. While he is eating, Benjiro leans against him, at first subtly then as if he is toppling over against his father. Leaning as far as he can, he presses against the arm Mikio uses for chopsticks. Without missing a beat, Mikio switches hands and continues eating his dinner with his right hand. He puts his fist on the floor to create a brace for his son's body. The little boy looks so content, leaning heavily against his father's body, she has to look away out the window. It is starting to rain.

Spirits dashed, literally, she is not surprised when Cynthia, also noticing the rain, says something in Japanese and then in English, "It has started to rain. We will go for ice cream tomorrow. Tea, Mother?"

Tea, again. Ivy sits in the corner of the sofa, looking out the window, remembering with swift recall another night when her fond plans were destroyed by weather. She had a walking date with her new beau, and her mother forbade her to go because it was raining. Jack appeared in the doorway of their small home, wearing his army greatcoat and a wet-weather helmet, his eyes gleaming with delight when he saw her. The gleam turned to quiet disappointment when he learned that he could not walk out with this English girl who had captured his fancy, as he styled it.

"Ah, well," he had said, doffing his hat and causing water to cascade everywhere, including on the new sweater Ivy had just finished knitting that very afternoon. The light-blue wool darkened with the water droplets, and he reached out to smooth the water away, almost brushing her breast. As if she were on fire, he pulled back his hand, and gasped an apology. Ivy giggled, certainly with a tone that caused her mother to call to her in agitation and annoyance. Something about letting all the heat out, as they had the three-bar heater on in the sitting room. Knowing it was useless to invite him in, Ivy had regretfully said good night, afraid she would not be asked again to walk out by this tall Canadian soldier with the gaunt face and merry eyes.

Ah, well. She considers the evening stretching before her. Cynthia brings her some tea, and then a wrangle breaks out in the boys' room. Cynthia's shrill voice, and then for the first time, she hears the raised voice of her older grandson. They seem to be in some sort of stand-off. Mikio intervenes and after several moments of shouting in Japanese, silence falls. She sits in the sitting room, arranging her expression to indicate she has heard nothing. Since she understood nothing, she might as well have heard nothing.

She looks out the window, her tea at the ready, now hearing the sound of a boy weeping. Surely not Keiijiro?

Bloody rain.

SIXTEEN

Tokyo, Saitama Prefecture. Sunday, April 8, 14°C, clear

She wakes on her left side, facing the wall. Sleeping always on the left side is bad for the heart, she heard on the radio a few months ago. Why, she did not catch. It seems to her if her heart cannot tolerate as benign a habit as sleeping on it, she's in more trouble than her body position in bed would solve. She always slept on the right of the bed, Jack on the left, and she slept facing out while he slept facing her, his arm draped over her hip. And yet it wasn't his heart that failed him, after all.

She glances anxiously at the digital clock. Relieved, she sees it is nearly six, and therefore she is not awake far too early to consider moving around in her room. She could murder a brew. Instead, she lies still, listening to her heart, counting the beats. Her heart always beats faster than it ought. She is also listening for sounds that mean morning in this household and morning in the street below. She hears the swoosh of tires on pavement that means rain, and the sounds of people, a few, walking. A person coughs.

She reaches out and touches the wall. The oyster grey, a fashionable colour, is dull in the dawn light. The rectangle that is her window is no longer infused with lights from the building next door. She touches the wall again, pressing hard with her fingers, so the blood floods away and her skin becomes ghostly white.

The window brightens and now she can see the speckling of the paint. Who had this room before she arrived? Who knows this view, this view from the bed to the wall, with the window high above? She lies listening for sounds that meant morning in her home in North Vancouver. Jack always woke before she did, and when she woke she would hear him making tea, the kettle knocking against the tap, the clink of cup, the cutlery drawer opening, and the sound of the cat and the man talking to each other. She closes her eyes. She sees the cat winding about Jack's legs, protesting the early morning, the apparent lack of breakfast, the dearth of birds. Each sound conjured specific acts. In North Vancouver, the dawn chorus in April would wake them both well before six. She hears no birds. No sparrow, thrush, woodpecker or flicker with its "I'm so sexy" rapping on the siding of their home. She strains her ears now to hear anything of Jack in this household, this solitary room, this place with no memory of him.

The curtain did not close, she discovered several days ago. No vantage point to peer in at her, so no need for a curtain to give her privacy. All she has to do is sit or lie on the bed and she is invisible to the apartment dwellers across from her. She reaches her fingers out and touches the wall again, imagining for a moment her hands reaching through the wall to touch the sleeping inhabitants of the next building. To touch another aged woman waiting for her house to begin to stir so she could go to the bathroom and pee without waking everyone up. How likely is it her magical extending fingers would tap another old woman on the shoulder? This is a society that reveres its aged — the guidebook says so. Where are they? Where is the polyester-clad splendour of Norma?

Thinking of another old lady needing to pee reminds Ivy's body it needs to pee with an urgency that startles her.

The apartment is quiet. Except for the sliding door in the sitting room, the windows do not open, so nothing disturbs the sealed-in spaces. Cynthia pointed out the windows when she was showing Ivy around, talking about how this tiny place had plenty of glass. No developer would design apartments without picture windows, Cynthia said. Right. Picture windows opening onto small — tiny — balconies that overlook more small balconies and picture windows. Ivy has discovered she could watch her neighbour's television with little effort if she chose to. Would Cynthia recall the picture window in their home in North Vancouver, a window six by ten feet? Did Cynthia remember the light pouring into the living room and dining room because of that huge window?

Small windows in the bedrooms, because no views. No movement of curtains. No random drift of air from an open window. Except for the balcony door, no windows open to fresh air. Ivy wakes up in the same air she went to sleep in, her mouth and nose dry, and she imagines her lungs welcoming the recycled air on its fourth, tenth, 100th visit. Surely it isn't healthy to breathe and re-breathe this air. She opens her eyes to the same lightscape she closed her eyes upon; dusk and dawn are the same, infused with the light from the street. No dark and no daylight. Gloom. She touches the grey wall, feels for the odd bubble of texture. Old wallpaper? It seems unlikely in any room Cynthia has control over. Everything is

110

neutral. Where are the splashes of crimson, of "Chinese" red? Purple? Gold? Not in this place and certainly not in this room.

No sounds of familiar or unfamiliar early morning activity. Only the light swish of tires and the occasional click of heels outside. What the household awoke to, most of the time, were alarm clocks embedded in the cell phones scattered around the apartment. The alarms are fragments of songs, none recognizable. Each one — there are five — sounds separately. Mikio's begins as a low hum that accelerates, so by the time she hears him moving the alarm is booming. His alarm is due soon.

She gets up and puts on her dressing gown and slippers. She looks at herself in the small mirror over her table and quickly combs her hair. These movements persuade her body *now* is the time to pee, and she sits down carefully, pressing her thighs together, trying to think about anything except the sound of water flowing. In her own home, she would stumble to the bathroom, hike up her nightgown, leaving the door open, talking to the cat, looking out the window at the garden, pee and then go about the business of gearing up to go into the kitchen for tea. Of all the things she has to get used to, waiting to pee was unanticipated.

Mikio is up. If she moves quickly, she can get into the bathroom and out before she gets in his way. She slides off the bed onto the wood floor. Her slippers are aligned carefully, pointing in the right direction. She slips her feet into them and tugs her sash tighter. Meeting Mikio in the hallway, both of them heading for the same place, is embarrassing. She pauses at the door, looking down at her hand on the door knob. The coast is clear, and she hurries to the bathroom.

How does Cynthia keep the bathroom so pristine? Ivy sits on the toilet, experiences the welcome gush of urine, and looks at the little plastic bins, in various shades of grey, holding face cloths, small hand towels, and small pieces of fabric whose use escapes her. The Tokyo equivalent of Kleenex?

SEVENTEEN

Tokyo, Saitama Prefecture. Wednesday, April 11, 10°C, rain

When Cynthia comes home, she sends Benjiro down to get the mail, and he comes up with some glossy flyers and a formal legal-sized envelope in cream stationery. Cynthia says, artificially bright and friendly, "Oh, look, Mother, here's the cheque."

Ivy looks across the small room at her daughter who is opening the envelope.

"A cheque? For what?" she asks, puzzled. "Is it addressed to you?"

Cynthia lays the envelope down, smoothing the ripped section.

"Sorry," she says acerbically. "Sorry. Yes, it is addressed to you. I'm just used to opening . . . "

Everyone's mail, Ivy finishes mentally. Two weeks in and the honeymoon is about to end, she can sense it. Benjiro also senses the plunge in emotional temperature because he disappears in plain sight, looking at his phone, "ears flapping" as Jack would have said, if he'd been here.

If he were here, his jokes would save them.

He wasn't.

Ivy reaches the counter and picks up the envelope. Cynthia remains standing close, her breathing loud.

113

Would it be so rude to retreat to her room? The three stand in an awkward triangle, Cynthia actually inspecting her fingernails.

Inside is a letter, a document of conveyance and a formal cheque embossed, signed by two people, for $789,642.87. Eighty-seven cents. How did they figure that? She peers at the numbers again and runs her index finger, which trembles, over the bumps.

$789,642.87. Nearly eight hundred *thousand* dollars. In Canadian money, which isn't doing so bad on the world stage right now. She puts the cheque down, causing Benjiro to look up. He touches the cheque, or starts to, but Cynthia snaps at him in Japanese. Why do her rebukes all sound like dialogue in bad martial arts movies?

Ivy turns the cheque so Benjiro can look at it, and Cynthia also looks at it.

"789,642.87," Ivy recites.

"That must have been quite the commission."

"I had no idea."

"Mother, you sold the house. Didn't you pay attention to the asking price? The selling price?"

"Yes, but — the forms were filled with numbers, and they all seemed fair. Percents and all. I didn't . . . "

"You probably could have got more. A lot more. Dad's hard-earned money."

Cynthia taps the counter with her inspected finger-nails. Ivy winces. Benjiro, in the gap, says quietly Seven Eight Nine as if reciting the numbers table. Seven Eight Nine in a rhythm.

Both women smile at him, surprising each other with the break in tension.

Ivy puts the cheque down. Cynthia picks it up.

114

"You have to deposit it. It's losing money—interest—by the day."

Ivy has the image of going to an insta-teller and depositing the cheque. The Bank of Montreal would probably blow up. Seven. Eight. Nine.

"Can you take me . . . ?"

"Not in Tokyo. You don't have an account. And you can't get one because you're a visitor. You cannot give them this cheque and simply get a savings account. There are rules. The bank won't let you."

"Well, I could just keep it. Until I do. Or . . . "

"No, Mother." Cynthia uses her bad martial arts movie voice. Or the bad woman in *Batman*. Or *Raiders of the Lost Ark*. She needs a German accent, Ivy thinks, then blushes.

Both women are red in the face now. Benjiro is looking from one visage to the other, perhaps interested in this colouring of his fair-skinned mother and grandmother.

"All that interest. It's a fortune," Cynthia protests.

"It's already a fortune," Ivy replies, hearing the querulous tone in her own voice, a faint passive-aggressive tone. She hates that tone when she hears it coming from her own throat. Hates old ladies who talk like this. She clears her throat. "What can I do, then?" Smarty-pants, she finishes mentally.

"I'll take it," Cynthia announces promptly, as if she has been waiting for this opening. She smiles her bright fake smile. She takes the cheque. "I'll deposit it. We'll decide what to do later." She seems to skip away, she moves so quickly.

Who's we? Ivy thinks, suddenly afraid. I haven't endorsed it. Surely the bank won't accept a cheque of that, or any, size without endorsement. Remembering with a vivid pinch Cynthia had learned how to forge her signature in Grade Eight. Maybe the Bank of Tokyo would also blow up today.

Their little North Vancouver bungalow that they loved and lived in for all those years. They bought it when all around them was forest on the North Shore, when the nearest house was at the bottom of the ravine, this cheque represents all Jack had to leave her. More money than even they could have dreamed. And now. Now Cynthia has taken the cheque away and it is done. What's done? Ivy touches the pages of legal document on the counter.

Benjiro looks up from his small screen.

"Seven eight nine," he declares proudly.

"Seven eight nine," Ivy agrees.

EIGHTEEN

Tokyo, Saitama Prefecture. Monday, April 23, 2007,
17°C, 40 km/hr wind

The next Monday, after ten days of hardly exchanging any words at all, Cynthia surprises her in the hallway at the peak of the morning hustle.

"Mother?" she asks, as if she wants her to get out of the way to the bathroom, or something.

Ivy tenses. Is this going to be about the cheque? She glances at her daughter, bracing herself for what's coming next. What comes next could have knocked her over.

"I wonder, I thought you might come with me today? I know we've all been so busy, you really haven't been out much."

Much? Ivy snorts indignantly and silently. *Much?* How about not at all for nearly three weeks. If I were a house-plant, I'd be dead now!

Oblivious to her mother's internal response, Cynthia continues.

"I thought we could go, well, you could go, I mean, you could come with me to school, that is, my school, where I teach. Then if you wanted we could go on to the bath."

Aside from noticing her daughter's unusual trouble with getting a sentence out, Ivy catches the welcome word bath. Beside real English Breakfast tea with real milk, a bath is on her ever-expanding wish list. Slightly above library and Lonsdale Quay market, right beside Peek Frean bird's nest cookies.

"And maybe lunch, if you wouldn't be too tired?" Cynthia flounders to a stop, just as Mikio appears in the doorway of their bedroom, fully and impeccably dressed. He gives his wife a fond nod of approval and he bows to Ivy, who begins to suspect this surprise is perhaps not the idea of her daughter.

Who cares where the idea came from. She says yes so fast they both laugh. Cynthia advises her she has only a few minutes to get ready, and they could get something at the station and Ivy is already flapping into her room to throw on anything remotely resembled clothing.

"Bathing suit?" she pokes her head out to ask, in time to catch Cynthia leaning against her husband's body. She straightens, looking at him, then turns.

"No bathing suit required, Mother. Not allowed, in fact. And the towels are provided. Just bring a washcloth."

Ivy dresses quickly, finding socks, a clean bra, her newest pair of underpants, a blouse that matches her slacks, and then she stuffs her money belt into her purse and brushes her hair. Ready. Carrying nearly five hundred dollars in Japanese currency, she is ready. She is breathless and hot, she is so excited to be doing something.

The trip through the subway station is bewildering. Benjiro is explaining something to his mother, and they are both speaking Japanese. She figures he is telling her he needs two-dozen chocolate cupcakes for school tomorrow, given how exasperated Cynthia looks. By the time the conversation ends, they are all wedged into a subway car and rattling forward. She can see little, surrounded as she is by more occupants of a subway car than she thought possible. The voice announcing stations is incomprehensible; she can't even tell what language the announcements are in. About ten minutes into this journey, with more people getting on and no one getting off, Benjiro suddenly disappears. Cynthia does not look alarmed, so Ivy assumes the boy has transferred to another line to get to his school. Or he has simply vanished into thin air, thin being the operative word. She wishes she could thin, as she feels the irrational desire to apologize for her size to all the silent, squashed riders around her.

Their stop arrives, and they are expelled with a whoosh of air. Flights of stairs later, with Ivy almost running behind her daughter, they arrive into the busiest street she has ever stood on. She hesitates and then plunges after Cynthia, afraid if she loses sight she will be lost forever. The noise. The colours. The melee.

Cynthia is heading toward a building with large neon letters apparently floating above them. The foyer provides sudden relief from the noise.

"This is where I work, Mother. This is the language school where I work."

Ivy smiles uncertainly, so Cynthia continues. "I teach English to students from around the world. They travel to Tokyo to learn Japanese, of course, and also to study English. I am on staff here."

The young people moving purposefully around must be students. Corridors lead to doors with signs and numbers. Elevators open and close constantly. It is like a small city. There is even what appears to be a food court. She spots the logos for brands recognizable from home. Just as the elevator door opens to take them away, she thinks she spots a Tim Hortons. Tea! And then they are several floors above, and Cynthia has turned into someone else.

Cynthia moves easily through the crush of people, many young and some her age, and is greeted warmly, especially by the ones Ivy thinks might be students. Cynthia is speaking in Japanese and English and — could it be French? Cynthia struggled over French classes in high school, unwilling to study, and indifferent to her steadily declining grades. French?

Even more astonishing, Cynthia introduces her to everyone. Her voice is light, warm, and she is smiling every time. Ivy is introduced in French, in Japanese, and in English. She is kissed (the French), bowed to (the Japanese) and hand-shaken. Smiles and exclamations of delight surround her and settle on her head and shoulders like so many — well — cherry blossoms. Without asking, Cynthia leads her into a room filled with students in their early twenties. These students all rise and call greetings to Cynthia, who then turns and introduces Ivy with what distinctly seems to be pride.

She doesn't know where to look or what to think. As she watches Cynthia speaking to her class, slowly, distinctly, every word beautifully enunciated, she feels as if she is glimpsing the woman Cynthia was meant to be, the woman Ivy had thought she might become once her annoying teen years were behind her. The students begin to sort themselves into groups, Cynthia turns on a computer that projects a photograph onto the screen in the corner of the room, and then says, "Mother, would you mind? The staff lounge is down one floor, turn left off the elevator, and it has a sign on it. I will be with you in fifty minutes."

Dismissed, Ivy retreats, repeating the directions, wondering if she can get down to the lobby and find the Tim Hortons. Instead, obedient to the new daughter she has encountered, she finds the staff lounge: Faculty Only. No Students. No Staff. Will someone accost her and chuck her out? She pushes open the door, and she enters a room crammed with magazines. They cover every table, there are racks of them against the wall and stacks under the copy machine. The galley kitchen displays a coffee maker, three kettles, and a large stand of tea boxes. Prominent on the counter is a large tin of cookies. She's died and gone to heaven. Fifty minutes? Leave me for the rest of the day, she proclaims.

She is sitting, holding four magazines on her lap and reading a fifth one when the door opens. She looks up, guilty, but the woman who has entered only greets her with a short word in Japanese and then Hello. She goes toward the galley then turns.

"You must be the honoured mother of our Mrs. Cynthia. You look so much like her. She is a beautiful person and you must be her mother." The woman speaks cautiously, standing with her hands folded into the sleeves of her sweater.

"I am," Ivy responds. Don't let Cynthia hear you compare us, though. That will not end well. "I am."

"I am Mrs. Yamamoto."

"I am Mrs. Birch."

"Ah, yes. The tree?"

Ivy nods, and then she rises. What happens next is something she thought could only occur in low-rent

121

American sit-coms. Mrs. Yamamoto extends her hand as Ivy bows; Ivy straightens and extends her hand as Mrs. Yamamoto bows. They both giggle, both women covering their mouths with their hands. Mrs. Yamamoto straightens, still smiling, and Ivy does too and then they both bow and then step toward each other to shake hands. Mrs. Yamamoto's hand is soft and small, like a child's, but her grip is firm.

"I am so happy to greet you, Mrs. Birch. Your daughter is a very good teacher. You must be very proud."

Ivy nods, hoping her confusion is obscured. Whoever this new Cynthia is, she is also pleased to know her.

Mrs. Yamamoto pours coffee, takes a cookie, offers one to Ivy (who takes it — her third), and excuses herself. Ivy sits down, takes up her magazines and spends the next half hour blissfully reading, drinking English Breakfast tea, and eating cookies.

Cynthia turns and Ivy sees her daughter naked for the first time since she was ten or eleven. Before she developed breasts. Once she developed breasts, Cynthia would not let herself be seen without several layers of clothes. Ivy cannot stop herself from gaping at her daughter, with her high proud little breasts, her slim unmarked torso, a scar faintly visible from her pubic hair to just below her belly button, her slender thighs, her blonde pubic hair, which does match her hair, so Ivy is confused. The hair is dyed at least on her head, isn't it?

Cynthia looks at her, sees her gawking, and turns away with a scowl. Ivy feels very naked, standing in her flip-flops, putting her clothes into the locker. Holding a small white towel the size of a face cloth, she enters the shower area in plain view of the women in the pool. The ticket taker, if she was inclined, could watch her showering.

Cynthia is scrupulously scrubbing herself. Ivy registers the meaning of the faint scar on her daughter's belly. Caesarean. At least one of her boys was delivered by Caesarean section. Ivy didn't know. She feels foolish. How could a mother not know this? The news of the arrival of her grandchildren came, as anticipated, by long distant telephone, and Ivy remembers asking, tactfully, "How was everything?" but does not recall Cynthia volunteering she had major surgery to deliver either of her sons. She remembers the giddy joy in Cynthia's voice, Mikio's cautious English, his attentive description of the first son. Only Mikio called when the second son was born, a call that began by frightening Ivy, who thought he was the doctor calling to tell her something terrible had happened. Mikio's voice was foreign, formal, and serious until he began describing this second boy, who looked just like his father.

Cynthia walks through the averted and yet probing glances of every person in the bath, and then when she enters the water, Ivy has to walk the same gauntlet of gazes. Feeling fat, dumpy, with breasts hanging so that her nipples point at the floor, she is ashamed. Shamed by the wobbles and bulges and ripples. Ashamed of the flawed porcelain of her skin. The freckles, scrapes, faint bruising and maps of veins on the back of her right knee.

She steps down quickly to immerse herself and hide her nakedness and then with a yelp leaps up again. The water is hotter than any water she has ever entered, hotter than the bath water at home — too hot to get into. Her legs flush hectic pink, and water sloshes about the pool.

"Mother," Cynthia whispers, and she begins to mime how to sluice water over her belly, her back, her breasts. She is sitting on a wooden shelf, and with the sunlight falling on her hair and then onto her body partly obscured by water, she looks so young, so hopeful.

Ivy copies Cynthia's mimed movements, and then carefully subsides into the water. Several women close to her draw away, nodding politely, talking quietly to one another.

A woman moves closer to Cynthia, and they begin to talk. Quiet is the tone, and with that and the warm air and hot water seeping into her bones, Ivy begins to breathe easier and her knee loosens up. Her breasts are floating, and she is suddenly thirteen years old and feeling fat for the first time at the seaside near Aldershot. During the war.

Searching for distraction for the creeping memory, she looks through the steamy windows at the garden. Late spring and the garden is an exquisite example of what she assumes is a Zen garden. Colour is subdued, and through the milky windows all that remains to be seen are shapes. Flowing shapes easing from one place to another. Small manicured trees assume shapes of connection. She has not noticed this connection before. Without her glasses, through the steam, through the quiet, something shifts in her vision.

She looks cautiously, to avoid gawking, at the women at her end of the pool and the men at the other. Cynthia is now sitting with a group of women, her head inclined, her hand covering her mouth, peaceful. She tries to remember when she last saw her daughter look so. The women with her are friends? She doesn't know. She knows nothing about this beautiful woman who is her only child. And the mother of her only grandchildren.

Tears pierce her eyes. Tears so sharp her breath catches. She goes to splash water over her face, to obscure the tears, then remembers her head and face are supposed to remain out of the water. Cynthia glances over, her expression soft as if the warm water has done its magic on more than Ivy's sore knee. Cynthia begins to move toward her, with two women apparently being towed in her wake. Introductions in a bath. Another first. If she bows, she better keep her face above the water.

NINETEEN

Tokyo, Saitama Prefecture. Monday, April 30, 17°C, rain

At 10:30 in the morning, she goes back to bed. She is tired anyway, the jet-lag that should have left her weeks ago is still with her, as if her internal clock cannot adjust to the fact this is 10:30 AM and not 2:30 AM. Every day stretches ahead of her, 10:00 AM feels like a hundred hours to dinner time. She rouses at noon, flustered and feeling sick, makes lunch, eats lunch, wanders around the apartment, and then goes back to bed at one. She lies on the top of the bedding for a bit, then pulls the blankets over her. Snugging them around her chin, she experiences the transitory bliss of snuggling down and waiting for sleep to claim her. She wakes at two thirty, befuddled and feeling sick. The mirror over her small dresser tells her she has creases in her face from the creases in the sheets.

She sits on the edge of her hard narrow bed, smoothing the cover with her hands, unable to put her feet on the floor. She cannot get used to the height of things in this apartment. This bed was built for someone six feet tall, and yet Mikio is not much taller than she is, and the fourteen-year-old is going to be about five foot eight perhaps, and Cynthia is at least four inches taller than Mikio, tall in this world at five foot seven, and she often wears shoes with a small heel. Ivy would never wear shoes to exaggerate her height if she were married to a man shorter than she was. It occurs to her suddenly that Cynthia's height, her white skin, her blonde hair, her English, make her a trophy wife. Was Mikio compensating by acquiring a trophy wife? Trophy wives, according to Ivy's information gleaned from entertainment shows, are supposed to be tall, thin, white, blonde, and beautiful. Cynthia.

She lies back and sleeps for another two hours or so, waking with a start, anxious not to be found in bed. It's four thirty, and Benjiro will be home soon. Then she remembers everyone would be in late, because the boys had tutorials on Mondays. She sleeps until six. The family arrives like so many shore birds, and she appears in her doorway, pretending she has been doing something. No one seems to notice her bleary eyes and mussed hair. The apartment is alive with activity for a few hours and there is no longer any talk of a walk after dinner. She sits in her corner of the couch, looking at the sky out the window, while the garish game shows play for a half hour. As is becoming her habit, she goes to her room at nine. Doing so means that at least for an hour or so everyone can speak Japanese, the tone and pace of the home relaxes, and all is well. With nothing to read and nothing to do, she finds herself crawling into bed before ten, her legs twitching and buzzing, and falls into a stunned sleep.

This night her legs buzz and her head swims with anxious thoughts, of accident, betrayal, ill health, disease, famine, death, her mind replaying mercilessly the final hours of Jack's life, the afternoon she realized he was really gone from her, did not know who she was, had forgotten how to swallow. Over and over, like some

127

demented movie. She sleeps fitfully, waking to hash over every negative thought she can find and then dropping into sleep alive with dreams.

She gets up at four thirty to pee, and she can barely walk. Her legs are trembling, she feels a roaring in her ears, she is so weak in her hands that when she uses her arms to support her as she sits down on the toilet, they fail her, and she topples noisily onto the seat and then sideways onto the floor.

Cynthia appears in the doorway with a key, annoyed, critical that Ivy has locked the door, embarrassed that her mother is sprawled on the floor with her bottom bare to the view of her grandchildren, who haven't woken up anyway.

Startled, frightened, Ivy goes back to her room and sits on the bed. She has been outside only once in nearly a month. She has not had a decent walk since they all went to the temple the day after she arrived in Tokyo. She will die, she realizes starkly, if she does not do something.

She resolves to run away.

TWENTY

Tokyo, Saitama Prefecture. Tuesday, May 1, 16°C, sunny with scattered clouds

The next morning, after everyone leaves, Ivy sits on her bed and inspects the bruise beginning to appear on her leg. It's going to be a good one, for sure. She sits for several minutes, holding her palm over the red area, and looking up at her window. Her choice is clear: she can have a nap or get up and do something about her resolution to run away.

She fetches the guidebook. In order to go somewhere, she has to have somewhere to go. She decides a museum would be a good start, because museums are designed for visitors — for foreigners. As she is, at this time. She opens the book and fans through the pages and pictures. She finds a map of the subway system. After looking at it for a few moments, she decides tea is what is needed next.

While the water comes to a boil, she stands holding the handle of the kettle, as if this will make the water boil more efficiently. Tea made, she sits on the plastic chair on the balcony and starts at the beginning of the book, "The Lie of the Land". Reading the manual, as Jack always teased her. He was the one who read the manual, all the way through, before he did anything at all.

"Tokyo is divided into 23 wards (ku). These are shown on the map on pp 60–1, with an overview of central Tokyo and the specific areas covered by this guide. All descriptions of attractions provide the name of the nearest station(s), the train and subway lines that serve that station, and the most convenient station exit(s). The street maps in the Sightseeing section start on p 57, with local sights and eating, drinking, arts and entertainment recommendations are clearly marked. See also p 8 Exploring Tokyo."

She turns to page sixty and stares at the map. She notes China in the inset area, and then locates Japan as a tiny string of islands until she realizes it is Philippines. Japan is obscured by the large red dot identified as Tokyo. So the Sea of Japan separates the island of Tokyo from China. Terrific.

She inspects the map of the wards and then locates a garden she has heard Mikio mention, Detached Garden. This garden is in Chuo-ku. She locates Chuo-ku and then realizes she will need to know exactly where she is in Saitama Prefecture to figure out how to get to Chuo-ku. She imagines what would happen if she walked to the subway nearby and attempted to get from here, wherever here is, to there. Wherever there is.

She looks up museums in the index and finds Tokyo National Museum. With a straight-forward name like that, she chooses this as her destination. The museum is in the Taito-ku ward, and she registers her smugness as she figures out how the book works. Taito-ku she locates at the top of the ward map on page sixty. There is a heading in each section that tells her "How to Get There" and she also discovers that the address of the museum includes the station, as in "Ueno station, (Yamanote line), park exit; (Ginza, Hibya lines), Shinobazu exit."

Now, if she only knew what any of that meant. She looks at the three pages of subway maps, each getting denser with information, and then spends some time sipping her tea and looking at the map of Mainland Japan. She was born in a country with a network of trains and buses and tubes once one got to London. She even has a tea-towel, had a tea-towel, of the London metro system, and she can still remember how to get around although she only went to London a dozen times. Tea finished, lunch time approaching, she finds the subway map of the Yamamoto line, which looks like a perfect oval, and she locates the station. Right, her inner cheerleader advises, now if only you knew where you were at this moment.

As if someone has tapped her lightly on the head, she hears a distinct "bing" and decides she will get dressed, leave when the housekeeper arrives, walk down to the subway station and . . . read the signs. When in doubt, read the signs. She can return, buzz the housekeeper, and get back into the apartment. No one will know, unless she fails in this simple mission and is found weeks later dead in a ditch.

Her heart is pounding so loud she can hear it in her ears. This pounding has even drowned out her constant tinnitus. Her palm lands consolingly on the bruise, which is now generating heat. The housekeeper is due in an hour or so, and thus her deadline is looming. In an hour or so she will slip away to find the name of the subway she sees from the living room window, the subway that daily swallows Mikio, Keiijiro, Benjiro and Cynthia in that order, one at a time, until they are all consumed. In order

131

to record the name, she will need paper and pen, and in order to reach the subway she'll need all the courage she can muster to wade through the stream of humans that rush toward and from that entrance every minute, like so much water charging around a storm drain in November.

A nap is beginning to look good.

The housekeeper arrives and Ivy tries to find out from her what the code is to activate the door into the building. Unable to communicate her question, she leaves, carefully noting the number on the door of the apartment. She gets into the elevator and stares with dismay at the buttons signalling floor selection. She chooses one that is at the bottom of the list on the right, hoping this is L for Lobby. She is correct, and experiences inordinate pleasure at finding herself in what she would call the lobby of the apartment building. Glass, tile, water running down the decorative wall (on purpose, Ivy determines), and then the doors. She cannot get the door to open by pushing on the bar that she assumes is the "push" bar. It has characters on it. Maybe it is "pull". Neither action works. Unable to believe she will be thwarted at the doorway, she spots and pushes a round silver button on the wall, hoping this is the automatic door opener. It is.

Both automatic doors swing slowly and fully open. She emerges from the building, blushing. She does not need this much space, is mildly embarrassed by the symbolic gesture of both doors and the expanse of space taken up when she could easily slip through an opening a quarter the size. "Wee, sleekit, cow'rin, tim'rous beastie" pops into her head, from a rhyme from her childhood, indeed her mother's childhood. Not even sleek, she acknowledges, as she steps into the booming environment of the street. She clutches one of the handrails on the wall of the apartment building entrance. Her legs are trembling, her wrist trembles, she can feel the wattles on her chin wobbling. She is a country mouse, daunted by the roar of traffic revealed by these slowly opening large glass doors. A Vancouver mouse, formerly an Aldershot mouse, originally a Leeds mouse. The doors slowly, eerily close behind her, finally clicking resolutely closed.

She advances, wanting nothing more than to return to her basket of crochet in the chair by the balcony window, the basket she is supposed to leave in her room. If she cannot successfully navigate this venture, she will be caught having left her personal "stuff" in the public space. She clears the overhang of the building, emerging into the light rain that manifests as large splashes on her unprotected head. Her hair will be as flat as a pancake; she will look — as her mother frequently observed when Ivy returned to the house after "walking out" and feeling quite glamorous — like a drowned rat. When she gets back, and she will get back, she will have to dry her hair and fluff it so Cynthia will not wonder how it is that her mother has wet hair — since she officially has not yet mastered the shower mechanism in the bathroom.

She reaches the street, discovering a large parking lot crammed with scooters. People are either driving in (scooting in? she wonders) or driving out, or standing around smoking. Several glance in her direction, nothing registering in their gazes. This she will have to become accustomed to. No one shows any emotion, as if it is an ordinary occurrence for a little old white lady to appear on the pavement as if shot from a nerf gun inside the apartment building.

She traverses the parking lot, steps onto the narrow sidewalk, looks right and left, and then sees the Tokyo Metro sign on a pole about twenty feet away. The pole has about ten signs on it, in several different languages, or at least that's the way it looks. She crosses a set of trolley tracks, inexplicably embedded in the pavement, reaches the island in the centre of the two-lane road, and waits for the light to change to green.

The traffic lights are horizontal, with what looks like green on the left. She searches for a Walk sign or something that might resemble a Walk sign. Irresistibly she conjures the racist cartoons of Japanese — Japs — from the newspapers and posters of her childhood in England. These cartoons always featured the men walking in an exaggerated manner, and she super-imposes the cartoon onto the bright yellow hand that reminds her not to cross. The red light flashes yellow and then green is lit. The cars stop in several directions, but no cartoon figure or any other kind of walking symbol appears. She does hear an insistent beeping, and she elects to scuttle across the street, hoping the beeping means she can walk safely or as safely as possible under the circumstances. Hoping that a random left or right turn arrow she cannot see is not directing vehicles toward her, she arrives triumphantly at the small sidewalk at the other side. Crossed! And not dead!

Finding the entrance to the metro is not hard, because the flow of people resembles nothing more than fall leaves flowing down a drain. She falls into step, walks about twenty feet, automatic doors whoosh open and she is swept through.

Okay. She breathes. Okay. She hears several phrases that she will come to recognize as, "*Sumimasen.* Excuse me. I'm sorry," because while pausing she has set herself as an obstacle to the crowd. Attempting to get out of various paths, she remembers the controlled chaos of Euston Station, and she edges toward a wall. Oddly, she hears Alastair Sim's, "Label. Label. Label." His chant as he searches for a way to direct the turkey he has purchased, after three visits from Christmas Past, Present, and Future. "Label. Label. Label," she mutters as she looks around. She sees no huge helpful sign suspended over the heads rushing by. No huge sign that says, "You are here." She suspects approaching a helpful stranger, even if she were to find one slowing down sufficiently to ask, "Where am I?" would yield nothing of value. Where am I, indeed?

While she's scanning for huge signs, she is noticing lots of English expressions. There is a huge poster nearby, with a cartoon of a young woman applying mascara with a wand — a practice she always thought was down-right dangerous when she observed young women applying mascara with a poky-wand while riding one of Vancouver's trolley buses. Did they expect there would not be an abrupt halt in their near future? This poster, she is comforted to see, has plenty of English in it. Next she sees the machines that can only be ticket dispensers. If there were to be an abatement of the queue to purchase a ticket, she might venture closer to see if there is a sign on the machine. No abatement is evident. She leans slightly against the wall, her legs trembling for real now. She feels the way she did when she toppled over on the toilet. Is she about to faint — carrying no identification, no credit card, nothing? What was she thinking? Her heart starts to rattle in her chest. She sticks her hand in her sweater pocket and discovers, like all ladies everywhere, as her mother always advised, she has a small embroidered handkerchief to hand. With her initial on it, she can tell by running her thumb over the surface she knows — well — like the back of her hand. She is not going to faint. She is not even going to swoon, equipped as she is with a handkerchief to press to her brow. She is not going to faint, or even stumble.

Because she is going to stand against this wall for the rest of her life.

She stares at the map of the subway system with dismay. She blinks rapidly and looks around the station, seeking perhaps Benjiro. He rides the subway every day to his private school. He'd know what to do. She has been cheerfully informed by the guidebook that they provide a subway map for dummies, so she is further alarmed at the complexity of this map, surely a map for smart people? She's heard tales about the fate of tourists who venture into Tokyo Metro, never to be seen again. The London A to Z looked like a map of the grid-like structures of Vancouver compared to this. She can't even figure out what line she needs to get to Asakusa, which is supposed to be "the historic district with the olde world flavour." Setting her sites on the Tokyo National Museum for her first foray seems now like an idea for — well — for dummies.

The map of the Tokyo Metro system covers one whole wall, and it appears to be moving or movable. Maybe if she touches it, she will find the "You are here" icon. Beside her is a plastic display holding pamphlets that can only be subway guides. She recognizes the format from the Sea Bus terminal in Vancouver. She turns, fondling her handkerchief and she finds among all the languages presented one UK English and one US English. Not daring to quibble where is the Canadian English, which draws a flicker of a smile on her face, she takes up the *UK English Guide to Tokyo Metro*. She has a guide, she identifies the ticket barrier, which looks exactly like the one for Vancouver's Sky Train, although it is, mysteriously, in two different colours. She finds these same colours on the ticket dispenses — ah, like the Oyster card in London. I can buy a pass, a ticket, or go to the kiosk and do either. Except there is no kiosk. Above the ticket dispenser is a row of hanging signs, small, a poster about — destinations?

But where is here? Baffled and aware her whole body is starting to flag with the unexpected activity of trying to figure out a metro station, she turns. She has to go back to the apartment before the housekeeper leaves. She has to get back. As she turns, she spots, above the entrance, which is obviously also the exit, Japanese characters, English numbers, and Wakoshi Y01 and then a word that is the name of the street she just came off. Wakoshi? Wakoshi. This must be it — and maybe the numbers are important too. They'd better be, because she feels as if she is a sand-dial, and her sand is just about running out. She'll be lucky if all she turns into is a pumpkin.

Wakoshi, Wakoshi, Wakoshi, she recites under her breath, adding a tune. If she were not seventy-eight, she might even be skipping a bit. Wakoshi. She's done it. And the metro station has many features she recognizes, so she feels, amid the signals of fatigue, optimism. She can do this. Maybe. But first, she has to get out of here, back across the street, and down the block, past the scooter parking lot, and into the apartment.

Emerging from the metro station, she faces the way she came, but the path's unfamiliar. She cannot return the way she came if she cannot recognize anything, so she resolves in future to turn frequently to see what "behind" looks like. Jack taught her this trick when he was teaching her how to navigate the streets around their first apartment at 10th and Oak Street in Vancouver. The old houses converted into rooming houses and the small apartment blocks all looked the same to her, and she would get lost easily. He taught her to turn around and look the way she had come, so she would recognize her way home. Freezing in fear and then, through the glimmer of fear, picking out the tall post with ten or more directional signs, reminding her of the wishful directional signpost on *M.A.S.H.* What direction would the sign Vancouver point? And if she followed the point, would she find her way home?

When she turns into the wide entry to the apartment building, the open door is slowly closing. With every bit of her remaining strength, she scurries forward in a lurching run, and manages to get through the door before it closes. Elevator, third floor, turn left, no, turn right, numbers ascending, and then she taps on the door, waits a few moments, taps again, and the housekeeper opens the door, smiles politely, and she has survived.

The housekeeper leaves, after making her a cup of tea. Both women smile and nod and bow, and the door to the apartment closes and she subsides on the corner of the sofa, holding her tea in one hand, and touching the talisman of her crochet hook with the other. She takes a big breath and exhales loudly in this empty, silent apartment. She looks out the window at the metro station and sees, in large letters, Wakoshi.

The next step is to get out the guidebook, which she has left on her bed, consult the subway map and figure out how to get from here, Wakoshi station, to the museum.

She sleeps.

TWENTY-ONE

Tokyo, Saitama Prefecture. Wednesday, May 2, 15°C, cloudy

The next day, her legs are stiff and her feet hurt when she gets out of bed. She feels the way athletes must feel the day after the marathon. I've done myself in!

The clatter in the kitchen assures her everyone is out of the bathroom for now. She hobbles in, pees, peeks in the mirror then endeavours to walk without limping down the hall toward the morning buzz.

"Mother? Why are you limping?" That sharp-eyed daughter has missed nothing.

"I — just — my toe. I kicked my toe when I got up. Nothing — "

Cynthia exhales loudly, fetches a box of Band-Aids and hands them over.

"Nothing bleeding. Nothing broken. No bother," Ivy repeats Jack's chant from Cynthia's childhood, hoping Cynthia will smile in recognition

No such luck.

She settles out of the way in the sitting room. Mikio leaves. The door barely clicks behind him when Keiijiro also heads off, tossing barbs in Japanese at his mother. It is not necessary to know Japanese to know this is a "you haven't had breakfast I'm not hungry you have to eat no I don't" exchange, and then he escapes, the little creatures bobbing on his knapsack, somewhat undermining the intensity of his "don't bother me" exit.

Today is not a good day to ask about the door codes.

More exits. No housekeeper will come today, Cynthia informs her as she leaves. We will all be home late is her final comment. Ivy is alone.

Without the codes for the apartment door and the building door.

She hobbles to the couch to sit down. It is not even 8:00 AM, and the day stretches ahead of her. Buoyed by her success getting to the subway — WAKOSHI the sign cheerfully informed her — she also recognizes she is very weak from her month of inactivity. She could spend the day walking up and down the hallway, but after one turn (thirty paces) she decides that is a bad idea. Her feet are very sore, the way they were when she had a bout of plantar fasciitis. That's all she needs, she tells herself, looking in the bathroom mirror. At least the pain in her feet has made the pain in her knee less noticeable.

She takes up one of the remotes. Will she find the Tokyo equivalent of *Coronation Street*? This remote has letters on it, and the words and symbols are English. She presses POWER. Nothing happens. She presses INPUT. Nothing happens. SYNC MENU PREV STOP NEXT are mysteries. She presses the POWER button again and suddenly sound comes from the TV. No picture but definitely sound. Music, even. Has she found the equivalent of CBC radio? In her excitement she presses another button and there is a flash on the TV and then nothing. The music has stopped.

It is quarter after eight.

141

By some minor miracle, at four thirty, on schedule, her younger grandson appears in the kitchen. She has been sitting for hours, rotating her aching feet on her ankles, flexing her fingers, crocheting, and trying buttons on the remote. She has also, she supposes, been in a sort of meditative state for some time, because the last time she registered time, it was one thirty. Nevertheless, here he is. She is not willing to question the miracle.

And she has a devious impulse. There must be a certain place in the afterlife for grandparents who take advantage of their grandchildren. She looks at this boy, who is looking at her as he is about to disappear into his room. He already has his phone in his hand. But for whatever reason, he looks expectant. Maybe this young Japanese fellow has a streak of the Celtic second-sight.

"Benjiro," she says, trying not to sound like the witch in Hansel and Gretel, "Would you like to go out and get some ice cream?" She has deliberately added "out" in case her clever daughter has a freezer somewhere with ice cream in it.

Benjiro does the Japanese equivalent of whooping with joy. Yes, he would, yes, let's go! Before she knows what is happening, they are standing in the hallway, and she is clutching a handful of Japanese currency. Benjiro suddenly seems daunted by the expedition, so she smiles confidently and offers him her hand. He takes it and together they set off to transgress several boundaries.

For example, it turns out there is a code for the building door so only one door swings open. She makes a mental note to write down what it is, although in the meantime she feels like a spy, watching his fast fingers on the number pad.

"Is it the same numbers coming in?" she inquires innocently, and the boy shrugs. What? They are trapped on the street with no way back in? He probably does not understand what she means, "The same numbers coming in." She barely understands that sentence herself. She will worry about the numbers when they get back to the building. At the moment, she is trying also to figure out how to persuade this lovely chap not to tell his mother — or more likely his brother — that his grandmother has broken a few rules and bought him ice cream before dinner.

It's an escapade!

The street, which seemed so puzzling yesterday, turns into a perfect straight line to the metro station. For an awful moment, she thinks they have to take the subway to get ice cream, but it turns out, when they get into the station, there is a mall-like array of shops angling off away from the ticket dispensers that had all of her attention the day before. They are both captured by all the goods on display in these shops; many of them feature candy, snacks, and small objects of desire. Benjiro has been speaking Japanese to her non-stop since they entered the station, and all she can do is nod and smile. She hopes she is not agreeing to buy him everything they both see. He is fixed, however, on ice cream and leads her into a section of the corridor that looks a lot like a food court at home. One of the stalls is selling ice cream cones, according to the pictures festooning the stall. The young woman facing them smiles at her and then addresses Benjiro. He says something to Ivy and she nods. The nod earns them both the biggest ice cream cones she has ever seen, and hers has at least three flavours. Benjiro's has more, and the grin he has could take in the whole top of the cone in one bite. Way too much ice cream for any single person, and way too much before dinner, but there you are. Ivy holds out her money, and Benjiro picks through it to select a bill. They receive coins and bills in exchange; she hopes he has not given the clerk the equivalent of a $100 bill.

Lumbered with these giant cones, it seems only sensible to continue walking and looking at the shops. Benjiro is still chattering to her in Japanese and he now has ice cream all over his face — no really — ALL over his face and down his school uniform. For he did not change before they set out, and she is sure they have broken another rule. At a certain point, she takes out her handkerchief and tidies up his face, and he smiles at her and then says, distinctly, "Thank you. Thank you for the ice. Thank you."

All is well. Now for the devious part of the plan. It happens that Benjiro's hands are sticky from ice cream and he asks her to enter the code. Which of course she is delighted to do. She compliments him on his English numbers, writes them down, and then enters them. The door opens. It is magic. Her grand plan has worked, and worth it even if she will have to spend eternity with similarly devious grandparents.

They get to the apartment door and Benjiro produces a fob that looks like something to open a fancy car. He waves the fob at the key-pad and the click tells her the fob is the key required to get into the apartment.

They have returned in time for Benjiro to change out of his uniform, giving her a chance to give it a damp facecloth treatment before he puts it away. She supervises his face and hand washing, and when the clicks of family members arriving begin, the two of them are sitting together on the couch, looking at one of his school books. She composes her face to persuade herself and everyone else they have been here the whole time, just as Benjiro, in precise English, tells his brother triumphantly Ivy has bought him the Colossal Cone, pronouncing it as if it were a thing, which Ivy supposes it must be, because where would this little fellow get those words if they were not the title of an item. It was a Colossal Cone, certainly.

Keiijiro does a very good impression of "tell someone who cares" and Cynthia simply smiles and tells Benjiro that he is lucky, because dinner is going to be late. Ivy cannot determine whether Cynthia has either not heard him or she really does not mind they have taken themselves out for ice cream.

She has the code. Now she just needs the fob.

TWENTY-TWO

Tokyo, Saitama Prefecture. Thursday, May 3, 22°C, cloudy

She will have to get her strength back before she attempts taking the subway to the museum. Aware she may be procrastinating, knowing how daunted she is by the thought of taking the subway anywhere, let along to a selected destination, she also knows her legs are weak and her feet are sore just from the short walks she's taken over the past two days.

So she embarks on a training plan. The housekeeper arrives and Ivy departs. Out the door, carrying her shoes, taking the elevator downstairs, she sits on the bench-like couch in the lobby to tie her runners. Runners. As if.

Out the door she goes. Recalling the strategies she learned when she arrived in Vancouver in 1947, she rehearses the turns.

Walk to the end of the apartment's walkway. Turn right. Walk to the first corner, turn right. If this works, she will continue to turn right until she comes upon the apartment building. Turn right again.

She hits a small dead-end street. Like a lane. Several small doors open onto the lane, and she hears the sounds of shops and restaurants. The end of the lane is a garbage bin. The pavement is broken, the buildings frayed on their corners.

She retreats. She walks another two-hundred feet and discovers a small strip mall — five or six shops in a concrete setback in the roadway. Traffic noises assault her, for beyond the small lot is a multi-lane roadway. It looks like Taylor Way on steroids, is what comes to mind. Well, she's not turning right out there. She walks ten feet farther and turns around, frustrated. There's no *there* here, she mutters to herself. How can people walk in this town? She hasn't gone far enough to be out of sight of the apartment block. All the apartment blocks.

This will never do, she declares, hearing her mother's expression of exasperation and determination. She retreats to the apartment building, hoping no one is noticing. She'll get taken in for aimless wandering. All right. Turn left. She passes the scooter parking lot, a car lot of some kind, a taxi stand, a stable for garbage trucks, a building of some bureaucratic nature, the glass shows her what looks like an official library. No one in it but a woman at a desk. A library?

Next is another cluster of apartment buildings and then a roadway. Left. The back end of the cluster, a small gravel lot with a short fence for dogs, according to the cartoon-like signs, a set of four shops of what looks like car equipment and building supplies and then a left turn.

By now, she is tired. Her head hurts. Her feet hurt. The pavement is uneven and her stride awkward. She is afraid she'll fall, or plunge into the busy road. She feels hot. She hears herself whining and smiles. Norma should see her now. And no cup of tea on offer at the food fair next to Sears.

Feeling foolish, hoping no one is watching, she retraces her turns and lands at the apartment door. She enters the numbers and the single door swings slowly open. She and a hoard of bad guys could enter. Should she stand guard until the door closes completely? She taps at the apartment door and is admitted. Smelly, hot, dishevelled, she forgets and wears her shoes right into her room.

She has been out for twenty minutes.

She re-groups, after sitting on her bed for what seems like an hour, mustering the energy and moves to take off her shoes. She spends the afternoon tidying herself and cleaning up the mess she made wearing her shoes into the flat. When she puts her shoes on the racks by the door, she sees how dirty they are, with bits of pavement and dirt on them. Then, at three or so, she subsides on the sofa and soon drifts into what she considers is a well-earned snooze. As she slips into sleep she has a sharp-as-crystal idea: she will ask Cynthia for a key fob when Mikio is nearby.

TWENTY-THREE

Tokyo, Saitama Prefecture. Friday, May 11, 18°C, sunny

Ivy is startled to hear someone buzzing the intercom, the intercom she has not learned to operate. She approaches it as it buzzes again — imperiously — and experiences the small triumph of figuring out the foreign symbols. As she waits at the door, she smiles down at her slippers. Foreign symbols. Actually, not foreign. The person reading the symbols is foreign, certainly.

The trunk has arrived. It takes up an alarming amount of space in her bedroom. The two fellows smile at her and then register dismay at her lack of Japanese. Hand gestures, smiles and nods do the trick, and they retreat, trunkless and also tipless, if they expected one for bringing this large brass-bound trunk up the elevator to the apartment.

Yes. The trunk is brass bound. Heavy metal and brass secure the leather straps holding all that remains of her life in Vancouver. When she opens this trunk and empties it, she will have everything she will have. It will be too late then to realize she left behind some artifact that means more than everything else. If she doesn't open the trunk, this potential discovery will never be made. She cannot close her bedroom door because the trunk takes up so much space. She backs into the bathroom, as if the trunk were a treasure chest protected by poisonous snakes. How long could a snake live in a trunk that has been travelling by ship across so many miles? Or has it. How did it get here?

She looks at the small mirror over the sink. How did I get here? She wanders toward the kitchen area, trying to decide what to do. The trunk needs to be opened, certainly, and before Benjiro arrives home from school. Experiencing shame, as usual, she goes back down the hallway to confront the behemoth lurking in the doorway of her bedroom. And — just as she feared — the door to the apartment opens and Benjiro enters.

"Good afternoon, Obaasan," he greets her as he has been taught. He stands facing her, his small body overshadowed by the size of his backpack. As she is standing next to his bedroom door, they appear to be at an impasse. He has no more words in English, they both know it, beyond formal greeting words and random vocabulary.

She says, "Excuse me," and turns to confront the trunk. "Excuse me," he echoes, and she feels the tremor of sorrow she always feels whenever she hears his small voice repeating words she has used, words he does not understand.

Maybe she will find something in the trunk he will appreciate. She unlocks the padlock and unfastens the straps. Benjiro has joined her to peer into it. Magically, among the stuff on top, are two board games, Monopoly and Sorry. The Monopoly game is taped shut but the Sorry game is not, so as she lifts them the board and pieces shoot out onto the floor. This makes Benjiro laugh, and when Ivy says, "Oops," and "Oh, dear," he repeats the words between snorts of laughter. They find themselves crouched on the floor, locating the game pieces and the mechanism that makes the game work. Sorry, indeed. Benjiro gets the board open in the hallway as she turns back to the plethora of items in the top layer, so much stuff, so many colours, textures, smells, her head is whirling. Memories surge toward her, as if she has unstopped the genii's bottle. The garden, the birds, the cat, Jack standing before the failed strawberry bed, discussing its demise with the slugs.

She puts her hands on the top layer, as if to stopper everything, listening to Benjiro chattering to her in Japanese, as he rights the board and assembles the pieces. Does he like board games? Is that possible, given the cell phone and video games everyone his age plays? Apparently yes. Well, she will teach him to play Sorry. Starting with how to pronounce the name of the game.

"Benjiro, would you like to play Sorry?" she asks, then realizes, as he continues to play with the pieces on the floor, he has understood nothing she has said, including his name. She taps his shoulder and he looks up. He does have the most lovely face, all open and goofy, with his missing teeth and big adult teeth making him appear bucktoothed. Like cartoons from the 1940s and 1950s, before common sense and decency obscured the racism the West held for Japan. She touches his chin gently.

"Want to play?" she tries again, holding up the Monopoly game.

He bounces to his feet, scattering the game pieces again. "Oops," he says, giggling.

"Oops," Ivy agrees.

He retrieves all the pieces, checking every so often to see that she has not put down the other game, anxious, she realizes, her attention might stray away from this unexpected offer. He is speaking Japanese, bundling all the pieces into his small hands. Pieces go everywhere again, and he says, "Oh, dear" so eerily similar to Ivy's expression they both laugh again.

They play Sorry. The coloured pieces, the dice in the plastic bubble that makes a satisfying snap when pressed: this might be the best part for Benjiro. He takes to the game, counting in English and coaching her to count in Japanese. He understands the objective, and when he lands on one of her men he methodically pegs it all the way back to the start, saying sorry every move. They have such fun, time flies along and it is Cynthia coming through the door carrying the fixings for dinner.

"Oh, I remember that game." She smiles at her son. "Sorry," she proclaims, not sounding the least bit sorry. Benjiro laughs and repeats the word as Keiijiro appears, causing everyone to laugh. As the laughter subsides, Cynthia tell her boys, "Mum and I would play that when we travelled. Mum had a small folding set. We would play Sorry while we waited in restaurants, in train stations, sometimes on the bus." This memory is lost on her sons, who are moving in three directions at once, it seems. The memory, and the softness it brings to Cynthia's face, is not lost on her. Nor is Cynthia's use of the word Mum.

After dinner, Benjiro goes to the trunk and comes back with the Monopoly set and Jack's lead soldiers. Canadian and Japanese. Before Ivy can stop him, he has the soldiers on the table. They are beautiful. She has always admired their intricate detail. Jack spent a lot of money on them and searched for rare ones to add to his collection. All she can do is mix them up as Benjiro sets them down, hoping no one will notice. Why Jack wanted Japanese soldiers was a mystery to her. He belonged to a group of military historians, and he would often take over the dining room table to set up a well-documented battle of the Second World War — that is, the war in the Pacific. Sometimes, she would find one or two Canadian soldiers set before twenty or so Japanese soldiers. In formation. Or twenty Canadian soldiers confronting two or three Japanese soldiers. She never asked. Did not know what memory Jack was enacting, what purpose these tableaux served.

Ivy opens the Monopoly game to distract Benjiro. He's entranced with the money and the cards. She finds the tokens, and shows him how to set up — one for him and one for her. She chooses the small ornament, a cat Cynthia gave her for her birthday when Cynthia was only five. The ornament has "Made in Japan" stamped on the bottom. She picks up the soldiers by the handful, indicates he could pick one to have as his "man." Although it's late and his attention is flagging, Benjiro listens patiently as she explains the game. They invent two more players, and Benjiro picks out the top hat for his second man and then hands Ivy the milk can. By the time they are organized to play, Cynthia is making throat noises that signal bedtime. Benjiro has transformed the capitalist board game into a form of Sorry, and soon there are several of Jack's soldiers stationed at key points. When Cynthia makes her expectations clearer, Benjiro reluctantly leaves the board, looking at it as if to memorize it.

"Tomorrow," she promises. "We'll play again tomorrow."

"Sorry," Benjiro says. Does he mean he is sorry or they will play Sorry or just what? He is tired, the poor gaffer, and so is she. Tonight going to bed early and trying to find something to do will not be a challenge.

As his son starts the many steps required to get into his bed, Mikio is looking at the board. Ivy is collecting the play money and putting it into slots when he picks up a soldier and holds it close to his eyes. Then another. And another. She wants to sweep them all into the box before he can figure out what he is about to figure out.

"Very beautiful," he says. He holds up one. "What uniform is this?"

"Canadian," she replies, still herding the tokens into their spot.

Mikio nods, his gaze now toward the glass doors that lead to darkness. He holds the Canadian soldier in his palm, looking out the window. His face gives nothing away, and he nods again. He puts the piece down on the board. He says, "Canadian," but so softly she might have imagined it.

Twenty-Four

Tokyo, Saitama Prefecture. Saturday, May 12, 20°C, overcast

She slept "like a log" after the exertion of yesterday, including the evening board games with Benjiro. A good night's sleep and noodles for breakfast are enough to resolve her faith in the world. A good cup of tea could always revive her, and the fun she had the night before buoys her as she greets the housekeeper and then goes out into the big wide world.

Once again, walking the block, such as it is, takes less than ten minutes. There are several apartment blocks like Cynthia's on the other side of the daunting multi-lane street. How do those people get to the metro station? While she's standing there, a man appears almost at her elbow. Like ants, people are stepping, somehow, from thin air. Emerging, probably, from an underground passage. She goes around to the side of this ant colony and looks down at more of those posters with pictures she has seen in the subway.

Checking the time, she decides to go against the flow of pedestrians and descend the steps. Eight steps and she is in a tunnel, with clearly marked lanes for people with and people without wheels. Prams and bikes and the like. Arrows tell her which way to go and she sets off. Her legs feel wobbly, and the change of lighting makes her dizzy but the escapade is giving her the courage to ignore her symptoms of inactivity. She walks for several minutes, often overtaken by pedestrians coming up behind her and edging her against the wall so they can pass. It's like getting into the moderate speed lane at the pool, by mistake. Still, even slow walkers deserve to walk.

She feels like one of those marmots on Vancouver Island, blinking as she emerges into the daylight on the other side of the roadway. Here, streets look like streets, with apartment blocks, with shops at street level. She sees the international sign for pharmacy, a stall with a display of fruit and vegetables, a fluorescent pair of scissors and a comb, a pair of chopsticks, crossed (which she knows is a no-no but maybe not on signs) and then she runs out of apartment blocks and turns right. Across another busy but not quite so busy road is a park. It has a waist-high fence and a tangle of brush that looks like wild roses. A road she can manage, if she can find the walk signal, and once across she can find her way into the park.

She checks her watch, and her level of energy and realizes she has to turn back. Feeling proud, though, and curious to explore those little shops — the day after tomorrow.

Once again, she enters the building with the code she has purloined from her grandson, and taps on the apartment door so the housekeeper can let her in. She knows this grand scheme will bite her one day, and maybe tonight she *will* ask for her own fob. In the meantime, she's in, with shoes deposited where they belong, her house slippers on, her bathroom needs attended to, lunch possible (noodles, again), and then — a well-earned nap.

Ivy wakes up at the sound of Benjiro coming into the flat. She quickly assumes her position on the sofa, her crocheting to hand. She is used to his plopping down beside her on the floor and opening his reading book with gusty sighs of resignation. They are supposed to speak English from the time he comes home until dinner, but often they converse in an odd mixture of English, his fractured English, and Japanese. Every time she tries Japanese, he giggles, covering his mouth and looking down. He looks so cute, she cannot help laughing and does not mind that he is making fun of her.

Today, however, he says something from the other end of the apartment, and she says, "Yes," although she has no idea what he is saying. It did sound like a question. Benjiro appears before her as she pretends to concentrate on a long row of crochet. He is holding a book, waiting. Benjiro is holding the *Collins Adventure Annual* she left on the edge of her bed. This book, a vestige of Jack's childhood, is battered and the spine is soft with age. On the cover is a colour picture of an Indian paddling a painted canoe. The Indian has a necklace of shells; a band about his shorn head holds what looks like a seagull feather, and his bare torso is partly covered by a shawl of many colours. He has a circlet of metal — silver? — clasped around his bicep. The water reflects the colours of the canoe, the sunset sky is gold and crimson, and a similarly painted canoe prow is behind him. It is a fabulous picture, and Benjiro traces the outline of the canoe in mystified awe. She knows she does not have nearly enough talent in English to begin to explain this picture to him. A picture from an imagined past in a country so far from him it might as well be Mars,

157

a picture that romanticized what Ivy came to learn was the truth about Indigenous peoples in Canada, a picture so laden with meaning it needed a ladle.

She opens the book, and discovers many more inscrutable illustrations. Benjiro is sitting so close he'd be in her lap if he were about two years younger. These pictures are intriguing, and she can feel his breath on her arm as he attempts to get closer. She hands him the book and puts her arm around his shoulder so the big book is across his legs and one of hers. He begins to speak softly in Japanese, tracing with his finger the pen-and-ink illustrations and then the nearby words, as if searching for meaning in the letters. The pages are loosely attached to the old binding and begin to come out as they inspect the book. Benjiro stops at a page with a dramatic pen-and-ink rendition of a man leading a horse across a log bridge over a canyon, facing a snake rearing to strike. Benjiro traces the picture while she tries to read the words to explain what is going on.

" . . . *yawning gulf, watching the turmoil of broken water racing through the narrow channel. A great tree trunk spanned the abyss from side to side . . . worn flat by the passage of generations of trailing Indians . . . the long brown sinister body of a rattlesnake gliding slowing towards him . . . Instantly the startled pony flung up her head, pawing nervously with her forefeet and snorting as she staggered unsteadily backward, tugging wildly at the halter rope. Then she reared, stood on her hind hoofs, missed her foothold and, stumbling, plunged over into the abyss . . .* "

No point reading any of that to this little fellow, even if he could understand. Let him learn the true story when he has English and is old enough to read it himself.

"This is a bridge," Ivy taps the log. "It is a tree."

She puts her fingertip on the sentence. "And this is a deep canyon. The horse and the man are crossing and a snake is coming toward them."

Benjiro is whispering, repeating her words. Snake. Horse. Tree. She bends her head to hear him.

"The man is leading his horse over the bridge. He is a cowboy."

"Cowboy," Benjiro says loudly, smiling. "Cowboy."

Well, one out of five or six ain't bad. She finishes the story with an impossibly happy ending, featuring the snake carefully going one way and the cowboy and his horse going the other. The fact the next page features the cowboy clinging to a rock in a raging river, after shooting the snake, spooking the horse, and falling off the bridge himself is lost on Benjiro, who turns the page back to the compelling image of the cowboy, the bridge, the horse, and the snake.

What kind of vocabulary is this for a Japanese child in Grade Four?

Benjiro wiggles even closer and they move on to "When Timmy turned . . . " which features a masked man with a revolver climbing onto a train caboose.

TWENTY-FIVE

Tokyo, Saitama Prefecture. May 20, 28°C, sunny

After breakfast on Sunday morning, Cynthia advises her, in the hallway by her bedroom, today they are going to have dinner with Mikio's family.

"This is a rather formal visit, Mother," Cynthia is almost whispering. "Do you have something nice to wear? A dress?"

Alarmed, Ivy backs into her bedroom and they both survey the trunk that yet again she promises she will empty so they can get it into storage in the basement. She finds a dress she bought a few months ago. It still has the tags on it, and she is afraid it might not even fit. It is a summer dress, with a pattern of wildflowers on a dark green background. It is a shirtwaist dress, and it does fit. With her only pair of sensible heels, she looks quite presentable. Not only to her own eyes but apparently to Mikio, who smiles when he sees her coming toward him, even though she is wearing her shoes and not carrying them. Cynthia appears, inspects her mother, goes back into her bedroom and emerges with a lovely dark green stole.

The boys are wearing dress shirts, grey trousers, and ties. Benjiro is also carrying the travel Sorry game.

They are off, looking like a family going to church. Cynthia tells her they are travelling by metro and then taking a short ride on the train. In the station, Ivy watches everyone, trying to catch how tickets are purchased. Each member of the family steps up to a dispenser, moving so quickly she cannot see anything except they are buying from the pink dispensers. She files that away. Pink it is, then.

Mikio approaches, holding out a small pink plastic card. "Here is your card," he tells her. "I have loaded it for you."

She wants to hug him. They have no idea how happy this little grey-haired grandma is at this moment, with the resolution to one big hurdle to getting to the museum. Her son-in-law, bless him, has just given her the keys to the kingdom. Well, perhaps not the keys, she still has to get those, but the pass to the kingdom certainly.

Now she has her own card, she is coached through the process of tapping in. Benjiro takes delight in explaining, mostly in English, what she has to do and she is excited to learn without anyone knowing exactly why she wants to learn.

Even if the rest of the day is a total bust, this acquisition has made her happy.

And the rest of the day is somewhat of a total bust. Benjiro and Ivy play Sorry on the metro and on the train. The train travels so fast she cannot catch the scenery. They seem to be passing through tunnels between buildings crowded very close to the tracks. Once again she is struck by the absence of green, of trees, of any vestige of nature, and that's all she gathers in the breakneck speed of the

161

train. Just as Benjiro crows Sorry and painstakingly moves her man back to Start, they arrive.

A man about Mikio's age, with a similar impassive demeanour, greets them on the platform. Everyone bows. Ivy is introduced. Everyone bows again and they set off. Cynthia tells her they will be speaking Japanese and she will translate when necessary. This man is Number One Son. He lives with his wife and children near his parents. They live with her mother. They walk for about ten minutes, making Ivy glad she has almost two weeks of walking-to-the-metro training behind her. The area they are passing through is a mixture of small one-car-width streets with no sidewalks and larger roadways with apartment buildings. They enter a four-storey block much older than the one Cynthia lives in.

While everyone is taking off shoes at the doorway, a man and woman about her age stand waiting in the sitting room. This apartment is more like those in movies and magazines; sliding panels of wood and heavy paper divide and create larger spaces. The boys step forward, Keiijiro first and then Benjiro. Both are very subdued; both bow deeply. Benjiro holds the folded Sorry game behind his back. Cynthia steps forward and greets these two, who look at her with cold eyes. They barely bend as they bow. Cynthia slips aside and Mikio steps forward. He bows also, very deeply, and then straightens. The woman, who must be his mother, narrows her eyes and looks him up and down. She says something to him. Mikio replies. It sounds like a criticism and an apology, although obviously she doesn't know for certain. This is not one of those times Cynthia needs to translate.

162

It is Ivy's turn. Mikio speaks to his parents for several seconds, then turns. Ivy also steps forward, and everyone freezes. She was going to bow, but it seems they were not and she doesn't know what this means. Mikio's father extends his hand, the left one, and Mikio's mother tucks her hands into the sleeves of her sweater. Ivy does not need a textbook in cross-cultural communication to understand what is happening.

They sit, everyone on the floor except her. She is given a chair produced from behind one of the sliding panels. Three boys in their early teens appear, there is more bowing and greeting, but friendlier now, and then they disappear taking Benjiro and Keiijiro with them.

The room is large, the furniture is beautiful, and one ceramic bowl is on a stand in the corner. The mat on the wooden floor looks like woven grass and it is also beautiful. Ivy looks at her hands, then smooths the fabric of her dress over her thighs. Cynthia is sitting so she can only see her profile. The colour has come up into her cheeks, as she listens to Mikio and Mikio's brother talk with their father. Mikio's mother is silent, and she is staring fixedly at Cynthia, who does not look toward her.

Ivy wishes the floor would open up and swallow her. She is miserable.

Mikio says something in English to her, but she does not understand. She turns to Cynthia, who is now looking at the ceramic bowl as if trying to conjure a genii.

At that moment, an elderly woman appears. Everyone stands up, quickly, and bows. The old lady waves her hand dismissively at them, and she makes straight for Ivy. She gets very close, her eyes cloudy with cataracts, and looks at her face as if looking for bugs. Ivy is still, letting herself

163

be inspected. She believes she can hear her daughter's breathing change, and this makes her lean into the inspection, the investigation. Everyone is silent.

There is movement on her sleeves, and she looks down. The old lady has taken hold of the fabric of her sleeves. Ivy takes one hand in her own, and the woman clasps both hands. She says something and Cynthia mutters, "She is asking for your mother's name."

"Marjorie. Marjorie Wentworth," Ivy replies.

Cynthia starts to repeat the name, but the old lady utters a word that could only be a rebuke. The two women stand almost nose to nose, holding each other's hands, while the room fills with their silence.

How old must she be? Mikio's parents look to be my age, so she must be — close to one hundred.

As suddenly as she appeared, the old lady lets go of Ivy's hands, steps back, and the sliding panel seems to swallow her. Ivy wishes she could follow her. The departure relaxes the tone of the room a bit, but Cynthia is still flushed and so tense she is almost quivering.

The men continue talking. No sign of tea or juice or cookies. In her culture by now tea would be on offer. Mikio's mother is now inspecting her with the same scrutiny as the ancient woman, and Ivy tries her very best "let's be friends" smile and lets the scrutiny be all that is on offer.

The boys break things up by jostling one another into view and apparently asking if they can have something. They depart for a mysteriously invisible kitchen, and there's the unmistakeable sound of pop cans opening. One of the boys was holding the Sorry game, so Ivy hopes at least Benjiro is having some kind of fun.

164

With no sign it is about to happen, Mikio says something to Cynthia, Cynthia says to Ivy, "We are going," and then a round of good-bye bows begins. Mikio's brother calls out to the boys, and they all hear a commotion in one of the rooms. Benjiro comes swiftly down the corridor, followed by his brother, who is looking focused for once on something besides his phone. Benjiro heads straight for his father and Ivy sees that Keiijiro is holding what is left of the Sorry game. He is holding scraps of cardboard and bits of plastic. He is holding the mechanism that makes the dice roll and it has been split in two. And Benjiro has a shiny nose brought about by tears he is trying to stifle. He would, in a different place perhaps, have buried his face in his father's coat but instead he whispers a complaint. The cousins are nowhere to be seen; their parents continue to look unconcerned.

She has heard nothing, not even the falling plastic bits that was the game she'd carried in her purse to occupy her daughter for so many years. Apparently destroyed deliberately, crushed under a house-slippered foot. Gone, now. She isn't mad about that. She is mad about the look on her grandsons' faces.

More rapidly delivered Japanese, more glares, for that is all they can be, from Mikio's mother toward Cynthia and Ivy, and then they are all doing the at-the-door shoe dance. Ivy is glad she does not have to use the bathroom, and she slips one shoe on. Mikio steadies her as she steps into the second one, and she catches the look of his mother at the sight of her son's hand on his mother-in-law's arm.

They exit, in silence. Mikio says something under his breath to Cynthia, and she replies. She looks like a little girl who has lost all her friends. Ivy wants to storm back into the apartment and slap somebody.

"Mrs. Ibee," Mikio says, forcing gaiety into his voice, an effort that makes her want to slap somebody else on his behalf. "We would like to take you to our favourite restaurant for dinner. Do you like fish? Please be our guest and join us."

Even if she didn't like fish, she'd eat ground glass for this pair at this moment.

TWENTY-SIX

Tokyo, Saitama Prefecture. May 28, 21°C, cloudy

Ivy has been practising for her excursion for almost two weeks, when she realizes she is doing block walks because she is afraid to try to make it to the museum. She enjoys her walks every other day, when the housekeeper comes. She hasn't screwed up once, and she still hasn't asked for a key. She reads the guidebook when she gets home, mentally rehearsing all the steps to get to the museum plus all the things that can go wrong. Then she picks up her crocheting and waits for Cynthia to arrive to make dinner. She has even stayed up past nine once or twice, when Mikio has found something interesting for her to watch on TV. She discovers David Attenborough's *Planet Earth* shows are just as beautiful and gruesome with a Japanese narrator as they are with his mellifluous voice. Why does the lion always have to get the baby gazelle in the end?

Perhaps she will experience a stroke of maturity and decide to tell Cynthia her plan. She would do it at the dinner table. Wait until everyone is eating, that is, everyone is chewing, and then she would drop her bomb.

"I am planning to take a jaunt into the city to the museum," she would say. Jaunt. Could she find a more unfamiliar word for this family trying to accommodate her lack of Japanese, out of respect? Jaunt.

They often eat in silence, Benjiro stuck for words except for horse, snake, log, and cowboy, and Keiijiro staunchly refusing to speak at all if he has to speak English. The boys would continue eating, knowing without knowing much English something unpleasant was about to happen. Mikio would set his chopsticks down on the little stand, his signal that fatherly intervention was about to occur. The first time this happened, she recognized the stand, because she had sent it to them many years before. Chopstick stands from Chinatown in Vancouver. What had she been thinking?

Mikio, as he often did, would try to save them all. While he was touching his impeccable lips with the rice cloth napkin, ready to say something soothing and conciliatory, she would burble on.

"I have a guidebook, and the route seems quite straightforward. I have found my way to the subway, and . . . "

"Metro," Benjiro would correct her, smiling at his use of metro in English. The fact most Japanese say metro in English anyway is not lost on Ivy, but she enjoys saying subway as often as she can so he can correct her. They may not have much English between them, but they are building up quite a collection of word skits.

"Metro," says Ivy. "I think I can manage."

She is wincing at her construction of the scene, trying to figure how to unsay what hasn't yet been said. Just taking the guidebook and giving it a try would not be as hard as asking for help, and she knows her own face would be flaming as colour mounted into her daughter's cheeks. Connected they were, by this unfortunate talent for blushing.

"I think I should get out for walks. Get some exercise. Have an adventure."

"You wish to visit the museum?" Mikio asks.

"Yes, the National Museum. It's the Ueno station, Yamanote line, park exit; Ginza, Hibya lines, Shinobazu exit. It's open every day."

Before Cynthia could undercut her request, Ivy would look at Mikio, appealing for help. Mikio would look at his chopsticks on their stand, then at Benjiro and Keiijiro.

"Boys, please assist your obaasan. She wishes to travel to the museum, by metro. She plans to have an adventure. This adventure will need some planning, and your mother and I want you to help your grandmother do so."

Benjiro would turn his phone to what looked like her metro map condensed to a four-inch screen. A little red dot pulsing. "This will be you, Obaasan," he'd say, bowing slightly. "With hope."

And they would all laugh. Cynthia would rise effortlessly to clear the table, and smile down at her.

She knew this would not be how the discussion would go. She would get into trouble with her daughter, the boys would start looking at their phones, and Mikio would maintain his composed folded position.

No, she is on her own in her foray to the museum, and there is no point in procrastinating further with more walks around the block. Even thinking about thinking about getting herself across this huge city gives her a stomach ache. She will have to get a key, however. She cannot count on getting to the museum and back in the short time the housekeeper is in the immaculate apartment.

TWENTY-SEVEN

Tokyo, Saitama Prefecture. May 29, 15°C, cloudy

The next morning, Ivy solves her key problem. She gets up earlier than usual, and stops Mikio as he is on his way out.

"Please," she asks, sounding more certain and more innocent than she feels. "Do you have a spare key to this door? I would like to go for a walk today."

Mikio straightens, giving her his best give-nothing-away expression. She pinches her lips a bit, catches herself and continues standing before him. Waiting.

He calls something to someone, speaking Japanese, which he rarely does in her presence. Keiijiro appears, they exchange a few words, he disappears and comes back holding out a fob.

Cynthia appears from her doorway — honestly, it's starting to look like one of those sitcom scenes — and says something to both of them.

"Why do you want a key, Mother?" she asks, taking the fob from her son's fingers.

Ivy takes a breath and straightens. Game on. "I want to go for a walk this afternoon. I know the code for the door. I need a key to get back into the apartment."

"Well, do you know your way about? Won't you get lost? Aren't you afraid of getting lost?"

Yes. Yes. Yes. Ivy looks at Mikio, who is holding the door open. "I have a pretty good idea of the block. I won't go far."

Cynthia relents. She gives Ivy the fob, and says crisply, "Don't lose it."

"I won't," Ivy promises.

It's done. Everyone starts breathing again.

She sets out for her first authorized walk at 10:30. Her usual walk is so familiar, and she is emboldened by her key acquisition, so she heads in a different direction. And promptly gets lost.

Stupid. She neglected to look behind her and neglected to count the number of turns. She remembers passing the scooter parking lot and the apparent dead end that looked like the back of several shops. Now she finds herself facing a row of shops, and when she turns to retrace her steps she cannot find the rabbit hole she dived into.

She has, as always, the address and name of the apartment building, written in Kanji and Japanese by Benjiro, so she looks at the shops to find one that might have someone who will speak to her. She has learned that at the sight of her, some shop keepers simply flee the counter, while others call loudly for some child to speak with her. The store she chooses has front windows completely filled with beach toys. Entering, she is delighted to discover she has found one of her favourite shops: a dollar store. It is probably not a dollar store, but rather a 100-yen store. She recognizes the layout, the aisles of stationery, hair products, kitchen doodads, wrapping paper, racks and racks of ribbon, tape, markers, toys. She smiles at the cashier, who appears to be the only staff in the store, and decides to look around first and ask questions on her way out. Having a key tucked into her cross-body bag makes her feel no pressure of time and — dollar store! She finds the section of knitting and crochet, and hanging displays of gadgets she recognizes, at least some of them. She finds novelty yarn, sock yarn, and good old knitting worsted. If she had a baby in her life, she could make a hat with the sock yarn. It occurs to her with a brief snap of pain she did no knitting for Cynthia's children, except for the crocheted baby blanket sent upon the advent of each.

Next to the gadgets are patterns, and here are the little animals she sees on the kids' knapsacks. Impulsive, she picks a pattern and discovers it comes with the yarn and accessories. The yarn is bright and not what she would have chosen, but it will allow her to make the exact creature on the front of the pattern. Who she will be making this for is beyond her. Maybe she will surreptitiously attach it to some unsuspecting child. And then get arrested. Because Japan probably does have a rule against such a thing.

On her way out, she identifies the logo for PK Tea, the tea of her childhood. She has not seen this brand for years, and she picks up a package. The packaging is in Japanese figures, and probably tells her it is not really PK Tea, but the look is so similar, perhaps the taste will be similar too. Beside the tea is a package that looks like a bad impression of Peak Freen cookies, with characters she doesn't understand. The packaging is suspicious. Is this one of those Made in China knock-offs, like the Louis Vuitton copies that still sell for thousands? Will she die of melamine poisoning? She now has the package of

172

yarn, the tea, and the cookies. And nearly 450 Canadian dollars' worth of yen to pay for this extravagance.

This will be her first purchase on her own. The clerk looks warily at her and Ivy guesses she is probably looking wary too. The items are scanned and the panel shows her Japanese characters, nothing that looks like numbers. The clerk says something then repeats in English the cost. Ivy takes out her wallet and finds a bill that is only slightly more than the amount, the transaction is completed and now . . .

"Can you tell me how to get to this address?" she says slowly but not loudly. She knows speaking English loudly doesn't help a bit. The clerk takes the paper, picks up a pen and makes some notations. She hands it back. It is a small map. A map she can decipher. The clerk smiles and Ivy smiles back.

"Have a good afternoon," the clerk says in perfectly intoned English.

"Thank you," Ivy replies. Thank you.

The map, turned the right way up, works. She finds the rabbit hole and emerges onto what she is coming to think of as her street. Triumphant, she enters the building, carrying her purchases, feeling as if she has encountered an old friend in an unexpected place. She is righteously tired, ready to get herself back to the apartment and have a cup of tea and a cookie and . . . a nap.

Twenty-Eight

Tokyo National Museum. May 30, 21°C, mostly cloudy

Yes, the National Museum. It's the Ueno station (Yamanote line), park exit; (Ginza, Hibya lines), Shinobazu exit. At least that's what it says in the guidebook, and she thinks she knows what those directions mean.

She makes it to Wakoshi, checking her bag for the key fob several times as she leaves the building and crosses the street. Every moment or so, she pats the money belt under her shirt, checks the key in her cross-body bag, and taps the pocket of her trousers for the notes she has made on an index card. She reminds herself of the catchers in the baseball games on TV, signalling to the pitcher. Jack spent a fair bit of his time watching baseball trying to figure out which signal meant what pitch, and when he guessed correctly he was so pleased. At this moment, she wishes more than anything she could be transported in time and space to her chair by the OttLite, with Jack across from her in his recliner, both of them watching baseball.

She is nervous, and thus she has the roaring in her ears. As rehearsed as she can be, she enters the station. The crowds surprise her, because it is after eleven on a weekday. She advances with her pink metro card. Card wielded, the gate opens and she is threading her way through the crowd, heading for the platform. The noise of announcements and the rush of the cars and the glare of the lights assault her. She can feel her heart tripping. She is about to throw up. Consulting the notes, stationing herself so she can see the board that announces trains, she braces herself. As saliva collects in the corners of her mouth, she considers abandoning her plan and returning to the apartment. Anything, including being sequestered in the tiny apartment with nothing to do all day, had to be better than this.

The signs light up, first in kanji and then in English. An announcement she cannot understand pours over the platform. This is the one. Reminding herself she can just get off at the next stop and either start again or retrace her steps and return to the apartment, she enters the car. It is very full, but not as full as it was the time with Cynthia and Benjiro. A young man gets up and leaves vacant one of the "old geezer seats" as Jack called them. She tries to establish eye contact to thank him but he is impassive, as if his act of courtesy was simply a happy consequence of his imminent departure. Sitting, she can see the electronic board announcing stops. She checks her notes again. She can do this, she tells herself so many times she is practically humming. She feels as if she is the only person in Tokyo trying to get from one unfamiliar point to another. Surrounded by Japanese travellers, she believes no one would help her if she asked for assistance. This feeling frightens her, and she scans the car for one of the young "foreign" travellers, perhaps hefting an overlarge backpack, who might be in a similar lost situation. Nobody.

She reads the notes over and over, looking at the board every stop. People get on, get off, sit down, stand up. Few are speaking to each other, most seem to be travelling alone. In spite of the cacophony of the announcements, the car is eerily quiet. Her stop is announced, and she stands up. Black dots cloud her vision for a moment, and she performs a geriatric monkey-bars routine, swinging from one stanchion to the next to reach the correct side of the car. Along with, it seems, every occupant of the car, she exits.

She may have got off at the right stop but she chooses the wrong exit. She retraces her steps through the busy station and finds the right exit. When she comes out above ground, however, she is not where she thought she would be. She cannot see the museum, which is supposed to be right in front of the station.

She falls into step with the hundreds of people walking in rows away from the metro station. The pavement uneven beneath her feet, she stumbles, and stumbles again, her ankle rolling over as her foot encounters treacherous uneven pavement. In lock-step with the crowd, at a gait far too fast, she grows breathless and desperate.

"Shit! Shit!" she hisses under her breath. All she can see ahead is a breaking wave of black heads, all she can feel behind is an inexorable crush. If she falls, she will be trampled and no one will even notice this little grey-haired grandmother ground to dust under the tramping feet of — yes — Asian hordes.

Ivy snorts with laughter at herself, spots a store entrance and dives in. Impossibly loud music pounds. Just inside are two old people sitting in leather armchairs.

Incongruous, to say the least. The old man has a cane held stately by his knee.

Waiting for a grandchild?

They look like Muppets.

Wishing they would leave so she could score one of the chairs, she leans against the glittering wall, pretending to adjust her shoe. Then she pretends to seek something in her bag. Breathing ceasing to roar in her ear, she peers into the street again.

The rush from the metro has subsided, or a walk-sign has intervened or some similar miracle has interceded, because the flow of people has abated. The museum should be right here. She's gone and lost the Tokyo Imperial Museum. Somebody has moved it. And surely not "Imperial". Didn't the Americans put an end to all that?

Maybe this is enough exercise for today? Maybe it is time to go home?

The word strikes her in the face, and tears spring into her eyes. It surely is time to go home, but home is not there anymore. She is not there anymore.

A cliché. A metaphor. A word meaning — back. Time to go back to the place she is now living.

"Home."

In a gap between people she recognizes the constellation of street signs and stop lights she saw in the guidebook. Beyond this massive crossing is the Tokyo National Museum. An absurd sense of triumph emboldens her and she steps lively, hearing Jack's sympathetic and teasing chuckle. "Just don't get killed crossing the road."

The museum entrance is like many others she has encountered in her life. There are signs and arrows and

177

kiosks and security guards who inspect her cross-body bag. Prepared for the noise and the confusion, she finds a wall and stands for a while before she figures out which queue to get in to purchase a ticket. She lines up, watching the people around her, many of whom are very young and many are not Japanese. She hears Italian, French, Russian, and English, as well as whatever language East Indian people speak. She hears Chinese. When it is her turn, she does not attempt any language but English; the clerk asks her something in English; she nods, and she is presented with a ticket. No money is exchanged. She has either made some terrible mistake or old ladies get in free today.

Her breathing has slowed. She is experiencing a glow of satisfaction because she has found her way to the museum, has a ticket, and can get a small guide to the museum for a suggested donation. Hoping she has not put a coin equivalent to five dollars into the Plexiglas box, she selects a guide in English and once again feels proud.

The museum is like a playground for adults. It is like the British Museum. Everywhere she sees something interesting and beautiful. She also sees signs for bathrooms, for shops, and the crossed knife and fork (surely it should be crossed chopsticks, except that's a no-no, but really?), which means tea, and maybe even international tea, which means English tea. Before she tackles the museum she will go to the knife and fork and see what there is.

Feeling like a kid who wants dessert before dinner, she follows the knife and fork signs and comes into a large cafeteria. Glass cases are on her left, a bank of machinery for making drinks is on her right and what looks like a thousand chairs are arrayed before hundreds of large tables. While she is hesitating, two people pass her, and begin the process. She follows them and picks up a small plastic tray. The glass cases contain more sweets than she has seen in her two months in Tokyo. Each plate has a description in kanji and the price. No explanation in English. The sandwiches and noodles are also displayed with only kanji notes. She will have to do this by eye. There's a cake that looks a lot like a bird's nest cookie, and the numbers beside it tell her it will not cost her all of the money in her belt. As she is looking in the cases, she hears a voice speaking English. English with an Australian accent. A young woman, very sun-browned and very blonde, is standing behind the case. "Yes, ma'am?" she asks.

Ivy could kiss her. "I want one of those."

The young woman nods.

"And tea."

"Ocha? Or Kocha?" The server laughs in a kind way at her alarm and says, "Ocha: herbal tea. Kocha: black tea. Or English tea. We have several kinds."

Ivy stores this information and asks, "Earl Grey?"

Miraculously, Earl Grey in a real teapot into which real boiling water has been placed is handed to her, along with a real ceramic mug. Beside it sits what the young woman has identified as a jammy dodger, words from Ivy's childhood. What seems to be a small amount of money is exchanged, and she is soon sitting in the sunlight from one of the huge windows, having English (kocha, she repeats to herself) tea and an English treat. She keeps looking around for the standing ovation she deserves.

Japanese museums do not provide much or any explanation in English. She was warned by her guidebook

179

about this. After her luxurious tea break she doesn't care that she is not sure what she is looking at. She wanders through the crowds and the rooms and the beautiful building, content to look. Time enough another day to figure out what the displays are meant to tell her. The museum is very crowded and yet people are moving easily around each other. There is little jostling or bumping, although often she does hear the word she recognizes: *sumimasen.*

She finds benches in every room and sits often, although when she does she can see nothing of the displays for the crush of people. She doesn't care. She is in a building with easy access to bathrooms, walking is easy, sitting is easy, she can buy herself a treat when she wants to and, most importantly and so exhilarating, she has made it.

Now to make it home.

TWENTY-NINE

Tokyo, Saitama Prefecture. June 4, 23°C, clear with a light wind

Ivy is invited once again to go with Cynthia to her language school. Anticipating the invitation, she has hung an outfit on the back of her door so she can get dressed quickly if she is given the nod.

They travel through the metro system without speaking. Cynthia's mind is on something, and she does not seem to notice Ivy handily managing the turnstile. The crush, still mind-boggling, does not warrant a comment, and they arrive at the stop, leave the station and enter the building without a word. Inside, Cynthia turns into a warm, cheerful, out-going person, and Ivy is invited to drop into Mrs. Yamamoto's class.

"We are all mothers and grandmothers, and learning English to travel," she is told, as she protests she would like to just spend her time in the lounge (with the tea, cookies, and magazines!). She is persuaded by a glimmer of the true Cynthia, however, and she follows Mrs. Yamamoto into her class. Everyone rises, so the twelve or so women only slightly younger than she is look and sound like twice that number.

Ivy hears words she does not recognize and for a panicky moment she cannot tell what language she is hearing. As she is introduced to this sea of faces, her mouth goes dry and her hands shake. The bobbing continues, and for a second she is reminded of bobbing birds balanced over water glasses. She takes the seat at the front of the room. Amid smiles, Mrs. Yamamoto announces, "This is Mrs. Cynthia's mother, Mrs. Birch. She is from Canada."

Eerily, several students pronounce Canada.

Some of the women are immaculately dressed and quite forbidding in their turn-out, while others are wearing casual trousers and tunic tops. There is a pause, as if she is somehow to get the class going. She flounders. "Ah," she begins, and many students repeat this sound. Reminded of Benjiro's efforts with English words and expressions she uses, she forges on.

"Tell me where you are going?" Ivy is looking in the direction of one of the students, who takes the question as a command.

She rises, her forehead furrowed with concentration, and she produces a sentence in English. Ivy can only catch one word: Ottawa. At least it sounds like Ottawa. She smiles, and repeats Ottawa, to hear a chorus repeating the word. It occurs to her Ottawa sounds like a Japanese word.

The next woman stands eagerly and announces she is travelling to Quebec to the city. Ivy hopes that's what she has heard, reverses the words and produces Quebec City. This call and response continues, with some serious stumbles over Cincinnati, which she cannot make out until several of the students repeat it.

One of the women announces she is travelling to a city in Korea, and there is a brief flurry of what looks and sounds like disapproval, quickly swept under the rug

182

of polite behaviour toward this old white lady with an apparent font of pronunciation knowledge.

The time passes much quicker than it does when she is reading two-year-old celebrity gossip magazines, and at the end of the class, as everyone bows in unison, Mrs. Yamamoto (please call me Eiko) is applauding.

Encouraged by this success, Ivy waits for Cynthia in the lounge, looking through magazines. Just before the time when Cynthia should be coming to get her, a woman enters. This woman is very slender, dressed in enviable business-formal, with perfectly coiffed black hair featuring one wing of silver. A woman with trouble written all over her.

"Please, who are you?" she asks, coming forward as if she plans to strip the tea and magazine out of her hands.

Ivy explains who she is, which barely appeases this woman.

"I am the owner here and the manager, and I should be informed when a stranger is in the building," she announces. Ivy agrees.

Cynthia arrives and the two women begin to speak very quickly in Japanese as Ivy gathers her belongings, puts on her cross-body bag, and washes her teacup. The discussion continues, both women speaking swiftly and almost, but not quite, interrupting each other. Although she knows she shouldn't, she cannot help peeking at them, and she notices neither is using their hands while speaking. This body stillness creates a silent-movie effect, leaving her to wonder if having still hands while engaged in what is clearly an argument is a Japanese thing. Cynthia does not have the last word; she is left standing facing the door as the manager delivers a final rebuke and departs.

The door would probably have slammed, if it had not been on complicated hydraulics and thus slowly closes after she departs.

Ivy begins to speak but Cynthia cuts her off by gathering her satchel and also departing. Ivy scurries after her.

"I've only been teaching for four years, since Benjiro entered public school," Cynthia says as they leave the building, speaking almost to herself. "But I've been speaking English and studying it since I was — oh — three."

They walk in silence for a bit.

"I didn't expect to stay home with my children. But when Keiijiro was ready for school, Benjiro was only two."

Ivy does not know what to say or even if Cynthia is speaking to her.

"I was out of the workforce for more than ten years. In the language school business, that might as well be forty years. My certificates were dated. The only people who were being hired were young travellers with degrees. Native speakers from foreign countries.

"She just enjoys finding fault. Because she and I know her English is not very good. You should see her written English. Appalling." Cynthia does not speak for a few minutes. "One day I'll tell her what I think and then I'll get fired. And we really need this job."

They have reached one of those enormous intersections. Cynthia moves to step into the street and then stops, realizing her mother cannot cross in the time remaining. Cynthia looks at her with wistful regard. Something gentle passes between them.

"Lunch, Mother. I'll teach you how to order ramen from a vending machine," she announces, and the moment passes.

The place is too crowded, so they find a food cart and take their bowls of ramen to a small table on the pavement barely two feet from the pedestrians and cars streaming past.

Perhaps it was the moment of gentleness or the insight into her daughter's work life, but for whatever reason, Ivy embarks on the topic of money. It is time.

"Cynthia," she begins, causing her daughter to look sharply at her. Whenever Cynthia began a sentence with "Mother" she knew trouble was coming. This time, however, trouble is coming in spades and Ivy is dealing.

"I would like to make some arrangements to give you and Mikio some money every month. I have my own money, I could contribute to the household. Pay my way."

"Oh, really, Mother, do you think we asked you to come here because we wanted you to pay your way?"

"I know you didn't. I would like to contribute to the household. You know, like paying room and board."

"That's ridiculous. First of all, whatever you think you could contribute would make a very small dent in the cost of our lives here."

Ivy flushes. She knows what not making a dent feels like. "Your father intended to leave me well provided for — his words. I have his pension from the railway, and my own CPP and OAP. I get survivor benefits too. I get — "

"I don't need to know this, Mother."

Ivy persists. "My pensions are deposited into my bank account. The money is just sitting there."

The two women concentrate on the task of using chopsticks to fish the last of the noodles out of their small bowls, as if that is the more important task. While fighting with the bowl, the slippery noodles, broth, and chopsticks, she considers her financial situation. She did not file an income tax return for 2006, although she knew they would owe her money and not the other way around. Still, the failure to file nags at her. As does the huge sum of money that has mysteriously vanished into Cynthia's bank account. Every time her mind brushes against the cheque for the house, she veers away.

"I could arrange for money to be deposited into your account from mine every month," she declares, not knowing if that is something her bank would do. "Or into Mikio's account," she amends, trying, and probably failing, to be culturally sensitive.

"Mikio would not accept money from you, Mother. It is his duty to take care of you."

"Yes, I know. And I appreciate. But I am getting money monthly from the Canadian government, at least as long as I am a citizen, and I would like to contribute my share."

"What do you mean, as long as you are a citizen?"

"I thought, if I am to stay here, I would become a citizen of Japan. Or a landed immigrant?"

"That is unlikely, Mother. And you cannot have a bank account unless you are a citizen. There are rules." Cynthia glances at her watch. The next stop is the *onsen*, and then groceries for dinner, a process she enjoys. She cannot let this topic drop, however, not now they are so far into it.

"Shouldn't I become a citizen, or a landed immigrant, or something like that? How can I live here without getting the proper status? I'm not even on a visitor's visa. What will happen if I get sick?"

"Oh, Mother, don't be so dramatic." Cynthia sighs, rising to collect their bowls, chopsticks and paper cups. "I will speak with Mikio about the permanent resident visa. I imagine your travel insurance will expire shortly. Can we talk about this tonight? And please — I would prefer not to discuss this when the children or Mikio are about. He is proud to host his mother-in-law."

"I understand. I do. It's just I want to help. To contribute. I don't want to — she is about to say "be a burden" and as if anticipating this, Cynthia walks away from her.

Ivy falls into step with her daughter, who demonstrates at the next two intersections she has forgotten to accommodate her mother's pace. Or is punishing her by rushing her through the crowds to get to the *onsen*. Ivy hurries along, mentally reviewing all the things that have to be resolved by September: some sort of visa, medical insurance, medical doctor, dentist, eye doctor, prescriptions. She gets tired just thinking about it.

THIRTY

Tokyo, Koishikawa Korakuen. June 6, 14°C. rain.

The housekeeper enters quietly. Ivy feels vaguely guilty that this woman cleans the apartment she could clean herself effortlessly. The heavy work is reserved for a team of cleaners who arrive once a month on a Saturday. On these days, everyone but Cynthia runs for cover, which is hard to find in the tiny apartment. In spite of the complete absence of clutter, this housekeeper dusts, straightens things, re-arranges the impeccable bathroom, and folds already-folded towels. The kitchen floor requires all of a minute and a half to wash. The bathroom floor does not require washing because, as Cynthia carefully explained the first time Ivy had a shower, it is a courtesy to mop the floor after the shower, using the small short-handled mop hanging near the toilet. The housekeeper does work Ivy could do and would do. It would please her to be of some use to this household.

Today, however, she consults her guidebook and discovers it is iris season in the parks in Tokyo. The guidebook tells her there are gardens, and she has plotted to go to one. Her excursion to the National Museum and her safe return have given her confidence. She is going to try getting herself to Koishikawa Korakuen — a "stroll" garden. Stroll sounds like a very nice pace. And the price is right: ¥300 which she calculates is about $3.50 Canadian.

This trip will mean taking a new route on the metro; the guidebook tells her she wants to get off at Iidabashi Station, Exit C3, and several lines will get her there: Namboku Line, Chūō-Sobu Line, Tozai Line, Yurakucho Line, or Toei Oedo Line. She's spoiled for choices, but she knows when she gets to the station her choices will be limited to the lines connecting at Wakoshi. It is a two-minute walk from the station to the entrance of the garden, although she is learning that a two-minute walk in Japanese terms is more like ten minutes for her. And there's a teahouse at the entrance, and the guidebook mentions benches and at least an hour to "stroll".

This will be her first journey in rain. Luckily, she still has one of those "old-lady" head covers, those plastic accordion-style covers designed to keep a lady's hair dry without flattening her hair-do. She tiptoes past the housekeeper, who is wiping the immaculate counters in the kitchen. They smile at each other; she has come to consider this nameless silent woman to be her accomplice in her escapades. Although, as she is sitting in the lobby putting on her shoes, she wonders if maybe every day the housekeeper leaves a note telling Cynthia about the wily old white woman and her absences. No, no. There would already have been a kitchen dust-up.

She steps into the street to be greeted by a stream of white umbrellas. The umbrellas are so big they look like tents with legs. Closer, she discovers they are not white, they are transparent. So people can protect themselves from the rain and not bump into anyone as well. Given that the umbrella was probably invented in England, and used in London, an equally crowded city, she is surprised at this ingenuity. The English just splash along, heads down and shielded by the black umbrellas, bumping into each other. Not the Japanese. Not only that, as the stream enters Wakoshi station, the umbrellas are swiftly closed and hidden about the bodies. No dripping umbrellas for these passengers. She is glad she only has her accordion head-gear, although she notices, after she successfully navigates the turnstile and finds the right platform, her hat is dripping onto her shoulders and probably on anyone standing too close, as they invariably do. Another cultural gaffe. Maybe that yen store has one of these transparent umbrellas and the manual that ought to go with it.

Her notes tell her to take the Tobo-Tujo Line to Ikebukuro Station (fourteen minutes) and then walk two minutes to Yurakocho Line (take Entrance 4) nine minutes (four stops) to Lidabashi Station. Cost ¥420. Walk 170 metres (two minutes). Her confidence is wavering, considering how difficult it is to locate the right platform and the correct side of the platform. But she was successful in getting to Ikebukuro Station and walking to the Yamanote Line to get to the museum, so she is hopeful.

She navigates successfully to the entrance of the gardens, which comes upon her suddenly, because she is looking beyond the entrance to the complex of buildings comprising the Tokyo Dome. The entrance is festooned with food carts and what look like bags of candyfloss sporting brightly painted characters. The promised teahouse is just beyond the entrance, and she is propelled forward by the crowd.

A "stroll" garden in the rain. Not the brightest idea she's had, but the crowds of people seem to disperse very quickly, and the rain is very like the desultory summer rain in Vancouver, when the sky is leaden but what is falling seems minor compared to a November storm. As she walks, holding the map she received with her ticket, she can hear the rain dripping onto her hat, and the hat is tied around her head so she can also hear her own breathing. Just like at the museum, it takes her a few minutes to drop the anxiety of travel and relax into the destination. According to the map, the viewpoints are designed to produce the effect of well-known vistas in China and Japan. And the paths have been engineered to bring one in an orderly fashion to each view. She sticks the map in her pocket.

The first view is beautiful, no doubt. The description in Japanese is quite long, and the one in English and at least two other languages are quite short. Since she doesn't know what the original view looks like or even where it is, she gives up on trying to match imitation to original, although several people around her seem to be doing just that, using the larger guidebook she had noticed at the entrance. For ¥4500.

The irises, as promised, are lovely. They are in fields, not orderly rows like the tulips in the Fraser Valley, and the grass is a spectacular green — a green-green, Jack had classified this particular colour. Green-green it is, and the many colours of iris create an impressionist painting. She has never seen so many colours of iris, and they are not grouped by colour or some other man-made scheme. It looks to her English-country-garden eye the iris have been planted at random. The effect is wonderful, especially because the sky is lightening and the flowers seem to be glowing.

The paths are even, and although there are a lot of people, it seems either everyone is whispering or there is some kind of acoustic trick to swallow sound. Most of the people are moving in one direction, so the garden must be organized as a loop. She lags a bit, falls behind the group ahead and is not yet enveloped by the group behind her. She is strolling at her own pace.

She notices the birds. Catching insects in the fields of iris. The trees, every one, are manicured in exquisite shapes. Some of the leaves are red, and she connects these red leaves to one of her favourite trees in Vancouver: a Japanese maple. These ones, however, have been shaped in different ways, creating the effect of bonsai writ large. The shapes are important aspects of each vista, and every single leaf on every single branch seems deliberate. This pristine pruning and the immaculate stones and plantings all create lovely effects, but she feels set aside, as if this were a landscape not intended for her. She feels more like an intruder in this garden specifically promoted as a tourist destination than she did at the museum. The clever idea to mimic a larger view on a smaller scale is impressive, of course, and she appreciates the feat of artistic engineering. But whenever she visited a garden in Vancouver, even the Nitobe Garden at UBC, she always came away with some idea for something she might do in her own garden. Here, each precise scene gives no clue about how the gardeners have done what they have done.

As promised, benches are available, and although the strollers impede any view when she sits, she doesn't mind. Her detachment, rain on the ponds, the sounds of running and falling water, all combine to calm her; she is reaching a stillness she has not experienced for months. Years, perhaps. Jack's decline gave her so much to do: special chairs, intricate clothes, new forms of eating utensils, medications, supplements. Every day a new task, something she had to fetch from a department somewhere, usually far across the city. And when she wasn't trying to locate offices and produce the correct slips of paper, she was sitting with her Jack, holding his hand, while he asked her the same question over and over. Can I go home now?

Fortunately, he only asked her once who she was. He either continued to remember until he could no longer ask anyone anything or some part of his loving mind saw the distress he caused her and prevented him from asking her that question but the once.

And then he dwindled. His brawny belly shrinking daily, it seemed. The skin on his arms sagging, the creases in his dear face taking on macabre furrows. His eyes, almost hidden by his drooping eyelids, lost their twinkle, the twinkle, if truth be told, that drew her to his side all the years ago and kept her there through the travails that beset any marriage. He looked, in the last few weeks, like a tired, cranky, ancient man. Wisps of hair, shaggy eyebrows, tufts springing out of his ears, the hair on his chest sparse and white. He became a grim caricature of the man she had loved for all those years. Sometimes, while she sat, he slept, and she stroked his old hand, the veins rising like ribbons through the slack skin. And she bid him go.

He would have loved this beautiful garden. He would have persuaded her to buy the expensive guide, the one that showed the original scene the gardeners had re-created. He would read the history aloud as they walked, exclaiming and chortling when he found a vantage point he was seeking.

She could almost hear him as she walked toward the famous bridge, she could almost sense him beside her. He wasn't, though.

Not here.

She comes to, sitting on a bench, now with a wet bottom, across from a pond covered with lily pads. She sees frogs jumping not only into the water but also from one pad to another. She has not heard frogs since last spring in North Vancouver. Did the peepers charm the new residents of her house the way they always charmed her and Jack? Each vying to be the first to hear frogs in the spring, and enjoying the chorus in the early morning and at dusk.

What would this decidedly beautiful park be like at the end of the day, when the crowds departed? The gardeners here must be something special. Like the gardeners for the rose gardens in Stanley Park.

She has been strolling, although mostly sitting, for nearly two hours. The teahouse beckons as well as the gift shop, although her money belt is getting thin these days. Before she tackles this teahouse, however, she goes into the gift shop and discovers post cards, some already stamped. Somehow she has concluded postcards are no longer produced, so she is pleased to see these, as garishly coloured as the ones from Butchart Gardens in Victoria, which never seemed to capture the true colours of the flowers. She buys one to send to Norma.

She arrives at the apartment at three fifteen, which is good because she has sodden shoes. She cleans them and arranges them on the shoe rack, hoping Benjiro will do what he usually does, kick his shoes off and thus obscure the tell-tale wet footwear of his grandmother.

THIRTY-ONE

Tokyo, Saitama Prefecture. June 20, 27°C, mostly cloudy

She has knit and crocheted all her life, beginning when she was eight years old. Her mother taught her to knit, and during the war they would sit together listening to the radio, knitting socks for soldiers. As her fingers aged, she mostly crocheted, creating blankets, hats, shawls, capes, slippers, hot water bottle covers in chunky, bright yarn. Her guidebook is unhelpful about yarn shops, although the book has a whole section on shopping for high fashion clothing and accessories in Japanese brand-name stores. She somehow doubts she would find size fourteen clothes in these high-end outlets.

If only she could figure out how to get a proper-sized crochet hook. The dollar store, her refuge on her walks around the blocks, has a lot of garish yarn and many huge knitting needles but no crochet hooks. The hooks she brought to Tokyo are not big enough for the kit she bought at the dollar store.

Among the gossip magazines in the staff lounge, she was surprised to find knitting magazines, all in Japanese. She notices hand-knit sweaters and accessories, especially on the young, and yet she has seen no one knitting or crocheting — but then where would she? No one is even supposed to use cell phones on the metro, and wielding a pair of knitting needles would be dangerous in such close quarters. Crocheting a slipper while walking through the museum would be culturally inappropriate, at the very least.

The pictures in the magazines were high-fashion items and what she could only identify as American nostalgia, such as sweater sets that reminded her of the one her mother knit for her as a going-away/wedding present. Nostalgia for the American occupation seems — weird.

She saw a man on the metro platform wearing a pair of casual slacks and a hand-knit sweater that was deliberately too tight, in garish green and khaki, with snaps along the bottom hem, random cables and bobbles, and large metallic buttons emphasizing the gap between the buttons and the button band. This sweater was worn with casual confidence. A Japanese hipster, if there were such a thing, as if she would know one to see one. Regardless, he obviously intended to be wearing it. No sentimental attachment to a sweater made by a grandmother, that's for sure. Maybe the sweater is a contemporary Japanese equivalent of the ugly Christmas sweater phenomenon just taking hold of the knitting scene when she left Vancouver.

She recalls the sweater she made for Cynthia when she was six, a cardigan that, when buttoned, featured a ballerina in a pirouette. The shoes were appliqued satin and the tutu was sewn on fabric that stood out from the body of the sweater. She embroidered the face on the ballerina. The sweater was pretty, and Cynthia loved it. She wore it until she grew out of it, and always took pride to button it up to create all over again the magic of the dancer appearing — and then disappearing when she unbuttoned the sweater. When Ivy was packing up the life of her home, she found the sweater, stored carefully in the bottom of the cedar chest. She took it to the thrift shop, hoping a little girl would fall in love with it all over again or maybe it would turn up — too tight — on an adult at an ugly-sweater party.

Puzzling over one of the magazines, she discovered an ad in English. Sheep Meadow: famous for its yarn, textiles, and crafts. The ad helpfully supplied a tiny map, informing her the shop was in Kichijoji, "just west of the city centre". Not helpful. She found ads in English in quite a few of the magazines. Yuzaway, the logo featuring a sheep with needles, was right next to Kichijoji and promised massive selection including inexpensive acrylic yarns as well as pure wool, silk and cashmere and the Japanese brands Puppy, Richmore and Reiko Dyed.

Her target becomes "the centrally located Okadaya, in Shinjuku", featuring eight floors, whimsical patterns, including Pokemon intarsia sweaters, and a few English-language knitting magazines. Buoyed by knowing what Pokemon is, she decides to make this department store — eight floors — her next venture.

This trip is more difficult than all the rest put together, because she has to plot her travel from Wakoshi to a station close to Shinjuku, without knowing what Shinjuku is. Is it a stop, a part of Tokyo, a store, a mall?

Small map and notes in hand, she heads out shortly after eleven. Although she has directions written down, she still consults the giant map in the metro station. She has learned to pay attention to small details of the route, such as Platform 1, Stop ID JA12 at the Ikeburu Station. This station seems to be the transfer point for all

197

of her travels so far, and she is getting to know what to do, especially when she makes a mistake.

She arrives at Shinjuku and accidently emerges at the smoking exit. She retreats into the station and consults the map again. This time, she believes she has to walk out of the correct exit, turn left, turn right at the first corner and then turn left at the next corner. Four minutes.

She walks for ten minutes, getting steadily more upset. She cannot find an eight-storey department store filled with wool. She cannot find anything that looks like a street sign. Anyway, she has learned in her travels over the past six weeks that the signs are usually in kanji and she couldn't read it even if it said, "You Are Here."

She retreats to the station, thanking Jack once more for his advice to always look behind her so she can find her way back. She starts again, talking to herself, reading the little piece of paper. This time, she makes the correct turns and finds herself at the entrance to Okadaya. As she hesitates, the automatic doors swoosh open, and she is standing in the largest yarn shop she has ever seen. At the door are large fabric carry-alls. She selects one. She has died and gone to heaven. Her stomach calms. All is well.

She goes through every aisle on two floors, touching skein after skein of yarn, blanching at the price of some and nodding appreciatively at the cost of others. On one of the floors she finds patterns and on another she finds every possible implement for crocheting she could imagine plus many she couldn't. In her large carry-all, she places a set of four crochet hooks, confident at least one will be the right size for the little dolls. She finds a sheet with instructions for a doll that looks very much like

Keiijiro's. She picks up a package of bright yarn in the colours that match the displayed dolls.

She emerges from the store at nearly one o'clock. Across the rather alarmingly busy street with no apparent intersections, is a storefront that looks a lot like a McDonald's. The colours are right, the logo is familiar, and when she gets there, having joined a group of about ten people who just step into the street in a gap in the traffic, she discovers it is a McDonald's. The display board shows her more kinds of hamburgers than she thought possible, and what looks a lot like French fries. While she is looking at the board, and deciding what to try to order, a group of teenage boys bowl through the door, laughing and talking, and almost spin her around. She is used to these collisions, which are usually met with silence and forward movement. One of the boys, however, puts his hand on her arm to steady her and bows in apology. Reverence for the old at last. She watches them order and steps forward to follow their lead. Because of Benjiro's careful coaching, she states the number of what she wants — grateful it is in the range of one to twenty — pays and stands, as the group of boys are standing, to wait for her food.

With the luxury of the yarn store behind her, and the knowledge there are lots of seats available, she feels a glimmer of contentment. She has made her way to the store, she has found a place to eat lunch, she has ordered and paid for her lunch, and she has lots to look at.

The boys take their French fries to the long table they share with about a dozen of their friends. Almost every one of them has a cell phone in hand, with the rapid movement of thumbs that mean texting. Surely they have all their friends with them. Who could they be sending messages to? Parents wondering why they aren't home studying?

She remembers the chips in the tea shop near the military base in Aldershot, how the men from the barracks would come in to order chips, calling them fries or French fries and laughing at her accent. She remembers the Canadian soldiers expected malt vinegar and salt and the American soldiers ketchup, which was not available. She offered the Americans brown sauce at times, if their complaints became persistent, but the response to brown sauce on chips was much worse than their complaints about the lack of ketchup. The first time she tasted ketchup, when she had arrived in Canada, she could not believe anyone would put this cloying bright red sauce on anything.

When she comes back to the scene at McDonald's she finds the group of teenagers eating their fries with chopsticks. The scene is oddly charming, as they hunker over their adolescent comfort food, cell phones in one hand and chopsticks in the other, showing each other pictures or texts, or perhaps a game, all the while eating. It makes sense. Eating French fries with one's fingers always seemed really messy, even when she was walking on the seawall with her beau, eating chips from a cone of newspaper. Although she notices more than one fellow wiping his hands on his trousers before doing something else with the phone.

She does not recognize several items on her hamburger, but the French fries taste just like the fast food in North Vancouver. She has no comment about the tea. The little restaurant is busy and noisy, with music playing over the din of people talking. She is happy.

She makes it home in time to sort herself out, get the kit out of her underwear basket, take it apart, arrange herself on the sofa and wait for Benjiro to come home. She wishes she could tell him, at least, about her day, but instead they spend the time before Cynthia arrives practising his cursive English hand-writing. He is making her practise kanji; she is mastering the kanji for Women's Bathroom. She is tempted to get the instructions for the kit and persuade her grandson to teach her not only how to copy the kanji but also what each symbol means. She doesn't even know what the kit is supposed to make. Amigurumi. Is that a creature, the name of a cartoon character, or what?

She has seen these little creatures everywhere. She's received a few glances that could almost be glares as she inspected those dangling close to her face on the metro. It looks like the pieces are crocheted and then sewn together. The pieces — head, body, arms, legs, ears — look like single crochet in the round. The kit has a set of googly eyes, strands of scrap yarn for facial features and fiberfill for stuffing. She could work out how to make one if she could get Keiijiro's to inspect and she has a reasonable explanation as to how she came in possession of the kit.

This business of secret travelling is creating a maze of misdirection and there is only so much she can hide under her nightgown in its wicker basket. When asked, How was your day, she has to stop herself from blithering on about the metro turnstile that wouldn't work, the boys eating French fries with chopsticks, the triumph she experienced crossing Shibuya intersection, and "Fine," she says, head down over handwork. "Fine."

201

After dinner, she lays out all the pieces from the kit and unpacks the small skeins of bright yarn. Benjiro gets interested and calls to his brother, who, rather miraculously, comes out of his bedroom. He and Benjiro speak quickly in Japanese, almost whispering so they will not get caught by Cynthia. Keiijiro retrieves his knapsack and takes the small creature off. Ivy inspects his doll, and the instructions she has from Okadaya, then makes a quick sketch to show him. Her sketch earns one of his rare smiles, and he assembles the small bundles of yarn and the google eyes she purchased on speculation and agrees he would like her to make one. He makes a few amendments to her sketch, and when Cynthia comes to see what they are doing, they are head to head over the sketch and material, with Benjiro translating.

She makes the doll that night while he is studying. Just as Mikio arrives, she holds up the finished creature. Everyone is amazed, including her. When Mikio replaces the clip and Keiijiro attaches his new creature onto his knapsack, everyone is beaming. Observing this, Benjiro gets out some paper and sketches a large dramatic anime creature, and presents it to her, to everyone's laughter at the improbable nature of the request. And — bonus — no one has thought to ask her how she came to have all these bits and bobs to make something so suitable for a fourteen-year-old Japanese boy. Although, she notices Mikio inspecting the package the crochet hooks came in, and realizes it has the bar code for Okadaya on it and the price in yen. Busted. He says nothing, however, and it is well past what she considers her bedtime, so she makes her escape before he can formulate a question.

She has learned to lull herself to sleep by listening to Mikio and Cynthia speak Japanese to each other and reviewing the day behind her, to seal the metro lesson she has learned. Reviewing often gives her a piece of the day she did not notice when it was happening. For example, it is not until she is nearly asleep that she understands the significance of the young woman in the bathroom at the cafe stepping forward as she left her cubicle, hesitating, and then stepping back to wait for one not recently vacated by a foreign woman. A white woman. An old woman. Ivy is at the intersection of several –isms, and she missed the meaning of this young woman's action. In the context of this successful day, this event is like a small invisible thorn. She can't pull it out and also cannot feel it unless she brushes against it. The day has been grand. And the evening, making something for the aloof teenager, is the first time, she thinks, her presence was a benefit and not a constant reminder her arrival has wrecked their lives.

Without a book to read herself to sleep, she has developed the habit of looking up at the ceiling, tensing and relaxing her feet, then her calves, then her thighs, then her belly, then her hands, arms, and shoulders. When she gets to scrunching her face, she is ready to laugh at herself and, shortly after, falls asleep. Her mystery trips wear her out, and her sleep is deep and dreamless.

THIRTY-TWO

Tokyo, Saitama Prefecture. July 1, 29°C, sunny with cloudy periods

It started out so well. Ivy and Benjiro were playing one of their intricate Monopoly games when Cynthia arrived home early — for her — and put some colourful brochures on the counter. She called to Keiijiro in Japanese, another signal of the unusual, and then said to the room, "I've found a really good place for our holiday!"

The boys and Cynthia grouped around the counter, while Ivy gathered up the Monopoly game. She picked up one of the brochures, but it was in Japanese, featuring large glossy photographs of beaches, skim boards, kayaks, paddle boats, restaurant entrances, and smaller photographs of kiosks selling trinkets, such as some sort of puppet.

Cynthia was fairly burbling, she was so excited. She even addressed Ivy directly, "With the bit extra we have every month . . . " (this was Cynthia's mode of referring to the money Ivy was now "giving the household," an oblique expression that made sense only to her and Ivy) " . . . we can afford this place, it's a really good deal."

The boys began to talk to each other, and the older boy had his phone out and was either looking up something or texting all his friends. He kept showing Benjiro the phone, and the little fellow was getting more excited by the minute.

Ivy pulled one of the brochures that had some English toward her. It was a pictorial description of the hotel, or cottage maybe. The photographs showed a big sitting room, a big kitchen, and the sleeping rooms. The shots of screens and tatami flooring told her it was a traditional Japanese apartment, which meant she would be giving her knees a workout, but she refused to let that major quibble interfere with her own quickly mounting anticipation.

"We will take the train," Cynthia said to the boys, speaking quickly, and Ivy wondered if either of them understood her. "Then we will rent a car. With a car, we can drive to the beaches and even go to the caves one day. Caves. Won't that be exciting?"

Her children did not answer her, so she switched to Japanese. As she spoke, they looked first at her then at each other, and even the fourteen-year-old was showing signs of some emotion.

Cynthia turned to Ivy. "The package includes the train, the car, the cottage, and two or three sight-seeing trips. The caves are extra, but — " she gestured to the brochure that was only in Japanese " — the package is so reasonable I think we can do that extra trip too." Cynthia actually bounced on her toes. "It will be so good to get out of the city while it is so hot."

Tell me about it, Ivy thought. The apartment was sweltering during the day, but since everyone left early in the morning and returned in late afternoon, she concluded they had no idea how hot it was at midday. On the weekends, Cynthia would turn on the air-conditioning for a couple of hours a day, reminding everyone how expensive heating and cooling bills were. On Sundays, when Mikio was home for much of the day, the air-conditioner was never turned on. The politics of air-conditioning were baffling. Ivy simply tried to do her part by enduring the heat, sometimes by going out, sometimes by sitting in her nightgown by the sliding glass doors, hoping for a breeze.

She contemplated how she would go about paying for the caving trip. It would take a brief skirmish, but she was learning how, when and with whom present she could get her way about paying for something. It was one of her minor goals to pay for a meal at a restaurant, and she was already scheming to invite them all out as her guests to celebrate her birthday. If she had to make up some cultural rule from her British background, she was prepared to do so.

Everyone but her was speaking Japanese, thank goodness. The stilted English conversations that existed while she was in the room frustrated everyone, including her. The boys were in the kitchen area with Cynthia, and for once she had a glimpse of how things were with her daughter and her daughter's sons when they were not trying to accommodate the presence of an English-speaking stranger. Keiijiro was even chopping vegetables, wielding one of Mikio's large, sharp knives, talking a mile a minute and gesturing with the knife perilously close, it seemed, to Benjiro's frequently bouncing body.

She looked at the brochures as dinner was prepared. She was starting to get excited too. She was planning how she could arrange to have them leave her in a sunny spot on a lovely beach while they did hang-gliding or whatever

206

passed for beach sports in Japan these days. She would buy a summer dress. One advantage of the ever-present "trunk in your bedroom" problem was whenever she bought something and Cynthia noticed it, she could explain she had "just found it at the bottom of the trunk." And as long as Mikio did not look at the labels, she would be fine. The idea of trying to find a store that sold bathing suits suitable for her body, age, and ethnicity was a problem she would solve another day.

A vacation. Wonders would never cease.

Wonders do cease about two hours later, after dinner, after a walk around the block to avoid the last hour of heat, after the boys are persuaded to do their homework while they are allowed to wait up for Mikio. He comes in about nine thirty, looking tired. He moved like a man many years older than his fifty-five-year-old body. He smiles almost regretfully at Benjiro, who nearly knocks his father over trying to hug him and be the first with the news.

Looking like a man who only wants a bit of dinner and a beer in the quiet, Mikio rallies himself and eats his dinner while his children tell him all about the holiday. They wave the brochures, Keiijiro shows his father the phone, and every so often Mikio looks up at Cynthia, as if to confirm the information he's getting from his excited children. Ivy hears more words coming from Keiijiro than she has for the previous four months, and the mixture of Japanese — the boys — and English — Mikio being diligent and Cynthia reluctantly following suit — add to the excitement.

Given the language melange, she is working hard to find a place to insert her offer to pay for the caving, since it seems, if she is understanding the details, the holiday has to be paid for within twenty-four hours, because it is a special offer based on a cancellation. As a consequence, she suddenly, with no reference to anything, says, "Let me pay for the caving. I don't think that's something I would do, so let me buy you all a present, and I'll pay for the caving."

Cynthia snaps, "Oh, I'm sorry. You've misunderstood. You aren't going with us. I'm sorry," Cynthia doesn't sound sorry. She sounds smug.

Ivy puts down the brochures she has been admiring. She's embarrassed. Hovering in the air is her excited tone, and hovering like a taste of sweetness in her mouth is the pleasure she had felt at the idea of taking a trip. How could she have misunderstood? Mikio, obviously too worn out to understand what has happened, continues to look at the brochures with the boys. Soon, the bedtime regime starts up, and no one notices Ivy stilled in the swirl of anticipation. Not going. Not wanted on the voyage.

Cynthia has noticed, evidently. As she is gathering up the brochures and Mikio is heading off to the balcony with his credit card, she puts on her bright voice. "We'll only be gone for a week. I'll bring in lots of food. I'll make sure you have some money, in case you run out. We'll only be gone a week, so that should be fine. You'll have your walks every day. You'll have the apartment to yourself, so that should be nice for you. Some peace and quiet."

Cynthia does not look at her and she just looks at the blank TV. She's so disappointed she feels sick. This might be the time to advise Cynthia about her excursions to the museums and garden and Shinjuku to get cash from the ubiquitous ATMs. A responsible grown-up might have done so, but at this moment she feels like a five-year-old who has been told she's not going to the PNE with the rest of the family. She's afraid to open her mouth because, much to her inner horror, she's tearing up. She nods, looking down as if to find her handwork. She hears Cynthia's customary snort of impatience, the moment passes, Mikio comes in smiling through his weariness, and the holiday is confirmed.

Ivy decides to run away.

THIRTY-THREE

July 21, 35°C, with a tropical storm approaching

Her family stands at the door, bursting with knapsacks, chatter, excitement, and four dutiful good-bye bows. Cynthia does not meet her eyes, but Mikio bows and then takes her hand in his, looks into her eyes, and almost kisses her cheek. They depart like a flock of starlings. She turns to face her "home". She always hears it in her head this way. Her "home". Before courage can desert her, she heads for her suitcase and her plans to travel to Kamakura and its shrines and sandy beaches.

She felt slightly guilty seeing everyone out the door, with her carry-all stashed out of sight packed for her own adventure. Metro to the high-speed train: check. Train ticket purchased: check. Orderly embarkation: check. Forty minutes to Kamakura: check. Then she would find her way to the ryokan, a traditional guest house, hoping her long-unused credit card would not be declined for "unusual activity" far from her customary purchases at Lonsdale Mall. The last one was the hotel near the airport four months ago.

Four months. She has been in Tokyo for four months and she is heading from one foreign place to another even more foreign. Suddenly, staying on her own in the apartment seems like a really good idea. Maybe she would learn to use the remote.

The piece of paper is in the pocket of her trousers. She stands by the front door, reading the list of steps again. Metro to train for departure at eleven. She feels keenly alone. She wishes somewhere on her list she is going to meet Jack. He had such a zest for these trips. He loved the West Coast Express and would talk her into taking it out to Maple Ridge then taking the bus home. Just for fun.

He loved riding the train. He loved the sea bus. He was Vancouver born and bred and never lost his love for the ocean. She would make this journey to the seaside for him, then.

She changes to her walking clothes and then she pees. She puts on her walking shoes. She makes her way out. A gust of wind blows grit at her when the doors of the apartment open, and she almost gives up. Turning, she sees her reflection in the glass — a little old white lady frowning, her hair behind her ears, the carry-all dangling awkwardly by one strap off her good shoulder. She hoists the bag and sets off, contemplating barrettes. Maybe she could find some in a tourist trap in Kamakura.

Her carry-on is alarmingly heavy — clothes for five days — and the weather too warm for her jacket. As she walks to the station, she recites all the things that could go wrong:

Miss station stop — Forget/lose her wallet
Buy wrong ticket — Leave her credit card behind
Get on wrong train — Get off at wrong station
Lose guest house — Find wrong guest house
Forget her bag on the train — Break a strap on her bag
Keel over and die of a stroke

The last one makes her smile as she moves through the metro station, flashing her card and getting a seat so she can see the next-stop billboard. She is on her way.

Kamakura, south of Tokyo. That's what the guidebook told her. The former capital of feudal Japan, famed for surfing and historic sights. The juxtaposition of these two activities is pleasing. She imagines surfer dudes standing before shrines, reading the descriptions and peering up at the stonework. She has pictured herself doing that many times. The reason Kamakura popped into her mind as she sat on the toilet recovering from the smirk on her daughter's face was the directions to get there were — now she was a subway genius — quite straightforward. The guidebook said "a good day trip" and she figured, as she looked at herself in the mirror over the sink, if a good day trip turned into a weekend and a bit, so what?

She gets off at the right station but takes the wrong exit. Like a meerkat in Stanley Park, she pops up, looks around and pops down to find the right exit.

Labelled in English as well as kanji, the exit features a long flight of stairs. Patiently, she tackles them.

The train station is orderly chaos. Having rehearsed this, she spurns the real person and heads for the automated dispenser. Steeled to the impatient behind her, she carefully selects English and then goes through all the choices to get a return ticket to Kamakura for a senior travelling on a weekday after 10:00 AM. Her joy when the ticket emerges is amusing even to her. Her credit card is still working; it's some sort of miracle.

The platform is announced. The expected surge sweeps her along.

She's one of the last to enter the train car, and the only seats available are in backward-facing rows. She sits down, patting her money belt as she always does and then the pocket her ticket is in. She puts her bag on the seat beside her and moments later a young man appears beside her and lifts the bag away from her and places it somewhere behind her. He sits down. She had selected one of the few remaining aisle seats, and now she has the feeling she has made an error of courtesy. She watches the last to arrive and notices the protocol seems to be to stash the suitcases and sit in an orderly fashion first in against the window, second in the middle, third on the aisle. Lesson learned.

The view is a blur because of the speed of train, and trying to catch a glimpse of anything makes her seasick. She folds her hands in her lap and waits. Waiting gives her time to worry about the next list of things that could go wrong. According to the guidebook, the ryokan is walking distance from the train station, in the shopping district. Since the guidebook was written for incredibly fit young people, walking distance sometimes means four kilometres, but this ryokan is supposed to be less than a kilometre from the station — assuming she gets out at the right stop and not in a town with a name similar to Kamukura, somewhere hundreds of miles up the coast.

She alights, panting with anxiety. Many young men are holding up signs that she disregards. She is not some dignitary, so none of these would be for her. She then remembers the fiasco at the airport and starts looking at the names. A young man is holding up a sign: Mrs Ibee. He bows and extricates her from her cross-body carry-all. Unburdened, she fairly bounces along beside her escort, who says little, but does walk slowly, and in about fifteen minutes they arrive at a concrete block with a small sign signalling the name of the guest house.

There is a queue to register, and as she waits her turn, she rehearses the cultural rules provided by the guidebook. Bathroom slippers. Socks in a tatami room. Queue before a selected door in public bathroom. Rarely toilet paper. Communal bath. Street vending machine. Rice is served at every meal to balance flavours, not doused in soy sauce. Chopsticks *o-hashi*. Put them down in front, facing left. Don't pour your own drink. Pour using two hands. Don't tip.

She steps up when it is her turn and says, slowly but not loudly, she has a reservation for four nights in the name Ivy Birch. Except she pronounces it Ibee, to save them all some trouble. Her reservation is found, she is advised the only Western room is not available, she accepts the alternative (not knowing what it is), she is given a book to sign like something out of a 1940s movie, and when she steps away the same young fellow is holding her bag and beckoning her. The guest house has no elevator, as she has noted, and she is happy to see that she is being guided to a series of wide low steps that take her the equivalent of half a storey. The fellow opens the door, gives her the key card, puts her bag down and leaves, closing the door quietly.

She surveys her home away from "home." She elected to stay at a ryokan — a traditional Japanese inn — because the price was right and she figured she was already living in a traditional Japanese home. This room features tatami mats on the floor, a low table, four cushions, two with back rests, a short floor lamp, a series of sliding screens that conceal the bed, and an alcove holding one slender pot on a very small table. The small cupboard holds a set of towels, a yukata dressing gown and a tanzen bed jacket that can be worn inside the inn and double as pyjamas. Just as the guidebook described, so far. On the table is a cup and a thermos of what turns out to be a fragrant clear tea. She slides open the screen to find the futon already made up. The room does not contain one Western-style chair. She turns back to the door, considering requesting a chair, and finds the room description, the map of the exits, and several lines in Japanese. The only English tells her the curfew is 11:00 PM.

She removes her shoes and walks into the room. It is simplicity. It is very small. The windows are set high on the wall, like the placement of windows in Cynthia's apartment. The bed is enclosed by the screens, and except for the first one, none of them seem to move. It will be like camping and sleeping in a tent. Which she and Jack gave up about twenty-five years ago.

Shaking off her persistent inner complaint department, she checks the time and finds she has four hours before dinner. The day that started out sunny, is now cloudy, but this change in weather may bring some cool and she decides to go for a walk along the promised narrow streets with all imaginable shops, leading to the Daibutsu.

A visitor to Kamakura in the thirteenth century would have been met by "gangs of sword-wielding Samurai strutting the streets in full regalia, en route to a Shinto shrine or a Buddhist temple," the guidebook advised. She would have preferred Samurai in full gear to the boys and girls in astonishingly tiny bikinis — both genders — wielding their surf boards, cell phones, and

215

digital cameras. The streets are jammed. She is reminded of Harrison Hot Springs on the Labour Day long weekend. Most of the tourists are wearing some version of beach wear, although she does spot several people who resemble her. Similarly buffeted by the crowds, it would seem.

She makes her way along the street, slowly, taking in the sights. She knows exactly how to get back to her guest house as long as she keeps going straight, and she has the address and map in her pocket just in case. She makes the stone gates that lead to the beach her landmark behind her and the end of the long street her goal. She threads her way around taxis, tour buses and sign-toting merchants. She passes girls wearing skimpy outfits pushing pamphlets and menus into her hands. It is very noisy, but very like Harrison Hot Springs; everyone is in a good mood, in spite of the darkening sky. If you're here for the shrines, temples, and world-renowned Buddha, you turn left, if the beach, you take a sharp right. Thus sayeth the guidebook. She resolves to continue left. Before she turns left, however, she does glance sharp right.

The scene at the beach reminds her very much of English Bay, except for the surfers. The freshening wind, signalling a change in weather, has created waves even she can see are good for surfing. Hundreds of people are on the beach, and before she moves on she registers a row of sandals at the entrance to the beach change rooms and toilets.

She makes her way to the Great Buddha, completely surrounded by crowds of people, everyone but her holding up a camera or phone. Carts with souvenirs move skilfully in and out the crowds. Stalls and kiosks sell replicas, cards, flags, towels with the image. The Buddha is very tall, and is sitting in the lotus position. The huge statue has eyes closed, as if exasperated by all the people. She doesn't blame him. The crowds intensify, although the mood remains cheerful and calm. It is impossible to see if there is a surrounding garden or smaller shrines, so she manages to get to the side of the crowds streaming through the stone gates and look up at this serene visage. A monument. Several hundred years old. Withstood tsunami, war, bombardment.

The sun is now obscured by clouds and the heat of the day is dissipating rapidly. She has been walking for over an hour, and it is time to find some tea.

The tropical storm bears down on the beach community. Flares light up the sky, warning surfers out of the water. The young gather in the transitory shelter of beach-front bars, until these close and shutter. Driven up the beach into the community — turning left — they are looking for their accommodations, clusters of surfers and bikini-clad girls consulting guidebooks. The storm intensifies, and soon the streets empty, as everyone seeks shelter. She retreats to her guest house, grateful she has a room, because when she comes into the small foyer, it is filled with people trying to get rooms for the night, to wait out the storm.

The guest house features a communal meal at the end of the day, to her surprise and dismay. She is the only non-Japanese guest, no wonder her hosts looked so alarmed when she arrived. The call display of Benjiro's phone must have mislead them, although there would have been no doubt an English-speaking person was making the booking. The office lady on behalf of her errant boss?

She seats herself on the floor at a table for six, trying not to make her effort evident. When she settles, the table becomes wrapped in silence because of Japanese courtesy not to speak Japanese before her. The meal reminds her of Cynthia's home. The long silences punctuated by careful questions in English (Mikio), attempts at humour in English (Benjiro), complaints in English (Cynthia), and silence (Number One Son). People at the table are kind but reticent, and she wants to tell them to speak Japanese — no need to include her. She doesn't.

"Are you on holidays?" the man across from her inquires. And so it begins, the twenty questions of travelling, most of which she cannot answer. Where are you from? Is this your first visit to Japan? How do you like the weather? Are you enjoying [insert tourist attraction here]? Where is your family today? Are you on a tour — or if perceptive perhaps — are you on a study tour?

She discovers if she answers, "This is my first visit. I live in Tokyo with my daughter," the questions cease. It seems Japanese people are kind and inquisitive until it becomes obvious she is a foreigner who makes her home in their home. Most Japanese people did not get much past the first question. Sometimes, giggling teenage girls would practise English on her, but usually she could not understand their English and they could not understand hers.

Soon, the table is filled with many small bowls and several platters. The colours and textures stimulate her appetite, in spite of her tea-and-cookies break less than an hour ago. Observing the cultural rules, she eats quietly, observing none of the habits she has come to appreciate in her grandsons. The younger taught her to slurp noodles, the two of them giggling as broth flew about their faces, spattered their glasses, bits of noodles shooting out of their laughing mouths. She would have loved a holiday with that little gaffer. Instead she decorously eats her dinner, noodles and all, without losing one iota onto her tunic. She frequently shifts her legs, extending first the right then the left, trying to ease the pain of sitting on the floor. She is relieved when everyone leaves before she does, effortlessly rising and walking out of the dining room, leaving her to unceremoniously hoist herself upright, shake out and wake up her feet and make her way to the small sitting room. The hubbub in the foyer spills into this sitting room, phones are ringing, people are exclaiming, and amid this jostle she finds some magazines to read and does so, or at least pretends to do so while she watches the kerfuffle.

Promptly at nine, she goes to her bedroom. She gingerly lowers herself onto the futon, and awkwardly unpacks while half-sitting, half lying on the bedding. She gets her clothes off and then lies naked staring up at the ceiling of this little space. The room is warm and quiet, although she can hear the wind and rain from the storm. Do tropical storms get names? Tropical Storm Ivy. More likely Tropical Storm Cynthia. Cindy. Tropical Storm Cindy.

She crawls off the bed and toward the short table. Using it to gain her feet, she gets out the dressing gown and puts it on, crosses the left over right. The communal bath opens onto the garden, and when she appears the two other occupants bow slightly and then everyone turns their attention to the wind and rain in the garden.

The koi pond looks like someone is tossing handfuls of pebbles into it. The hot water soothes, the benign indifference to her presence comforts her. For a moment, like a breath, she feels accepted. In a few minutes, she is alone, thus spared the anguish of rising and stepping up the few steps, her bare bottom exposed in all its glory. She rests a few more minutes then gets out, wraps herself in a provided towel and watches the miniature landscape of the garden beset by wind and rain.

Tea and hot water will be in her small room. She has a book. Tonight her review of the day will be close to a ten. She has done it. Escape: Day One.

Thirty-Four

Kamakura. July 22

The storm held its position overnight and there is news it might last for at least two more days. She learns this sitting in the dining room, watching the large TV rolled in during breakfast. The channel selected is Japanese, and so she gathers her information about the weather by watching the screen behind the weather reporter. After breakfast, she suits up in all she has for walking in a tropical storm and she goes into the street. It is marginally less crowded; the narrow streets continue to be filled with people walking toward the Great Buddha or shopping. The wind is quite strong, but nothing compared to winter storms in Vancouver, so she walks once again toward the stone gates, passes through the gauntlet of sales, finds a wall to stand against and looks up at the now rain-lashed figure.

He looks sad. His closed eyes signalled impatience yesterday, but today she reads in his expression stoic acceptance. Waiting. Enduring. The rain streaking down his body. The grey turning to a darker steel grey, rain pooling in the folds of his clothing, his hands forever poised in a thumb to finger pose. Indifferent to the hordes. Indifferent was probably not the right word. Oblivious? Detached? This massive figure will wait forever, sitting in a spiritually significant pose she does not understand. She understands nothing about the religion, the faith behind this figure. Who created it? The sculptor, long dead, was he proud of his masterpiece? Happy to get such a large commission to feed his family? Did he expect it would endure so long? Somewhere on the statue is there a tiny signature, the feudal Japanese equivalent of "I was here"?

Did anyone involved in its first few years expect, contemplate, the commercial enterprise, the concept of tourist attraction?

She stands for a much longer time than she intended, looking up at the face of the figure. The wind has kicked up, the rain is falling harder, and people are starting to take shelter in doorways, restaurants, bars. Shutters are going up. Carts are moving. She walks away from the figure, turning every hundred feet or so to look at it, now left alone, with eyes shut, contemplating — what?

Something about the statue makes her feel very sad. Tears, which have been standing in her eyes for a long time, begin to spill down her rain-spattered face. She is keenly aware she is a very old white woman walking too slowly down a rapidly emptying avenue, into the wind, not adequately dressed, crying. And there is nothing she can do to pull herself out of the mood.

She passes the entrance to the beach, now eerily empty. The waves are extraordinary; she has seen nothing like them. The beach has emptied as if there had not been hundreds of people on it less than twenty-four hours ago. The memory of sun is all that remains.

On her way back to the guest house, walking on quiet streets, watching merchants shutter their shops, she sees a little restaurant with a hand-written sign in kanji and

English: Open. She steps into the small space to find a few people sitting at Western-style tables. The menu is on the wall, and a smiling woman greets her in Japanese and then English. Welcome, come in, please, sit, we have lunch for you, she says cheerfully, as if a storm is not booming down the beach toward her place. Everyone smiles and nods at her, and when the next customers come in, two young European women, everyone smiles and nods at them too. She feels like they are all survivors from the storm and happy to be inside a warm secure space, together, with food available. She orders a Western-Style Salad as it is described, with tuna sashimi and a cup of clear, hot soup. The tea is ice-cold and fragrant and at the end of the meal, over which she is dawdling, she is offered a small cake filled with cream and coated in syrup.

She returns to the guest house feeling comfortably fed, and proud of her outing. The staff smile at her, and she is emboldened to ask for a chair, a Western chair. She is barely in her room when a tap on the door leads to the young man smiling, nodding, and bringing her a Western kitchen chair. She is so grateful she could either kiss him or tip him, if such actions were allowed. Maybe the next tap would bring a Western-style fold-out bed. She sits to take off her outer clothes, and in her smalls eases herself down to the floor and crawls into the bed. As she drifts into what she considers a well-deserved nap, the visage of the statue floats before her. Calm. Assuring. Advising her not to be sad.

At dinner, she enters the dining room to find it transformed to accommodate the extra guests. Two Western-style tables have been added, and one of the people from the night before waves her to join them.

The common "How was your day," gives her a chance to talk about walking up the deserted streets to get to the Great Buddha. A lively conversation ensues, with her at its centre and focus, and then when she talks about lunch she has to repeat the directions — draw a small map as Benjiro has taught her — so her companions can try it tomorrow. The meal passes in convivial conversation and laughter and she is talking so much her throat starts to feel raw.

At the end of the meal, she is invited into the sitting room, and the group has expanded to include a couple and their son, who looks about Keiijiro's age. He makes a point of sitting next to her; he has brought one of the Western chairs.

"My son, this son, he is going to Canada in September," his mother says.

Ivy turns to acknowledge him, and then says, "Oh, that's grand. Whereabouts?"

"Vancouver. He is accepted into the degree program at British Columbia University in Vancouver."

"I live — I lived in Vancouver." She is about to explain North Vancouver and its relationship to Vancouver but changes her mind. "Have you been there before?"

The mother answers, although they are all looking at the boy, "No, he has never been away from us."

"Well, Vancouver is a very nice city. The university is like a small town. It is beautiful. There is a garden, Nitobe Garden, which may remind you of home."

The boy and the mother exchange a few quick sentences in Japanese and then the woman says Nitobe as if to correct Ivy's pronunciation. Everyone smiles as the name of the garden is confirmed.

"Where will you be staying?" Ivy asks and the boy looks confused. "Where will you live?" she tries again.

He smiles and then says something she doesn't catch, and his mother explains, "In the residence. In the first year "quiet study" residence. No parties."

"No parties," Ivy repeats, with just a touch of skepticism in her voice. They all laugh, and then the boy excuses himself.

When he returns, he is carrying a carafe of tea, cups, and a Vancouver guidebook. It is the same publisher as her guidebook, and she looks at it and pronounces, "Lonely Planet" just as he does. More laughter.

The next hour passes pleasantly. The boy has put sticky notes on several pages, and he has questions about the metro (Skytrain, she corrects), bicycles (absolutely, with helmet, she advises), Chinese food (*Chinese?*Yes, authentic Western Chinese food), Sea Bus (you will love it), Grouse Grind (don't know) and much more. The parents sit in happy silence, watching their boy converse — as he warms up — confidently with this foreign lady. By 9, she has a sore throat and yet is filled with energy and sparkle. She says good night to the family, wishing she could give him a piece of paper with her address and phone number on it, so she could look forward to visits from this young fellow sometime in the fall.

The *onsen* is crowded, and many of those in the pool are not familiar with the protocols. Ivy sits with a view of the garden, now getting a serious thrashing from the storm. The lights are flickering, the wind can be heard when it gusts, and although they all know disaster is not possible in this low, concrete building, when a particularly ferocious gust rattles the windows, they look at one another and grimace playfully.

She goes to her room. She sits for a few minutes in the chair, looking up at the windows. She cannot see what the sky is doing, because it is dark and the windows are too high. She closes her eyes, pretending to be the Great Buddha.

What is she thinking?

THIRTY-FIVE

Kamakura. July 25

She spends three more days at the guest house, and because no one can go anywhere for most of the time, a sense of community builds. Guests exchange books and magazines, give each other tips about the few restaurants open, share snacks, and the sitting room becomes a story-telling circle. The third evening, Ivy produces her crochet, and two other women bring their handwork. When, on her last day, the news confirms the storm has moved off and the trains are once again moving on time, she is sorry to see the end of her vacation. She has, she tells herself as she climbs once more to her feet from the bed, had the best time since she came to Japan. And she doesn't feel guilty about acknowledging that. She will, however, have a hard time not blurting out a story or two about her grand adventure.

That afternoon, she makes her way back to Tokyo, retracing her steps. She will arrive, she calculates, three days before Cynthia and crew, giving her enough time to straighten everything out, discard the groceries — a plan about which she feels quite bad — and arrange herself as if she has not done more than her daily walks around the block, with perhaps one trip to the dollar store.

Imagine her surprise, then, when the apartment door is opened as she is getting her key out, and her daughter is standing there, so angry she is vibrating and white around her lips. As both women open their mouths, she notes the two boys and Mikio slipping behind Cynthia to the shelter of their rooms.

"Where."

"I was just."

"We have been so — I have been so worried. I thought."

"I decided to take a trip to the museum, you know, the one I have asked you about," Ivy begins, hoping Cynthia, in her fury, won't notice the carry-all on the floor in the landing.

"We've been home for *four* days, Mother. Four days. Where have you been?"

"I — um — I — " and she feels her head start to wobble and her voice falter. She thinks now would be a good time to have a stroke, although of the two of them Cynthia is probably the one most likely to experience an explosion in her head.

And then the most extraordinary thing happens. Cynthia grabs her by both arms and yanks her into the apartment. She slams the door, hard, leaving the luggage in the hall. Ivy yelps in pain.

"Where have you been? I have been frantic. We called the *police*. We walked around the block for hours, thinking you had fallen somewhere. I called the *hospital*. Where have you been? I looked in your room, and your bag isn't there. I thought you went home."

Cynthia is pacing wildly from the kitchen area to the sitting room, to the sliding glass door, and back. Ivy is leaning against the wall beside the shoes, trying to get her shoes off. Once again, Cynthia grabs her, this time by one hand and pulls her into the sitting area. The only reason she doesn't throw her onto the sofa is Ivy is already falling on to it, her hand sending off alarms of pain.

Oh, my god. My daughter has broken my hand. She is unable to form any answers to the shrill questions pounding down on her, and she is afraid. For the first time in her adult life, she is afraid someone is going to hit her.

Rescue of a sort arrives in the form of her son-in-law. He comes from behind Cynthia and says something in Japanese; it sounds like the sort of command one hears in martial arts movies. This gentle man can assert control in his household, it appears. Cynthia, still shouting, replies to him, and he speaks again — sternly, though not raising his voice. He puts his hands on his wife's shoulders, she stiffens, and then falls against him, still complaining.

Mikio looks at Ivy over his wife's head. He doesn't smile but neither does he look like he's going to hit her. He looks down at her hand, which she is holding protectively against her belly, touching her money belt. Her luggage is outside. Maybe in the lull, she will stand up, straighten her jacket, and march decisively out of their lives.

She doesn't, of course. She feels to blame, is sorry, and is registering again her fear of her daughter. Of all the things she anticipated about coming to Japan, being hit by her daughter was not one of them. Neither she nor Jack ever raised a hand to Cynthia, in spite of the many tempests during her life with them. Maybe a good smack on her bottom would have taught her more than all their calm and patient correction.

"I'm sorry. I am sorry. I thought I would be back before you, so I did not leave a message. I am sorry I worried you." Cynthia still has her face pressed against her husband's shirt. "I took a trip. I took the train to Kamakura. I stayed at a ryokan. I was safe there during the storm. I had money. I had my cards. Your address and name is in my purse. I'm sorry."

Cynthia whirls. "You'd better be," she shouts, taking a menacing step toward her.

Ivy flinches, Mikio takes hold of his wife by the shoulders, and the three of them freeze in place, as if playing a high-stakes game of Simon Says. For a flash, Ivy remembers playing Simon Says in the back yard, on the velvet green grass, she and Cynthia moving orderly, or sometimes not so orderly, toward "Simon." She can almost feel the cool slipping down from Cypress Mountain, on those fine, long evenings at the end of the summer. Simon Says, "Take a step." Jack loved playing Simon Says. She can hear his voice ordering, "Hop on one foot" in his military style, the command so compelling everyone always fell for it. And she hears his laugh. Hears him laughing as if he just stepped out of the room and would be right back to sort out the long-standing conflict between the two women he loved most in the world.

Simon Says, "Speak."

"I saw the Great Buddha," Ivy offers. Her hand is starting to send up flares of pain. "The storm wasn't too bad. The guest house was well prepared. I took the high speed train."

She hears her voice and she stops. She sounds obsequious. Pathetic. A foolish old woman.

"I have been going on excursions for weeks," she confesses. "I started following the directions in the guidebook. I never once got lost," she adds, lying through her teeth. Still, if she's sitting here, she didn't get lost, really. "I knew what I was doing."

Cynthia opens her mouth in a face bright red with anger. Her eyes are blood-shot, and her usually immaculate hair a mess. It looks like she hasn't brushed her hair or washed her face in . . . four days.

"I should have told you," Ivy says. "I'm sorry." She will say no more until Cynthia responds.

"Why," Cynthia says, although it sounds like a statement not a question. "Why would you do such a thing?"

The hours, days, weeks of inactivity and boredom, the effort not to look too hopeful if a walk was proposed, how sick she had started to feel, all come boiling up. She now wants to shriek, and punch, and throw something. Maybe the ceramic bowl through the sliding glass window. The words seethe, the sentences, all the things she wants to shout at her daughter, who has been so unkind, so just plain mean, for weeks and weeks.

"I'm sorry," she says. "I wanted to get to know Tokyo. I didn't think any harm would come."

"Were you just going to pretend you had not been away?"

"Yes."

"Mother," Cynthia starts, and then subsides against the body of her man, who is still holding her shoulders. She shakes her head slightly, says something to Mikio, and leaves them.

This is worse, in a way. Mikio has never been anything but kind and gentle. Even when he is obviously bone tired, he will often be the one to suggest an outing on a Sunday. He doesn't deserve this. He is probably as in the dark about her behaviour as anyone could be.

"I am sorry," she repeats. She sits up straight and removes her second shoe. Mikio steps forward, takes it from her, and brings her the house slippers. She knows he will not ask her about her hand, because to do so will verify what has just happened.

My daughter has broken my hand.

"Please," Mikio says, as he sits on the floor. "Please do not leave the home without telling us where you are going. Please."

She nods. This would appear to be the negotiations for peace.

"We will bring you a phone, so you can send us messages and we can send you messages."

"Yes."

"Please stay here unless we are advised. It is not a good thing for you to travel alone in Tokyo. The city is very large and very confusing."

She is about to contradict him, but refrains. "I would like to go to some of the museums," she observes, lowering her voice. Both of them can hear Cynthia making noise in the bedroom. What she could be doing is beyond contemplation. Throwing wire baskets of underwear on the floor?

Mikio nods. "We will discuss plans for you to visit the museums."

"And the library," she suggests, not having any idea if there is a library in Tokyo or if they have any books in English. But the captivity, for that is what it has begun to feel like, is closing in on her. If she cannot leave the apartment except when she gets approval, approval she will have to get from her daughter, she will go mad with inactivity.

Mikio nods. They both sit, looking down.

"Please do not go far unattended," Mikio asks. This is the final request. He is asking for a promise.

She nods. If she could place her hand behind her, with its crushed fingers, she would cross two of them.

The next time she runs away, she's going home.

THIRTY-SIX

Tokyo, Saitama Prefecture. August. Average daily temperature 31°C, eight days of rain

Her daughter has not broken her hand, but she was awake most of the night with the hand throbbing, getting hotter and hotter, and swelling until she could barely distinguish her fingers. Even her fingernails looked bruised. When she fell asleep in the early morning, she missed the morning hustle, so when she puts in an appearance, with a long-sleeve blouse pulled down over her hands, no one is in the apartment. The housekeeper arrives and holds the door open, expecting her to be leaving. Ivy retreats to the bathroom and inspects her hand. The swelling has gone down, and she can move her fingers. She stands at the little sink, cold water running over both hands, stalled by the events of the evening. Never afraid physically of anyone, she does not know what to think about what happened. She decides to think nothing.

About noon, Benjiro comes into the apartment, wearing shorts and a T-shirt. His hair is wet and he is carrying a towel and a book. Unlike his usual greeting, he nods and disappears. She concludes she is in trouble with all of them, or her daughter has ordered the grandchildren not to talk to her.

Not as terrible as that — it turns out the boys are on school holiday for the month of August, so Benjiro is not required to sit with his grandmother from four thirty to six. What he does do is snack all afternoon and watch television for a while and then play a game on his phone. His frequent excursions into the kitchen give her something to do; she tidies after him and in the process discovers how to make ramen for herself. At about four she goes for her permitted walk, telling Benjiro, whose head is down over his phone, she will be back by five.

It is blistering hot outside, the pavement radiating heat upward. She decides to go to the metro and walk along the corridor as far as she can in thirty minutes. Her money belt is thin but she can still afford a small ice cream, and she walks along, not paying attention to the shops. At the thirty-minute mark, she turns about and returns home.

Cynthia arrives and it becomes obvious in a minute or so she is not speaking to her mother. She asks Benjiro something in Japanese and then she turns her attention and activity to making dinner. Ivy sits on the sofa, with the sliding doors open, glad for the evening breeze bringing cooler air. To say the situation is awkward would be an understatement. She sits, looking at the blank TV, waiting.

August is a month of waiting. The shock of the quarrel wears off but the consequences do not. It feels as if she is confined to barracks. Dinners are excruciating, and she is only glad Mikio misses all of them, coming in as he does much later. Every day she goes for a walk, around and around the block or up and down the corridor of the metro. By the end of the first week she has run out of money and by the third week she has only five thyroid pills left.

The arrival of the promised cell phone gives Benjiro and her a chance to interact without earning a scowl from his mother. They spend a couple of hours figuring out how to use the phone. It is unlike any she has seen her friends using, and Benjiro barely has the vocabulary to teach her. He does, however, and the two of them laugh when she successfully calls his cell phone and he answers it, the two of them less than two-feet apart. He also shows her how to enter search terms into a little box; although he is not able to explain what he has taught her to do, she understands she can now "surf the web" and she even knows what that means.

Cynthia speaks fewer than four complete sentences to her and Mikio comes in too late for her to enlist his aid in conversations.

One evening, having learned that the boys have gone out after dinner "to play" (whatever that means in this ultra-urban landscape), she bides her time recalling Cynthia going out in the summer evenings to play with friends in the park near their North Van home. When it was time, Jack and she would walk together to fetch her, usually finding her on the swings or sitting on the top of the monkey bars, talking with her chums. They always wrecked her day, as she often told them, by coming so early to round her up and bring her home. Where do Cynthia's boys go? Since they rarely seem to speak to each other, she has a hard time imagining them together playing on swings in the park.

Cynthia is doing dishes, a task she refuses to share with anyone, so Ivy decides to take the plunge.

"Cynthia, I wonder if we could — I am quite short of money, cash, and the past three — "

"Weeks I haven't given you any. I know. I haven't. I don't want you wandering off, so I haven't gone to the bank for you." Cynthia continues with her scrubbing, her head down, moving efficiently.

"Yes, I understand. I have been walking every day, with no trouble, and I do like to have money in case I need something."

"Like what. Tell me what you need and I'll buy it when I shop on the way home."

"But I don't have anything to do. To read." Ivy catches the whine in her tone and straightens up, so she is standing at attention at the end of the counter. Cynthia plugs in the kettle for their ritual tea after dinner, a ritual that has been agony for the past three weeks.

"Benjiro will take you to the library. It is quite close."

"I would like to have my own money," she repeats.

"If this is about the cheque."

"No. No, it isn't. I — We had an arrangement that you would give me some of my own money every week, on Mondays, after you went to your bank. I am asking you for some of my own money."

Cynthia slams cups onto the counter. The teapot takes a serious hit going from the cupboard to the counter top. "I just don't want you going anywhere."

Ivy finds, to her horror, she has tucked her hands out of sight in her pockets. "I won't. That is, I agreed I would not go anywhere without discussing it with you and Mikio." She slips in his name, hoping doing so will calm her daughter. Turning on the game show and getting out her crochet seems like a good idea.

"I don't want you going somewhere and getting lost. We thought you were lost."

"I know. I am sorry. I am not asking because I want to go somewhere . . . "

"What do you need money for, anyway?"

"Well, everybody likes to have a few coins to rub together," she replies, mimicking Jack's expression. She can almost hear his voice now, cajoling her to wait for another, better day.

If you don't give me some of my own money, I am going to Shinjuku myself and get some from the ATM, she warns, silently. Because she has determined this is what she will do if her daughter remains unwilling. I will go to the Canadian embassy and tell them I am being held captive by my daughter. I will call 911 and tell them I've fallen in Tokyo and I can't get up.

This threat brings a smile to her face, just as Cynthia glances at her.

"I suppose you think this is funny?"

"No. No, it's not funny. None of this is funny."

"None of what? What do you mean? None of what?"

The door opens, and rescue is at hand, but it's only her grandsons, and they quickly assess the situation and retreat. Their door closes.

Round Two.

"I always managed my own money, Cynthia. You know that. I would like to be able to buy a magazine, a package of crisps, an ice cream." A ticket home.

She hears her voice, placatory, pleading almost. If she can only keep the whine out — it is the best she can hope for now. The idea she will get some money is as remote as finding something sensible to watch on TV.

Cynthia picks up the tray and brushes past. She puts the tray down, settles on the floor, and pours herself tea. Cultural rule violation number seven.

Ivy sits on the sofa, facing the TV, and waits.

Cynthia is inspecting her fingernails. Her hair could use a cut. She is losing weight. She looks tired, and her lower lip is trembling almost imperceptibly. Only a mother would notice.

Sounds rise from the street. Night is coming on. In North Vancouver at this time, birds would be singing their "We're so sleepy" songs and Jack would be saying "What's that one," as he always did. And she never knew.

She has travelled so far down memory lane she doesn't, for a second, know what they are arguing about. "I will not go anywhere without discussing it with you. I promise."

Cynthia does not respond.

It's a draw.

Mikio takes the remote from its location on the highly polished table. Ivy learned not to leave anything on this table, including her crochet materials, the night many weeks ago when Mikio picked up her tools and placed them back in her bag. Only the remote and one highly polished pot sit on the table, the pot reflecting the surface of the table and the table reflecting the pot in an endless loop.

At the commercial break of the game show, Mikio uses the remote to go to a blue screen with Japanese symbols. He moves deftly through several screens, reminding her of Jack programming the VCR so they could tape his beloved football games.

Benjiro appears and comes to stand silently behind his father, leaning slightly against his back. She is now attuned to such gestures, and she finds them touching. The boy and the man have such similar profiles, the hair falling in the same way, neither of them aware of her scrutiny.

Task done, Mikio replaces the remote precisely and nods at the TV. Beneath the picture, a black box has appeared, and in this box scroll English words. Mikio's second son exclaims and plops himself down beside her so quickly she bounces. Mikio utters a quiet reprimand and Benjiro says quickly, "*sumimasen*." She replies, as she has learned, "*donmai*," the equivalent of the English "no bother." They sit, transfixed. The captions are a bit ragged, and the game-show English reads as demented as the host appears to be. The interpretation contains much jargon, but she doesn't care. She sits, mouth agape, handwork stilled in her lap.

August 30, with no money in sight, Ivy breaks her promise and — in the guise of going for her daily walk — takes the metro to Shinjuku, locates the bank of ATMs that will take her foreign debit card, withdraws thousands of yen and returns to the apartment. Not until she gets in the door and ascertains her absence has not been detected does she take a proper breath. She has also squandered some of her money on two magazines and a paperback mystery by Louise Penney, items she will have to hide in her room, probably under the mattress, as she once did with a contraband copy of *Lady Chatterley's Lover*, achieved at great risk. Only bad girls read *LCL*, as it was coded, and she and her friend read the first few pages in the movie theatre, hiding the cover, and looking for the naughty bits. As she recalls, the naughty bits were obscured by Lawrence's language, and when she did find them, she didn't understand them.

She knows she will have better luck with the Louise Penney mystery.

THIRTY-SEVEN

Tokyo, Saitama Prefecture. September 1, 33°C, sunny

September hoves into view and the children prepare to return to school. New uniforms arrive home with Cynthia, who has been working all summer except for the one-week holiday. She does not speak to Ivy except to direct questions about provisions she might need to get through the days. The boys have been out and about for most of August, and the daily Monopoly game or reading of the Collins compendium have been on hold until school starts up. Cynthia has not suggested further Monday trips to her language school. Ivy walks every day, at the required time, in the blistering heat. When everyone is out, the apartment is stifling. She sits by the open sliding glass window but there is rarely a breeze. The streets are hot, heat rising in waves. When she goes to bed, every night at nine, her room is also stifling. She lies on the top of the bedding, in her underwear, her nightgown folded over her stomach, and reviews the day.

Mikio has been coming in later and later and often she has dozed before she hears him. The boys stay up late, though, often watching something on TV with Cynthia, and sometimes the family talks in lively conversation. The situation would be intolerable if she had any way to make it tolerable, but she doesn't. She is unable to figure out what to do. She has now run out of her thyroid medication, and since she doesn't know what will happen if she stops taking it she decides to wait and find out.

She will keep quiet. Observant and quiet. With no one to talk to, she talks to no one, exchanges smiles with the lady at the ramen shop, who has taken to waving at her as she passes on her daily walk, but otherwise there is no one to talk to. She wishes her phone would let her call Norma, but what could she say to her? How could she tell anyone that her daughter has taken the cheque for the house, and is preventing her from gaining access to her own money? If she were to call Norma, she is afraid she would burst into tears and be unable to say anything.

They've forgotten about you, she tells herself, appreciating she is being maudlin. She sent Norma the postcard weeks ago, and there has been no reply. No mail for her at all. No catalogues. No leaflets advertising gardening or pop-up markets at the quay. No form letters from the government advising her to register to vote or recycle correctly or put her compost bins out the day they are being collected and not the night before (*bears*). When she and Benjiro start reading the *Collins Boys Annual* again, maybe she will tell him a few of her bears in North Vancouver stories.

No letters from home. Is this what Mum experienced? She did write letters, and after her mother's death, these letters were offered to her. She didn't want them back. Now, she'd kill to have those letters, to match with the ones from her mother, scraps of information, masters of allusions.

This month of penance is like the time after Jack died. Her friends gathered around immediately after, and she was grateful. Friends called, invited her for tea, brought her food, flowers, wine. But then, sometime in the third or fourth month, the phone stopped. It was about the six-month mark when she realized she had lost almost all her friends. Even women like her, widows, seemed to have dropped her. She admitted she wasn't much fun to be around, with Jack — the entertainer — no longer taking the lead in conversations.

She is sorry now she used to make fun of the old codgers gathering at fast food restaurants or the food fair in the mall: romeos, Jack called them. Retired Old Men Eating Out. She is so lonely she might even try to join one of these groups, if Tokyo had such a phenomenon. She is used to seeing clutches of teenage boys and herds of high school girls, but groups of romeos or roweos are nowhere to be seen. Where do they put the old people in this city and culture that revere the elderly?

Aside from wondering what the effects of suddenly not taking thyroid medication is having on her body, she has another pressing concern. She is unable to trim the toenails on the toes second to her pinky toes. She has not been able to cut the nails on the second-last toes of each foot for nearly five years. If she were feeling really flexible, she could tackle it with a nail file, but lately the contortion required to get her foot close enough to her nail scissors or nail file is beyond her. Last year, she found she could put her foot on the bathtub edge and reach the problem toes with the force of gravity, and some squishing of her belly and breasts. This apartment has no similar ledge, and she knows doing such personal care at the *onsen* would be greeted with horror.

The nails are growing at an angle as a result, and the sharp edge is digging into the middle toe on each foot. She bought some bandaids at the dollar store, and every day she applies the pad between the sharp nail and the middle toe. Doing so is awkward; she can't really see what she is doing. What she can see, when she sits on her bed and extends her feet for inspection, is both middle toes have raw, red spots. Great. She applies ointment from a tube of something she thought might be similar to Polysporin and boldly purchased from the convenience store kiosk at the metro station. She will get a blood-borne infection and die of flesh-eating disease, all for want of a pedicure.

If an under-active thyroid run amok doesn't get her first.

THIRTY-EIGHT

Tokyo, Saitama Prefecture. September 10, 28°C, sunny
with cloudy periods

Well past the ninety-day point, her visa's expiry date, she
decides to make her first visit to an Immigration Bureau
(*nyukoku kanrikyoku*). Using the search function on the
phone, she discovers the address and then uses the metro
map to get the directions. The ninety-day point has drifted
past, and the six-month mark is rapidly approaching. She
will be out of travel insurance and out of blood pressure
medication. While she does not seem to be any the worse
for not using thyroid medication, blood pressure control
is another matter.

Mikio no longer comes home in time for dinner.
Whether he is avoiding the tension in his home or it is
simply the demands of work, he isn't home until nine or
ten. With the start of the new school year, the boys are
hard at homework every night, with or without a squabble
from their mother.

"Cynthia, I plan to go to the Immigration Bureau this
week to see about my visa," she announces as they are
having their evening tea.

Cynthia for once does not look about for something
to clean or straighten. She looks instead into her cup as
if there might be leaves there by which she could tell her

fortune. "Yes," she agrees, almost placidly. "We need to get that sorted for you."

Ivy takes such a large gulp of hot tea she has tears in her eyes. Not wishing to break the moment of cordiality, she rattles on, even though she can feel the tea landing with a crash in her stomach. "I can get started. I know you are busy. I will go to the place and get the forms and find out what I need to do. I have the directions and the hours."

"Can I see?" Cynthia asks.

Ivy goes to her bedroom, wondering if somehow today a stranger has possessed the body of her daughter. Passing the boys' room on her way, she glances in and finds them both on their phones, so probably not doing homework. Another storm this evening.

She hands over the index card with the stops and the exits. Cynthia takes out her phone and does a few moves with her thumb and then nods.

"I think maybe this other exit will take you to the better intersection."

They both sit for several minutes in silence.

"Where did you go?" Cynthia asks.

"The museum, mostly. It's a complex. There's a lot to see."

"Why?"

"Why?

"Why did you go and not tell us?"

Ivy has no answer, and Cynthia's tone indicates she expects none. There she is, just for a moment, just past the bristling surface: her daughter. Why, indeed?

While the women are finishing their tea, the boys come in with an obviously rehearsed request. She seldom

247

sees Benjiro and Keiijiro together, and this is the second time she has heard an extended statement from the older boy. They are speaking Japanese and Cynthia is replying in English. Benjiro looks so like his father he could be his brother, with no sign, not one sign, of his mother's genes. Unlike the older boy, who has the exotic appeal of a *hafu*, with his dyed hair, his aquiline nose — Mom's nose, actually — his smoky blue eyes, his body. With his slender frame he looks so like Cynthia when she was the same age; it was as if she would never get the secondary sex characteristics so sought after by girls as they grew into their teens. The clothes this boy wears perfectly suit his body type. He could be a model, like the ones on the sky-scraper billboards in her journeys through the Tokyo landscape.

He could be a model, as Cynthia desperately wanted to be when she was fifteen, loudly complaining about her parents' inability to pay for her to attend "modelling classes" with two of her friends. A school barely disguised as a dance school, with sky-high fees and no guarantee the students would gain work as magazine or even catalogue models. She remembers overhearing the girls reviewing the flyers that came in the local paper, making fun of the discount store fashions, their treble adolescent voices dismissing the white-bread good looks of page after page of children and young people wearing the latest fashions according to Sears or Zellers. This was "back in the day," before the internet introduced children to the Gap, Macy's, Old Navy. Cynthia would — it turned out — steal the fashion magazines from the corner convenience store, and Ivy would find them, with annotations on some of the models and, worse, pen marks where Cynthia had re-drawn the already skinny flanks and thighs to be even smaller.

It transpires the boys want to watch a music special, which they can get on their computer but would be more exciting on the big TV. Cynthia agrees, after everyone promises all the homework is done. Ivy is happy to have ducked out of the rest of the conversation about immigration. They all settle to watch. After a few minutes Benjiro turns on the English captions, and Cynthia produces some snacks that taste a lot like pretzels. When Mikio comes in, looking so tired, she wants to exclaim, "See? We can get along."

An office lady in a grey suit jacket, stylishly short thus not meeting the waistband of her skirt, a white blouse with a complicated front, extravagant hair, makeup far from the "you have some slap on" of *Coronation Street* — all this Ivy registers as she waits her turn. Stomach abroil. Holding the printed pages Cynthia gave her at breakfast. Will they send her home? And if home is an apartment in Saitama Prefecture, what then?

Three clerks, three chances, but Ivy knows she will get the perilously young office lady in her expensive suit, who greets her with the ubiquitous phrase in Japanese, even though it's clear from the startled alarm in her eyes she knows what is coming next.

"Do you speak English?"

"Yes, please."

"I live here in Tokyo with my daughter and I need an external resident's visa."

"You must get one of these from your home country."

"Yes. I know."

"May I see your air or vessel ticket, please?"

"I lost it. I . . . no . . . I . . . " Ivy looks at this young woman, not much older than Keiijiro and sees no avenue to her sympathy. The unviable lie hangs between them like a sock on a laundry line, barely twitching.

"It was one-way. I intended to return within ninety days, and so my husband, that is, my daughter's husband is ill, and I've . . . " she falters, superstitious, "I stayed on."

Crisply, Ivy's interlocutor nods and next she is sitting in a small cubicle in one of four chairs facing an unadorned divider covered in grey carpet.

What if they ask me when I arrived?

They do. Or rather the man who examines her passport knows because the date is stamped right on it.

Or when did Mikio fall ill?

Not exactly that. Or rather worse than that. A form exists on which the details of Mikio's illness are to be completed by his doctor. Ivy takes this form, scared now her lie is going to unfold into a narrative of such instability she will find herself deported. Cast out. Leaving behind the money in Cynthia's bank account.

More forms follow. Terse questions to which she has no reasonable answers, such as where does Mikio work, where does Cynthia work, what is Ivy's cell phone number.

"May I see your traveller's insurance?"

Ivy produces the card, with the date of expiry stamped on it. September 27, 2007. If she was planning to stay for ninety days, why did she purchase twice as much insurance?

"May I see your record of earnings?"

This is Japanese tact; she is obviously well beyond sixty, the usual age for a Japanese woman to retire. She smiles

250

and meets the impassive expression she knows well from her travels on the metro. When a Japanese face gives nothing away, it is actually an expression of disapproval.

"No. I have the Canada old age pension."

"Old Age Security," he corrects her. "And your husband?" His eyes on her wedding ring.

"I have his CCP."

Swiftly, using a form with columns for figures to be entered, he and she together determine she is indigent, not collecting sufficient money to live independently in Japan, or at least in Tokyo. Another form appears, this one to be completed by Ivy's guarantors, her daughter and son-in-law.

Ivy's smile falters, her lips tighten over the scene of getting these forms completed.

"Any other assets?"

A bank draft my daughter has taken. Over half-a-million Canadian, indeed nearly 800 *thousand* dollars.

She does not speak these treacherous words, blinks against her own dismay. She would confess nearly everything to this officer of Japanese foreign affairs, everything but this — that her daughter has taken her money.

"I have money coming from the sale of my house."

"Where is this house?"

Oh, not another form. "Vancouver."

A slight shift of eyebrows. "North Vancouver," she amends. "North," she says again.

"You will need this, a form for permission to open and maintain an account as a Foreign Resident."

All forms in Japanese and English. All to be completed by October 1, the deadline on the application, an Extraordinary Request — for Foreign Resident status.

Sometimes being "a grey-haired old grandmother" has its advantages, perhaps. Or he is being kind. Or there is no line of plaintiffs outside his cubicle.

Jack's years of paying the mortgage has saved her. Saved her for a life in a land that does not want her. Saved her for life in a household beset —

As she assembles the forms, she drops one, drops her reading glasses, bends over and nearly bangs her head on the corner of his desk, his hand appearing to cover the corner and her forehead a whisper away from his skin.

She leaves terrified and sorry. Realizing she had hoped and wanted to be unceremoniously, or perhaps ceremoniously, clapped in irons and escorted off the premises, that would be off the island, that would be away from Japan.

THIRTY-NINE

Tokyo, Saitama Prefecture. September. Average temperature 28°C, sunny

"What is it?" her grandson asks her, as they are eating what they all refer to as Western cereal in the kitchen at breakfast.

"Pardon?" she says.

He wrinkles his nose at his bowl. "Excuse me?" he says, laughing so that milk dribbles out his mouth.

She knows he doesn't understand her constant apologies. "Sorry," she offers, causing threat of choking in her grandson.

"It. It is hot today. *It?*" he explains.

She is fair baffled by that herself. Maybe Cynthia could give her some quick explanations for these expressions and usages. Although Cynthia herself does not care for her mother's expressions, such as "that girl" and "our Cynthia", expressions of endearment, like dear itself, a word Cynthia asked her to stop applying to her friends when they were all fourteen or so. Good thing she has already given up "love" and "pet". Perhaps when Cynthia relents and takes her to the language school again, she can ask Mrs. Yamamoto. Does she ever ask after Mrs. Ibee? What does Cynthia say? Does Cynthia have a friend to whom she confides her frustration with her mother?

Cynthia's version of the story of her deceitful, probably slightly ga-ga mother.

Her cookies, on the other hand, are a big success. She found the ingredients in the dollar store, so goodness knows when they passed their best-before date, but she made sugar cookies anyway, figuring she could eat them and perhaps be carried off by the mealworms happily living in the flour. No such worms are found, however, and the sugar cookies come out of the toaster oven six at a time, golden brown with a dusting of berry sugar. Benjiro is thrilled, eating two at a time until she manages to stop him. They read the ingredients together, justifying the consumption of another two by reciting sugar, flour, shortening, vanilla, milk, and egg. The other person who seems bowled over by the cookies is her perennially cranky daughter.

Ivy looks in the dressing room mirror. In the wide-legged cotton trousers and long white tunic, she looks like someone else. Who knew those tiny Japanese women got wide in the waist as they grew older? With the draw-string and elastic, the pants move with her, and the tunic is a beautiful, soft, heavy cotton with embroidery on the sleeves. She looks as if she's wearing a Halloween costume. All she needs is a coolie hat and canvas slippers like the ones in Chinatown. Is there such a place in Japan? Why, with all the Japanese who lived in Vancouver before the war, was there no Japantown? Maybe somewhere in Tokyo there's a Canada town or, more likely, an America town. Although after the war, the occupation of Japan by American troops turned the whole place into America town, one would think.

She decides to buy the clothes, especially when she realizes the trousers have extra padding on the knees.

The shop girl comes into the curtained area. She smiles and bows slightly, like a miniature applause. This is her first purchase of clothing in Tokyo. She asks if she can wear them out of the shop, and after a few minutes of confusion, her request in English is granted in Japanese. Proud of her achievement, she accepts the bag with her old clothes and leaves, tucking the map and directions into her purse. She has quite a collection of "how do I get there" index cards.

Few streets in Tokyo have names. When she first asked a fellow in one of the ever-available police boxes how to get to a museum, he had asked her for the code of the building. The only way he could help her was to look at her phone, to ascertain the Japanese name for the place she was trying to get to. She has also learned, with Benjiro's coaching, how to use the GPS on her phone, which would project her position onto a map. Once she learned which way was up, this feature of the phone saved her more than once. When she did spot street signs, often when she no longer needed them, they were small plaques usually attached to a building and therefore almost tucked out of sight. She still has no idea what the series of digits after the name on the plaque mean. More than once in the past month she has found herself not where she intended to be, and when she was questioned at the end of the day by Cynthia she had to explain her change of plans without letting on she'd been unable to find the original destination. Everyone else on the streets seemed to have no trouble, although walking with a phone out was a very, very common sight.

FORTY

Tokyo, Saitama Prefecture. October 1, 24°C, cloudy

Ivy's goal today is the Institute for Nature Study. The
guidebook promises a primeval forest in central Tokyo.
She is warned admission is limited every day, and so she
hopes the time of year will be good fortune for her. She is
also promised turtle-filled ponds and strolls.

When she gets there she discovers three tour buses
lined up near the entrance. These buses remind her of the
buses at Royal Oak Mall, although with reverse ethnicity.
This looks like a tour for the aged, she concludes, as
she watches more than one person with a cane. The
groups are marshalling before their tour guides, who are
holding aloft colourful umbrellas. She takes a chance,
darts around the groups as only a seventy-eight-year-old
woman can dart, and fetches up at the ticket booth ahead
of the motley crowd.

She is admitted. Her ticket is time-stamped and is
number sixty-two. Within steps, the sounds from the
entrance fall away and she finds herself in a forest that
in many ways is like Capilano Canyon. She hears crows in
the upper storey and some sort of whistling insect close to
the ground. The promised ponds are not manicured as
were the ponds in Kamakura, and in the warm high-cloud
afternoon, turtles are basking on logs jutting into the

water or large rocks semi-immersed. Dragonflies. Wild fields of grasses. Flat crushed gravel walks and wide, deep steps very kind to her knee. The trees are varieties she does not know, and many leaves are starting to change colour. From every angle lines of trees are receding as far as she can see. Some look familiar to her, but none are the massive cedar and fir she is used to. At times the path narrows so the trees are enclosing her. It is enchanting. She is enchanted. Even the little tea kiosk with picnic tables does not disturb the calm of the forest.

On her way out, she encounters a black tree with four elongated limbs, very close to the path. Like the huge cedars in Capilano Canyon, this tree exudes strength and almost perceptible personality. The tree must be very old, although it is not as big as the old-growth trees in Vancouver. Standing close to it, she can almost hear it breathing. What stories you could tell. She looks up at the greenery, trying to identify the tree, and then — with no one in sight — she reaches over the rope and puts her hand on the trunk. Her hand, brown spots, light-blue lines visible in the faded skin, puckers, her wedding ring imbedded in her finger; the tips of her fingers encounter the rough bark of this tree. Beyond is a surround of greens, as if sheltered by this old beauty. From her fingertips, she feels warmth radiating up her hand, like the warmth from the *onsen*. Her bones seem to exhale. She exhales, as if she has been holding her breath for all these months. If someone told her the tree has been electrified she would not be surprised, because she feels tingling between her fingertips and the bark. Her eyes closed, she stands for many minutes, listening to the tree. It is only when she hears the hushed murmurs of an approaching group that she steps back and drops her hand. In spite of the tour crowd descending, she remains there, looking up at the limbs of this tree. If she were a youngster, she would be tempted to climb. The small sign in the crotch of the tree probably says "Do Not Climb," but since she cannot read kanji, she does not know what the sign says.

She walks on, determined to keep ahead of the tour group with their umbrella-wielding guide. She will tell Cynthia, at her inquisition, about the forest but not about the tree.

It is time to find her way home. Her index card tells her she will walk for ten minutes along busy Meguro Dori to Meguro Station. McDonald's is her landmark. From there she will get to Yamanote Line, and it will take her toward Wakoshi.

The tour buses are now grouped along the busy street. She emerges with the tourists who are showing one another their gift shop purchases and park guides.

They see a Tokyo she does not see. And then they go home. She literally steps back in shock at the homesickness, like nausea, she experiences. They get to go home and tell their friends all about their trip. She will never do that. Never go home and show her pictures to her friends at the mall, give them goofy tourist gifts, hear everyone laugh.

Maybe they won't notice one more grey-haired grandmother. Not one wearing this peasant outfit. Next time she goes out, she vows to wear the two-piece polyester pantsuit that whistles when she walks. Can't hear herself think in that get-up. In her new outfit, all she can hear is the sound of her own breathing.

She stands through several light changes, a temporary rock in the river of foot traffic at the intersection of Meguro Dori by the forest of Tokyo, watching people slowly climb aboard their buses and the buses pull away — without her.

FORTY-ONE

The fruit is displayed lavishly. She looks about for apples and once again cannot find any in this large fruit and vegetable market. Are no apples to be found in Japan? With a climate so like Vancouver, and southern BC, how could there not be apples? Her first encounter with BC apples was when she and Jack drove into the interior on the old Yale Road, to fruit stands overflowing with cherries, pears and peaches. After the hard rationing in England after the war, she thought she had found heaven. They bought peaches, pears, cherries, and tomatoes and hauled them home in their old green Ford. She canned for days, with Jack stoically peeling fruit.

These memories warm her like candles warm a cold room. In the fall, just before the snow, they went back to the Okanagan and bought apples. Beautiful bright red glossy apples with flecks of green: McIntosh apples, Jack's favourite. Soft skinned and easily bruised, not practical apples, by the bushel they bought apples. Bigger than her two fists together, these apples were a show-off version of the apples she'd had at home. At home in England, that is. She quickly learned to modify her "at home" because if she didn't, Jack would cock his eyebrow at her and a smile would nearly touch his lips beneath his moustache.

In this open-air market, holding an orange, she struggles to remember when Jack stopped wearing a moustache. Not remembering frightens her. In the mid-eighties? In protest after Cynthia left home? When did Cynthia start calling Tokyo home?

She expected to find oranges in Tokyo. During the fifties in Vancouver, around Christmas, Japanese oranges arrived in stores, in wooden boxes, each orange wrapped in bright green or orange paper. Perilously expensive, these oranges signalled the beginning of the Christmas season, and Jack always brought one box home, usually in mid-December, purchased in Chinatown. She remembers Cynthia's querulous, "What's mandarin?" noticing what her parents carelessly called "Jap oranges" were actually Chinese oranges: mandarin oranges. At the time Cynthia pointed this out, Jack and Ivy were side-tracked by their delight she had read the box, being only seven. About the time she figured out Santa Claus was "my parents' imaginary friend", she began asking imperious questions of these adults who were evidently not capable of raising a child, especially a child like Cynthia. She was probably right.

Ivy had always been charmed by her daughter's constant poking at the surface of the world, at the words and their contradictions, and the difference between the way things were and the way folks pretended they were. Now, she is simply frightened by that incisive mind and open contempt. In a country where the elderly are revered, Cynthia seems callous to a degree that never ceases to amaze her.

Whatever has she done to deserve it? It's something bad, she knows. She has no idea what, however.

When she does find apples, they are presented like precious cargo, each wrapped in extravagant packing, imported from who knows where and costing hundreds of yen.

Considering their extravagance, she remembers with a pinch the apples of England, the blossoms in the spring, the trees growing in orderly rows in orchards, or wild in the roadside, apple trees flinging their ripe fruit to the ground with abandon in autumn, collecting these apples, fighting off the drunken bees, taking apples home to make apple butter with her mother. Small, tangy apples, whose skin was tough and whose flesh was bright white and stayed that way all through the winter in the cold cellar, only slightly wrinkling toward the end of March. She can taste those long-ago apples. Do farmers in England still grow apples?

She touches the skin of the elegantly proffered apple, wondering why they are intended to be purchased in singles, why so huge and why so expensive.

And that night Mikio brings home a large bag of Fuji apples. Of course. *Fuji* apples.

Early evening, after a subdued quarrel in the boys' bedroom, Cynthia appears in the sitting room with Benjiro behind her. She is holding a piece of paper that she thrusts at her mother.

"Mother? Please help Benjiro with his spelling. He is not doing well in the written spelling tests in English. He gets a list at the beginning of each week and then a test at the end. He has to write the words the teacher dictates.

He has to recognize the word and then write it in English. And in cursive."

Benjiro looks miserable. He has his head so downcast he looks headless. She sees only the collar of his shirt and the top of his head.

"Let's have a look, Benjiro," she says, knowing from experience that the way she pronounces his name makes him smile. Cynthia leaves them.

Benjiro holds out the paper. There is a number in kanji at the top of the page but the large red *X*'s tell her what she needs to know. Four out of fifteen. Under this page is another one with a list of twenty words. These then would be the words for this week. And tomorrow is the end of the week.

She says the first word on the list. Corpulent. What kind of word is that for a nearly eleven-year-old to spell in a foreign language? Did people even use the word corpulent anymore? She says the word again, and Benjiro looks defeated. He clearly has no idea how to begin and he remains standing, twisting his pencil in his grimy fingers. She scans the list for a word he might understand, or she might be able to explain in English. Aluminum. Locomotive. Annoyance. Aerodrome.

Back to corpulent. She asks him for another sheet of paper and he disappears. Many minutes later he appears with several sheets. It is obvious he has not only been crying but also eating a candy, because his face is a mess of tears and sticky sugar.

She takes the pencil from him, writes the word corpulent on the top of the page and draws a cartoon stick figure. Her cartoons were not bad, back in the day when she would sometimes leave notes for Jack with cartoon illustrations. Her stick figure is a caricature of a fat man, with bulging cheeks, thick thighs, and a ponderous belly and bottom. She turns the page toward Benjiro. He is a great lover of cartoons, and his eyes light up. He smiles. He sounds out the word, tracing the figure with his finger as he does so. Corpulent, she repeats, so he will know it when he hears it on the test. He writes the word in his untidy cursive across the bottom of the page. Cor-pul-ent he says, making the second syllable sound like pew and the last syllable ant. Close enough.

She looks for nouns for the next cartoon. She writes annoyance across the top of the next sheet and makes a quick sketch of a little boy poking at a larger boy. She even manages to make a likeness of Keiijiro out of the older boy. Benjiro makes a few quick strokes and he has transformed the younger boy into a good likeness of himself. Annoy. Ance. She says. Benjiro repeats the word, still admiring the cartoon. He then writes annoyance easily, although his cursive is still wobbly.

The game is on. They have twenty words, and most are not nouns or adjectives, but they manage twenty cartoons and twenty words and have been at it for nearly two hours when Cynthia appears to prod him toward bed. Ivy and her grandson have made a mess on the table, and Ivy asks if she can give Benjiro a few of the words as a test before he goes to bed.

She picks some of the easy ones and some she knows he understands. He writes, head down, still snickering. He gets six of eight words correct.

Off he goes and a moment later comes back for the pages of cartoons. After he has gone through all the bedtime routine, she can hear him giggling in his room.

On the next week's list, Benjiro has already done some cartoons. As they work on the words and the drawings she spots a test sheet: four red crosses. Eleven out of fifteen.

FORTY-TWO

Tokyo, Saitama Prefecture. October 23, 19°C, cloudy with rain in the afternoon

A firestorm destroyed Tokyo in March 1945. One hundred thousand people died in a single night. The city was decimated. Ivy stands still, hunched into her jacket. Her eyes are the eyes of the foreigners who bombed the city until there was nothing left but famine. How the city resumed its former life she knows, because she watched her people do the same. She spent an afternoon in London with her mother in 1943; she saw the smoking ruins of the great old churches, the roads gutted, the tenements gap-toothed with floors above miraculously intact while floors below were gone. She knows the stoicism of her people, the Londoners who walked to work the morning after the subway bombs of 2005, undaunted. She wonders about the people of Tokyo. She wonders about Cynthia's in-laws, especially the old lady who stared at her with piercing intensity. Is she a survivor of that firestorm?

She examines the photographs of the devastation and feels the rueful connection with these people, her former enemies. Civilians are civilians no matter where they are placed on the game board called War. School children are evacuated. Parents stand on railway stations, seeing their children off to a safer place, knowing that the requirement for such a drastic action means they might not see their children again. Tokyo mothers and fathers look at the bundled children before them, with labels attached to their collars, the older (the eight-year-old) holding the hand of the younger (the five-year-old). Both terrified. All terrified in different ways. Every time her mind lights on one of the photographs, she turns her attention elsewhere. They stood there too, these old people she sees in the parks, doing Tai Chi. The graceful movements of their bodies enclose all their memories. They sent their children off, they lost everything by fire, they suffered famine, they endured the occupation by Americans of the country they revere.

She was spared that. Jack returned to Aldershot for complicated demobilization in 1946 and said nothing, after gently telling her that he had "taken some time to get away" from his internment. And except for a tendency to have a lingering cough after a cold, Jack had no lasting effects. Except perhaps that was why his mind departed so easily. He didn't want to remember the war years, and so, when the opportunity presented itself, he didn't remember the war years or — at the end — anything. She remembers the last time he looked at her and saw her. Ah, he said joyfully, taking her hand, greeting her. Ah, ah, he almost moaned, so joyful. She realized, as she kissed his soft old cheek, he thought she was his mother. He had forgotten she was Ivy, but knew she was someone precious. Someone who loved him and would love him and would keep him safe, no matter what. She sat beside his chair in the tiny room in "the home" and heard old ladies singing in the sitting room; she held Jack's hand, and was grateful at least he knew she was someone.

She was in England when the Americans dropped the bombs on Hiroshima and Nagasaki. She remembers the headlines in the newspapers. She knows about bombs falling on cities we love. People we love. Children. Women on their way to get tea. She looks away from the large photographs and takes in the big interpretive signs telling the story of the firebombing of Tokyo. The language is indirect; bombs were dropped. She goes blank. The walls of the museum, the hush in the galleries, the sombre regard from others in the vast rooms — she wants to speak, to inform everyone she is not American. Is not making her pilgrimage to resolve curiosity and perhaps some guilt for dropping those bombs on the population just going about its business. Is not one of those with an explanation that, no matter what, does not make sense.

Jack had been in Japan when they dropped those bombs. He may have been in Tokyo when the city was firebombed. She knew the name of the camp, but did not know what Tokyo Camp 3D – Kawasaki was, did not know its location, and waited for months to hear from the Red Cross that he was well after months in hospital, and was headed for Aldershot to be demobbed before he went home — which meant Canada.

Vancouver, Canada, she used to recite when anyone asked about "her Canadian soldier." He had been, before he left for the Pacific theatre, as they called it, one of the kind, older soldiers who kept a protective eye on her when she was fourteen, a mere slip of a girl. She accepted his request to write to him, and she wrote several letters, spending hours puzzling over what to say to a man old enough, she thought then, to be her father. She only received two, one from the Red Cross in 1944 advising her he was believed to be a POW "somewhere in the Pacific", and one written in 1946 with the Japanese postmark, written in pencil with Jack's customary style.

When he came back to Aldershot and found her at the bakery he was thin, so thin, and all that remained of the gallant man she remembered was the twinkle in his eyes.

He never talked about the war. Never talked about the camp. Only got angry once, when their optometrist declared, "I know about them. I was at the camps!" and launched into a diatribe. Jack reached his hand across to cover the quivering fingers of the other man, almost patted him, and said, "No, mate. Not in front of the wife."

Ivy leaves the museum without looking for a place to sit down and have tea and a cookie. Descending the stairs, she notices writing on the T-shirt of a white man coming up the stairs toward her. Attuned to English anywhere, a glutton for English expressions, she is accustomed to reading odd words and images on teenagers' chests and bottoms. She has often earned the indignant glare of a teenaged Japanese boy who has discovered her staring at his chest, trying to understand the English expression she found there.

She understands the words on the T-shirt sported by this man in his sixties, one of the Tilley-shorted, Tilley-hatted, many-bagged tourists she is used to seeing, folks who do not want to have anything to do with her, because she is clearly not-Japanese and therefore knows nothing about Tokyo.

The T-shirt declares *2000–2004*, beneath the silk-screened image of a cocker spaniel. *Remembering*

Sparky, the next line declares. And beneath, in larger letters, *I miss you boy.*

She could imagine Jack's response. Four years and compelled to print a T-shirt to commemorate his love and loss? Four years?

She translates the relevant information onto her T-shirt: *1946-2006. Remembering Jack. I miss you, lad.* She cannot resist adding the missing comma. She scrutinizes the man. The orange T-shirt is faded, and he is obviously travelling, so this shirt is not the result of careless T-shirt selection on laundry day.

What possessed him to create this T-shirt? What had the encounter at the T-shirt shop been like? Had anyone thought to add the comma? Had anyone suggested to the owner of the dog and presumably the creator of the T-shirt that advertising such a loss is somehow foolish? Silly. As in empty. Now, nearly four years later, as long in loss as in life, does he even notice the shirt or remember Sparky? She will not live long enough in loss as she lived married to her lad. She cannot, also, imagine donning a T-shirt as the sign of her loss and wearing it carelessly all day in the society of Tokyo.

FORTY-THREE

Tokyo National Museum. October 28, 10°C, raining.

"May I sit here?" the voice inquires. Ivy takes a moment to realize she does not need to translate this question into English, frame an answer in her limited and halting Japanese, and reply. She looks up, spilling her tea, into the face of a white woman about her age, wearing glasses, with thin grey hair askew on top of her head.

"Oh, of course. Please. By all means." And so on, the clichés of her English upbringing spilling out of her. The woman sinks gratefully into the chair across from her. "It's such a challenge — finding somewhere to sit when you're . . . " she pauses and brings out a fair version of *ohitorisama desuka.* "I am grateful. Thank you so much." She places her tea and noodle bowl in front of her and then there is the tourist equivalent of setting hen, as she puts the cutlery down, and the napkin, and slings her bag over the back of her chair, puts her purse crosswise on her chest, puts her coins into her jacket pocket.

Canadian? Ivy is not sure about the accent. Not Australian. Kiwi? Her table mate looks around, avoiding eye contact, not wishing to intrude. The signs indicate she will be ignored if she does not make the first move.

"Are you?"

"Travelling alone? Yes. Yes, I am. Travelling alone. I tried a tour two years ago, to China, and we spent one night in Tokyo. One night. We arrived in time for the preset dinner, and then we had two hours 'to explore' possibly the largest mall I've ever been in, and all I could do was sit on a bench watching the world go by. Then we left the next morning at five thirty, and I didn't even see one of the bridges. Although I must have crossed one to get to the airport. Ouch!" Her headlong babble is stilled by her gulp of too-hot tea.

"I've done that," Ivy confesses, wagging her head from side to side. She smiles with what she hopes is a commiserating grimace. "It's amazing how hot the tea can be, when the soup is often stone cold. Even when it's not supposed to be. That one, though," she peers into the bowl, "is supposed to be cold."

"Is it?" her table mate says in dismay. "Oh, I was trying to get the hot soup. I don't like cold soup with noodles. Blecch. I'm sorry. That was rude. Expressing revulsion at a national dish is not appropriate." She sounds as if she is quoting the very guidebook Ivy has in her bag, set between her ankles. Both women laugh ruefully, and silence hovers.

"Pardon me. My name is Vera. Bera, as everyone here says. Vera Withnell. I'm from Canada." Vera holds out her hand. She has a pleasantly strong grip.

"Ivy. Canada."

"Ivy Canada? What an unusual name."

"No. Sorry. Ivy also from Canada. Vancouver, actually. You?

"Edmonton."

"Oh." Ivy resists the traveller's impulse to ask Vera if she knows so-and-so from Edmonton. "You know, if you want hot soup, you could pop that bowl into the microwave over there."

"I could? Oh, thank you. I could." And off she goes to confront the Japanese notations on the microwave provided for frugal Japanese who bring their lunches to just about everything. Ivy watches Vera at the panel, watches her look about in consternation, watches her figure it out, watches her return triumphantly, bearing now-steaming noodle soup.

"Well, I do appreciate that tip. That would work with stale buns too. Good tip." Vera picks up her chopsticks and begins the task of eating noodles with them. Re-heated cold noodle soup isn't the best dish in the museum cafeteria, but it beats some of the other choices, like the lasagne on offer and the sandwiches. "I learned early not to have lunch in restaurants. Dinner if I have to, but not lunch. The cost." Vera purses her lips around the noodles, miraculously avoiding slurping. Eating noodles is hard enough without someone watching you, so Ivy looks away. She looks down. She opens her guidebook to the section on the museum.

"What brings you to Tokyo?"

"I live here. With my daughter and her family. My grandsons, that is, and my son-in-law."

"My goodness. So you must speak Japanese?"

"No. Not so far. I'm learning, from my younger grandson. He's teaching me Japanese and I'm tutoring him in English."

"Engrish," Vera jokes.

"Yes. It's tough. Of course, I'm sure I mispronounce everything. So far, I can't be understood when I ask for subway tokens. Or order noodles."

"How long have you lived here?"

"Seven months."

"And, how are you — that is — how is — do you — " Vera flounders to a stop.

Ivy shakes her head, and smiles vaguely at the room brimming with tourists, many of them Japanese. "It's okay. My son-in-law is a very pleasant man. My grandsons are typical ten- and fourteen-year-olds. The fourteen-year-old doesn't like anyone much, and he mostly ignores me." She feels the temptation to tell this stranger everything, starting with the cheque. "Do you like travelling alone?"

"No. But I like travelling, and I've learned the hard way that most of the people I think I would like travelling with are lousy companions. No one wants to do what I want to do, and everyone complains. There I am, complaining. So, I travel alone. I've been to Viet Nam to count the butterflies, to Spain to preserve the cave paintings, and to Scotland to map a cemetery. I skip all the big things and try to get to the out-of-the-way things."

"Mapping a cemetery in Scotland? Are you Scottish?"

"My great-grandparents are. I do family research. When I retire, I plan to spend a month in Edinburgh at the National Archives."

Retire? She looks well retired. As if reading her mind, Vera says, "I retire with any luck in two years. In the meantime, I get these gigs through work. Well, sort of through work."

Vera's use of the word gig makes Ivy smile. When she uses such words, her grandsons think she is pretty funny too.

Vera smiles back, and says, "Well, are you finished with your lunch? Would you like to poke about in the museum with me? I promise not to complain. You can pick the floor. Maybe we can figure out what we're looking at."

"What about the fabrics and needlework?" Ivy asks.

"I'd love to!" Vera declares, swiftly collecting up her stuff.

Somewhere in their poking about she will have to warn Vera about leaving her bag on the back of the chair, given the swift hands of Japanese pickpockets. Or in this case pickbags.

FORTY-FOUR

Tokyo, Saitama Prefecture. December 6, 10°C, clear

In September, she began to crochet an intricate lace tablecloth of the cotton/silk she'd kept for all these years and could not bear — her thrifty soul — to throw away. She began the project imagined nearly thirty years ago, when Cynthia was grown and gone, and she was looking for something to do.

Now the sun rises at 6:36 and sets at 16:27. By five o'clock in the evening it's dark. She sits in the living room in the pool of light cast by the one lamp she feels she can turn on, leaving all the rest of the flat in darkness. She learned to do this one day in October when Cynthia came home, exclaimed at all the lights on, and turned off every one, almost including the one Ivy was sitting beside. From dusk onward since then, Ivy sits beside the one lamp and listens to BBC International on the television, distracted, for hours at a stretch.

She sits, crocheting with thread fine enough to be cobweb. The dimensions of the tablecloth will be six feet by six feet when she's done, but the progress is infinitesimal, measured in half inches. She dreams as she crochets, the thread flowing through her fingers, her wrist moving, the tiny hook on the end of the stainless steel barely visible. Without her reading glasses on, she cannot actually see the hook. Her fingers tell her when she has made a slip, and sometimes she has to go back to repair a missed double crochet. The pattern is deceptive; it is not difficult, although the results look very complicated. The weight of the cloth, after four months, is still barely as much as a kitten. She crochets and dreams and sometimes when the door opens she cannot remember who she should be expecting.

One day, Mikio brings her a crochet hook the same size, in silver. An antique. She cannot imagine finding such a treasure, with intricate carving on the shaft, worn by the hands of a Japanese woman crocheting. Did they call it crocheting? Jack used to call it crotchetting, just to make her laugh. She smiles into the dim room, at times, when the memory of something small and silly comes upon her. At times in the day, she misses him so much she feels a pain in her chest. Deals with the devil made no sense to her until Jack died and she knew he was truly dead. She would have agreed to any deal offered, anything, to see him again, to hear his tread on the stairs, to see him in the yard trimming the hedge, talking to the cat, looking at the blue jays. If he were here, what fun they would have, travelling around this perplexing city.

It turns out this household does not celebrate Christmas, even though Tokyo has taken on all the trappings of a commercial Western Christmas. Stores are lit up with Christmas symbols, from US mythology, and Merry Christmas stencils and decals are everywhere. Most stores play Japanese versions of American Christmas songs, usually performed by girl bands and played at high volume. Because of her obvious ethnicity, Ivy is frequently greeted with something that sounds like Merry Christmas.

She asks Benjiro what people are saying and if she should reply the same way and he sounds out the expression and then writes it on a card for her: *meri-kurisumasu.* He rehearses her several times and then makes her say it to her harassed daughter coming in with groceries for dinner. When she says *meri-kurisumasu,* Benjiro snorts with laughter, but all Cynthia says is, "We don't celebrate that, Mother."

Christmas Day passes without notice, and she feels sad. She would have enjoyed shopping for presents — even if doing so seems a fool's errand in this family. They don't celebrate birthdays either, unless everyone has one in January and February. She will be seventy-nine a few days into the new year. Cynthia's birthday was in early August, when no one was talking to her. No Christmas. No birthday. No Mother's Day.

New Year is a different story. A big family event is planned, and they all must go. She remembers keenly the fiasco of the last visit, but since no one is seeking her opinion she gets with the program. All dressed up, they travel by train on a bitterly cold day with most of the population of Tokyo, it seems. Her coat is well up to the challenge, but she notes Keiijiro is wearing a thin jacket open to the elements — and showing off his tight unadorned T-shirt — and flashy shoes. Too cool to be cold.

This event is very different in tone. All of Mikio's brothers are present, and all of their wives seem eager to meet her. Number One Son's wife, acting as if the previous visit had not occurred, takes over the role of introducing the novelty, Ivy, as if she were a new house pet. Ivy asks the gathering to speak Japanese but they all demur (after

278

a flurry of comments in Japanese that sound a lot like "What did she say?"). The children, and there are a lot of them, leave to go to the party room in the building, carrying two boxes full of snacks and drinks. Keiijiro stays with the adults, and he seems to be getting advice from every adult male, starting with his grandfather. The meal is extravagant, and she is grateful she has learned, in her travels, what many of the dishes are and how to eat them. Although hardly vivacious, the spirit of the gathering is at least convivial. Mikio is a different man with his siblings, smiling often and doing what sounds a lot like teasing his father. Cynthia is on the edge of all the conversations, and Ivy notices she rarely starts one and when she does she is sometimes ignored. Everyone is polite, but she is ignored. Her daughter is subdued, and Keiijiro is watching her. Protective. This family may not realize what is happening, but they are creating a resentful boy who will become a man with no time for any of them. Their exclusion of his mother is his exclusion too.

Mikio's grandmother, the fierce old woman, sits in the place of honour, and her grandsons and their wives bring her small treats from the table. She nods at some and dismisses others, her bearing regal and sombre. She also never takes her eyes off Mikio, and an imperceptible softening of her visage tells the truth. Number One Son may be the first born and have the privilege of that status, but this old woman loves her fifth grandson. Does he remind her of someone? Her husband?

Ivy has the tablecloth in her handbag. Her plan was to give it to Number One Son's wife, as she is the host, but instead she approaches the old woman. The conversation flags just a bit, enough for her to wonder if she is making some huge cultural gaffe. Too late: she is committed. The old woman looks into her eyes, the two staring steadily at each other for so long the room becomes silent. Cynthia has arrived at her elbow, in time to see her give the table-cloth to the grandmother.

"I made this for you. I hope you like it," Ivy says and hears Cynthia doing a rapid translation.

The old woman does not put out her hands, so Ivy lays the cloth on her knee. One of the wives steps into the frame and says something to her grandmother-in-law. She picks up the tablecloth and the fabric unfurls, looking spectacular in the soft lighting of this room. The old woman touches the fabric with one finger, and everyone, apparently, has stopped breathing. Seconds pass. Is she about to fling it on the floor? Another wife appears, folds the cloth and lays it on her shoulders. A shawl, it's a shawl, must be what people are exclaiming in Japanese. A shawl, then.

More wives come forward, adjusting the cloth and tentatively patting her aged shoulders. It does look good, draped around her and folding across her wizened chest. Her hands, thick and knotted with arthritis, lie incongru-ously among the folds of delicate lace. Rapid comments are flying, and Ivy feels the smallest of touches on her shoulder. Cynthia has touched her.

At last the old woman speaks. She gives a command to someone, who disappears. She says something else, and Cynthia translates: "Honourable Great Grandmother is telling you she has done this kind of work. Before. In the past." Someone has brought a Western chair so Ivy can sit beside this venerated woman. Together they inspect the pattern of the shawl. The person who has been sent away returns with a photograph. It is an old photograph, in a tarnished metal frame. For an awful moment Ivy thinks, "It's been through the firestorm." The photograph is of a man in a military uniform, a boy he seems. Impossibly young to be wearing a soldier's uniform. A son? She racks her brain for this word in Japanese. A cousin? Father?

It is her husband, Ivy concludes, fumbling now in her wallet for the photograph of Jack, taken on their Alaskan cruise. That Jack is an old man in her photograph and that this man is a boy is not lost on her. The two women regard each other's photographs, as a hush seizes the room. This man, the father of Mikio's father. Lost to them. Lost to her. An impossibly long time ago. We are not enemies, she wants to say, but how can she? And what a silly comment to make, anyway. We were never enemies, you and me. You lost your man and I found mine. In a situation where words fail one, it's helpful at last to have no words. She says the only word she knows that might be appropriate. "I'm sorry." And she hears Cynthia's whispered translation.

The old lady bows her head, and tenderly holds the photograph in her hands under the corners of the shawl. There are tears in Cynthia's eyes, and behind her the implacable regard of her son. The mood, like the sea, changes, conversations start again, tea and sweets are offered, and she sits in silence watching. When Mikio's mother comes to bring her mother-in-law tea, Ivy sees her run her hand surreptitiously over the intricate pattern.

FORTY-FIVE

Tokyo, Saitama Prefecture. January 20, 8°C, cloudy with
wind

Ivy sits at a small plastic table on a small plastic chair, at
the end of a garden in Tokyo. She has travelled by subway
to get here, but she's not really sure where here is. In her
previous life, she would sit in public places and listen to
conversations around her. After Jack died, she took great
pleasure in eavesdropping, especially with her back to
the speakers. It's impossible to eavesdrop when everyone
within ear-shot is speaking another language.

She's managed to buy herself a Styrofoam cup filled
with tea. The next person who blithers on about the
much-vaunted tea ceremony in Japan is going to get an
earful from this ex-pat. Or rather ex-pat ex-pat. What
do they call people who give up the country of birth to
immigrate to the new world and then immigrate again, to
what could only be described as an old world, if not her
old world?

Stupid. That's what they call them. She sips her tea
and stares ahead at the ground, blocking out the feverish
hubbub. Blocking out the bray of the subway announcements. Blocking out the babble of voices out of which
she cannot detect one single word. Of course, that's
sheer melodramatic nonsense, really. Because she can

distinguish the ubiquitous *sumimasen.* The polite request to move aside. Thank you — *arigatou gozaimasu,* which she does not need to look up to see is accompanied by a bow. *Arigatou gozaimasu. Arigatou gozaimasu. Arigatou gozaimasu.* The ground bubbles and blurs as tears cloud her vision.

Hopping into sight, a common English sparrow. Hopping placidly about, pecking at specks of detritus that mean food to this contemporary dun-coloured, drab, citified version of the sparrows of Aldershot. One of her sparrows. One of the sparrows that kept her company at Lonsdale Quay when she sat for what now seems like most of her life waiting for Jack to return from his visits to the specialists — sparrows she would watch by the hour.

"How did you get here?" she asks the little bird with its little brown dust cap, its tame, inquisitive gaze, startling herself to hear an English sentence in this vast Japanese soundscape.

She would not have been more surprised if the bird answered her. Birds in Japan so far have been unfamiliar; the gulls look odd, small and scrappy, the jay-like birds large and avaricious, and no ravens to insult her and try to capture the beaded barrettes she used to wear.

How *did* you get here?

She wishes she had purchased something to eat so she could scatter crumbs before this bird, this harbinger of another place, not here.

Worn down by her solitude, she talks to this wee bird. She leans down and tells this bird all the things. She was the chatterbox in her marriage, the one who spoke first and often to fill the gaps. Sometimes she caught the glances of exasperation as she prattled on, breathless with the strain. Endless talk. Jack listened and sometimes nodded and over all the years enjoyed his babbling brook, as he sometimes referred to her. Her volubility matched his reticence. Or did the one create the other? And if so, whose?

She still sees the warm gaze of her man, from the first time over tea when she explained the entire reconstruction of the collar of her dress, to the last day when she held his IV'd hand and stroked his thumb nail with her thumb and talked non-stop until she fell asleep. And then they woke her to tell her, "Mr. Birch has passed."

Passed. All the expressions that mean away, not here with her. Off somewhere, as he was for those years in the war. Not dead, simply not here. She wishes for him to be gone for a moment, in the Men's room, and he'll be back and together they'll tackle the Tokyo subway map. She asking the question, and he understanding the answer. Ivy is gone too. Passed over to another land, where her life carries on although her friends no longer know of her. Is this death? Is she caught in the space between, and when her daughter called her and began the process that changed her life, was that the flash of life passing? Is she in the dying fall, the mythical moment between life and death?

She shudders in the sparse sun and the little bird flies away. Sitting in noodle shops, on benches under trees, at galleries and museums, watching crocodiles of school children filing by huge murals of ancient Japan — are these lines of obedient uniformed children called crocodiles in Japan? — she has learned to be silent. She watches a world she does not know and has no one to make her observations to but this familiar transplanted bird.

FORTY-SIX

One minute she is walking, threading through the crowd to get into the subway car she preferred; the next minute she is falling, landing on her right knee. The bad one. Up with the bad, down with the good flashes through her mind like so much trivia. She should have fallen on the good.

The pain is astonishing, and tears are running down her face. Not from the pain so much as the shock of the pain. She is writhing in agony, trying to get away from herself, from the terrible pain in her knee. She can't get up, she can't move away from the pain in her knee, and she is cursing steadily. She feels hands on her, trying to assist her, and she shakes them off, not willing to suffer the shame of so many small people hoisting her heavy body upright. When she manages to crawl to a step and sit, she looks up into the faces of strangers, the blank, inexpressive faces of strangers with black hair, with black eyes that lead nowhere, with not one glimmer of sorrow or sympathy or assistance.

She closes her eyes, feels her head wobbling in frantic pace with her heart, and hears the babble of the foreign language, except it isn't foreign, is it? It is the language of the country she is now living in, and she doesn't understand one word. The few words her younger grandson taught her vanish, and besides, this isn't the time to ask where the bathroom is, or where she might buy a cup of tea. Glass of tea. Kocha. She is badly hurt, her knee now sending out signals of panic, her heart roaring unevenly, black dots dancing in her eyes, and she doesn't know where her purse is. And the heels of her palms are registering pain as well. She's alone, without means, without a way to get hold of her daughter, with little ID, and her passport is tucked safely away in Cynthia's bedroom.

The roar of the next train and the wind that precedes it bring starkly to mind that all she wants right this moment is for the magic wand to wave so she will be able to get up, pick up her purse, step smartly into the waiting crowded train and make her way "home" before Cynthia. She doesn't know if her knee will even hold her if she is able to get up, and she knows she can't get up without the help of these strangers still standing uncertainly around her.

Rescue of a sort arrives in the guise of a young woman in a subway-station uniform carrying a red bag with a white cross on it. She makes a mental note to think about the ubiquity of the red bag with the white cross some other time. The young woman expertly rolls up her pant leg and together they regard her reddened knee. The skin is not broken, and the flesh around the knee seems to be in the correct location. The attendant places her warm hand against the knee — light-brown fingers, tapered nails, subtle but beautiful nail polish and the incongruity of small decorations that glitter. Stars? Before she knows what is happening, the attendant has wrapped a tensor bandage around the knee and stood up. She motions to a man standing nearby and together they offer four hands. They get her onto her feet.

The attendant says something in Japanese. Ivy shakes her head, tears bubbling out of her eyes, looks toward the arriving train and declares in Japanese, "*Sumimasen, nihongo ga wakarimasen.*" Benjiro's best lesson. She always considered delivering this sentence was silly, since if she doesn't speak Japanese what use is admitting it in Japanese. If her hair, skin colour and eyes do not give her away, her accent does, of course. The sentence is very helpful when she answers the cell phone on the kitchen counter, something Cynthia is constantly telling her not to do.

"*Sumimasen, nihongo ga wakarimasen,*" she confesses again, and the attendant switches to English. Within moments, with the assistance of the man, a phone call is made to who knows who and she is moving her leg, realising she can move, even walk, and she persuades them to let her board the next train. Her train.

During the fourteen-minute journey, she locates her purse, still slung across her body under her jacket. She has lost her shopping bag, and cannot remember what was in it anyway. She had bought something in the dollar store, something for Benjiro, something to make his eyes dance, something for them to talk about. She remembers determining the price, navigating the purchase, and leaving the shop with her re-usable shopping bag, all without speaking a word. It is gone, whatever it was.

She takes the seat for old people offered her and lowers herself cautiously. Her knee is throbbing. It feels hot through her slacks. She looks up for the subway map that is her constant companion, looking for the red letters streaming across the screen, notifying them all of the next stop, the date, time, and weather. Finding these landmarks, she also catches sight of her face in the relentless reflection created by the window of the train, as it moves through the tunnels. She looks — old.

She snorts with captured laughter. Old. She hears Jack snorting too and feels his hand tenderly cupping her knee.

When she reaches Wakoshi, she stands up and yelps in surprise and pain. Her knee has stiffened, and feels impossibly hot as she makes her way as quickly as she can to the doors. She's engulfed as always by the flood exiting the car, swept into the larger streams from other cars and then whooshed up the escalator, almost borne above the floor, weightless, even though she knows her feet are touching the ground and she is walking. Communal forward motion, this flooding out of the car.

She reaches the surface, crosses the street, and makes her way to the apartment. She can tell from the lights and action that she is not late; no one but Benjiro is home, and all will be well.

FORTY-SEVEN

Hina-matsuri (Doll Festival). March 3, 12°C, rain and thunderstorms

Ivy is busying herself, helping Mrs. Yamamoto (Please. Call me Eiko) with tea, so she doesn't really tune in until she hears the Japanese-inflected words "Miss Tee Canada." She looks through the kitchen pass-through to the school's party room to see her daughter displaying a doll, an English/Caucasian doll. The women begin the cooing admiration that is a collection of words she cannot begin to sort out. The admiration, however, is unmistakeable. Cynthia lifts the doll out of a beautiful wooden box and also brings out the outfits. Each one immaculate: the wedding dress, the knit suit, Chanel jacket, the silk gloves, the peddle-pusher trousers with a matching striped boat-neck blouse, the evening gown. All finely made, by hand, nearly forty years ago. The tiara and miniature matching necklace and earrings are admired, and so is the bathing suit with the banner proclaiming Miss Teen Canada as well as her black hair and impossible figure, reminiscent of Barbie. Ivy remembers buying the Miss Teen Canada doll, produced to counter the grip of the Barbie doll on Canadian little-girl culture of the 1960s. The doll had dark eyes and dark curled hair, and she came with a pageant dress and a sash. She also bought many more clothes from the Hospital Auxiliary Gift Shop: a suit, a jacket, a boa, another evening gown, tiny heels, a bathing suit, a nightgown laced with trim, all handmade with a handmade carry case. Not satisfied, she proceeded to make several more outfits, some of them crocheted.

She looks away out the window so no one will see her tears. For whose hands but hers had created the clothes, made because Miss Teen Canada came in a box wrapped in hard plastic, wearing only a bathing suit, heels that wouldn't stay on the plastic feet, a tiara, and a bouffant hairdo. She sewed for hours with the fiddly patterns and fabrics, by hand, adding lace to undergarments, sparkles to the crinoline of the fancy dress, using scraps of fabric, cheered on by Jack who appreciated, as he would, the miniatureness of it all.

Except Cynthia hated the doll. It was not a Barbie. Her friends would make fun of her. "Mum" had ruined everything. Or words to that effect. She grudgingly took the doll and the clothes into her room by command of her father, but her pout lasted for the whole birthday party and well into the next few weeks. She was ten. She'd wanted the Barbie that had just been introduced and heavily promoted in Canada. Barbie was the only fashion doll worth having; her accessories and clothes commercially produced the only items worth bringing out when the girls assembled to "play dolls". Cynthia turned eleven, her period started early, her buds of breasts became bra-worthy, and the doll disappeared.

Ivy, bewildered and remembering Jack as if he were standing at her elbow, stops in the doorway to the kitchen, holding the tray of teacups, wondering about the story of the doll. When had it become worth saving? When did Cynthia realize that it was worth showing off? When she left to travel the world and instead stayed in the first country she visited? Had she taken this doll and all its accessories with her?

Here it is. Exquisitely preserved. Cynthia clearly revelling in the admiration of her friends. A doll worth bragging about. Does Cynthia remember who made the clothes? Does she remember how bitterly she rejected the gift? Does it matter?

Ivy can't breathe. She remembers holding up the dainty skivvies for Jack's approval, and he winked at her and made a lusty joke. They ended up having sex on the couch while the evening news talked to them of the assassination of Martin Luther King Jr.

And yet. Here is her Cynthia, smiling at the doll, holding the edge of a carefully crocheted skirt. Cynthia's friends and colleagues are excited, passing the small garments around, holding them up. One woman takes off the pageant gown and banner and sorts through the clothes for the pedal pushers and boat-neck top. She says, "Pedal pushers" and they all giggle. Cynthia is sitting happily, with her hands folded over the crocheted cape and knit skirt. She looks as if she has never seen the doll before, looks the way she should have looked when she received the present more than forty years ago.

Ivy proceeds into the room as Cynthia says proudly, "My mom made all of the clothes," and the cooing praise increases in volume. She sets the tray down, Eiko sets down the cookies, both women moving in concert, and this simultaneous action amid the coos taps at her heart. She smiles her polite company smile and then, as one of Cynthia's friends holds out the kimono, presumably bought recently, feels her heart give way; something tight releases, and she truly smiles. What matters is the doll; the doll is loved and appreciated now.

She looks at her daughter. However it has happened, no doubt when they were far apart, Cynthia has found joy. In this and many other ways.

FORTY-EIGHT

Tokyo, Saitama Prefecture. March 10, 14°C, partly sunny

The cell phone on the counter in the kitchen keeps buzzing. Helicoptering, Benjiro has told her. Helicoptering. Hopping about. Buzzing like a bumblebee in a bottle. Ivy considers the device. She has never answered the house cell phone, because when she first encountered this mysterious buzzing and reached for it, she was rebuked: "Mother, that's probably for Number One Son."

It irritates her beyond belief when her daughter uses this appellation for her older boy, considering Mikio suffers under this ancient rule, suffers because he is not Number One Son, but Number Five. So far down on the list he might as well not be a child of his mother and father. Exiled from any consideration whatsoever. Except she has seen the fond gaze of his grandmother, who regards him whenever he enters the room as if he is the only person in it. That she loves her Number Ten Grandchild is obvious to everyone.

It turns out the helicoptering cell phone is attempting to communicate with her — the foreigner who is persistently disregarding it. She discovers this to her chagrin when the neighbour comes tapping on the door, to ask in polite old-fashioned English to please (indeed, he says prease) to pick up the cell phone and press the

293

small green old-style telephone receiver and place the ear then to the screen and listen to the message from the daughter.

The message tells Ivy her daughter will not be home for dinner, because she is at the hospital. The hospital — as if in Tokyo, in this vast unknowable city, there is only one. And will she wait for the boys and tell them not to worry.

Not to worry about what? Ivy bleats at the small screen, which is displaying Japanese characters in a rolling stream. Even if she could read these characters, she cannot read these characters. She holds the phone less than an inch from her eyes to confirm that she cannot read these characters, could not even if they were in full-block English letters. Too small. Too old, her eyes are too old.

She sits down on the couch, stomach on fire.

Mikio in the hospital. Tubes in his nose, wires running into his veins, a bag beside the bed filling with bright yellow urine. His skin ashen. Cynthia sitting beside him, her hand resting next to his hand mottled blue and scarlet, punctured by IV lines.

He looks like death warmed over, she hears her mother's voice, a statement she heard last when Jack lay *in extremis,* no hope left, unable to swallow, when all that remained was to die. Jack's heart was the last organ to go; Mikio's seems like the first. And he not yet sixty. With two not-grown sons. A wife who sits haggard by his side, not quite touching his hand.

Mother, will you take the boys home?

Ivy, unnecessary, is led away, escorting two boys who have been travelling on Tokyo Metro alone for years. She

294

feels keenly how unwanted her presence is. Her physical presence is a stigma; the older boy, at least, would prefer to die to avoid being seen with his *gaijin* grandmother.

As if every gaze does not discover his *hafu* identity, his *hafu* legacy. As if every gaze does not linger over his eyes, his nose, the shape of his skull, the colour of his nut-brown hair. Even when he dyes and streaks his hair, there is a straight line connecting this boy to the elderly woman at his side. It is one thing to look like a foreigner; it is another thing to be forever a foreigner in one's own country, as this boy is.

She is beginning to understand how deeply Keiijiro is affected by the choices his parents have made. A member of this world yet forever at arm's length to belonging.

He should move to Canada, she considers as they await the train. Vancouver. He would find a place in Vancouver.

She imagines him setting out, settling in, making a life on the North Shore, and assuming the life Cynthia fled. She sees him, grown, secure, laughing, sees his children, his wife a red-haired child of the west coast of Canada.

It will be all right, she wants to tell him, as they board the car and hurtle through this vast city with no place for him.

At the apartment, he makes for his room and shuts the door on his brother. The little fellow stands stranded in the corridor, up past his bedtime, bereft. She reads his shoulders and the back of his neck, calls to him, using the tone and modulation his father would use.

"Tea?"

When Cynthia arrives, it is nearly midnight, Keiijiro has not appeared and Benjiro is asleep on the inhospitable sofa, his head resting on his grandmother's leg, both of them covered by the granny-square afghan.

How is he? Voices low, almost murmurs.

Out of danger.

Do they?

He will have tests tomorrow. They think no permanent damage to the muscles of his heart.

Do they know?

"Why? No." Cynthia shakes her head and looks vacantly at the TV. Both women know why. Mikio is working too hard, working himself to death, caught in a trap not of his making, unable to provide for his family in this pricey impossible city.

Ivy doesn't even know what he does and she knows that.

FORTY-NINE

Ivy turns. Cynthia is standing at the other end of the balcony, facing the setting sun. She is looking down at the leafy wonder of the park, the trees shot with light. Something about her body, the set of her face, is suddenly that of the little girl she was, their longed-for precious daughter. They tried for years — and she can hear Jack's common rejoinder — "Trying wasn't so bad, eh, old girl?"

Cynthia continues to look down at the park with the pond, and beyond, the cityscape light and airy. Her face softens. Are those tears in her eyes?

"It's too much. We cannot afford this one." She exhales, no longer looking young and hopeful. The glimpse of the little girl vanishes, leaving a woman who does not love her, perhaps will never love her. Ivy has a startling image of the two of them, living together without the buffer of the boys and Mikio. Is it possible? That they would be the survivors? Cast adrift together. How horrifyingly ironic.

She shakes herself, throws off the Celtic dread.

It is perfect. It will take all the money, but in that moment comes Jack's chortle of encouragement. "Why not, old girl. Let's give it a whirl, what do you say?" She followed him to Canada, in spite of common sense and most of her friends, telling her to be sensible, cautious, safe. Time to do so again. What is she saving it for?

Let's give it a whirl, as Benjiro appears with his father, exclaiming about the room — his room — Mikio has just shown him. And a games room downstairs. And a pool in the park. And —

"We should get this one," Ivy says to Mikio. "This one."

It was perfect. A longer but easier commute by train for Mikio. A better commute for Benjiro and Cynthia. Keiijiro is standing in the living area, texting. Who is he telling what? Benjiro takes her hand, holds it in that way he has and asks her to come with him to see the bedroom, his room. The feel of his small hand in hers. Their contrasting skin tones, which are beautiful to her now.

Cynthia comes around the corner of the balcony and turns into the woman she is now. Years of frustration. Years of fear. Years of loneliness. Saliva floods Ivy's mouth. Regret bites deep into her body, resonating in her knee. Feeling sorry for her daughter causes her knee to ache? She really is turning into an odd old woman.

Benjiro is chattering to Mikio, about the room that could be his. Two mats wide, it suits his buoyant body perfectly. He is installing items from their old home already. All the small purchases she could make in her dollar store to equip this new room. If they buy this apartment. If.

Keiijiro stands near her, engrossed in the screen of his phone. The apartment will cut his commute by forty minutes, unless he gets into the school his parents are hoping for. She has no idea what Keiijiro is hoping for.

Mikio appears in the sitting room, his face suddenly superimposed on his younger son, a trick of light and position. His eyes seek hers. Her lips tighten and she nods almost imperceptibly. He returns her slight gesture with one of his own.

It is perfect. The park, the sense of being in a treehouse, the extra room, all dimensions just that much larger. Large enough to make up for the space displaced by a twelve-stone woman. Buying this apartment would wipe out their mortgage. Buying this apartment would wipe out Ivy's "cushion" as Jack always called their savings. A cushion for landing, perhaps. For running away? For the long-postponed trip to Hawaii. Although Jack had no desire, it turned out, to travel anywhere any more.

"I've done my bit to see the world," he would laugh when she made one of her efforts to produce travel brochures. Now, now, so long after it matters, she is beginning to understand what he meant.

FIFTY

This is not what happens, of course. Mikio is in hospital for less than a week and then discharged "to rest" for a month. Not even a week later, he goes back to work. Ivy is afraid to ask, but she assumes his return to work is a result of inadequate medical leave. His salary keeps the family afloat in this, the most expensive city in the world. A few days after that, Cynthia asks her to wait up for Mikio because, "We have something to discuss with you."

They, or more likely Cynthia, have put an offer on an apartment north of Tokyo. They, or more likely she, has used the money from the sale of Ivy's home to qualify for the mortgage. Mikio's face is grey under his usual golden brown skin, and he is too tired to say much. Ivy wants to say a lot, but somehow, in this moment, she is unable.

"What will be left?"

"Some. Enough for moving expenses. The mortgage will be much less; we will have it paid off in eight years."

She is stunned; all that money and the equity of this apartment and there will still be a mortgage. In eight years I will be dead, she thinks, knowing her intuition is accurate. In eight years I will be dead, she repeats, looking at the papers on the table. Mikio is sitting on the floor, not on his usual folded-fan stool, and he looks like he wants to rest his head on the table. Or his wife's shoulder.

She looks out the sliding glass door. She could put up a fuss, they could have one of their all-too-common quarrels, and yet nothing would change. For months she has avoided the confrontation over the money Cynthia put into her own bank. It is too late now. Too late.

"I will continue to keep some of my pension?"

"Of course, Mother. What do you think?"

I think you have taken all my money and made a decision about using it without discussing it with me. I think you have done this at this time because you think — you hope — I will not contest these decisions. Because of your husband's illness. I think I am screwed.

"Do you have some pictures?"

Mikio produces his tablet and shows her the real estate photographs, which capitalize on the colour, simplicity and location. The street looks like it will be quieter. There is a park six blocks away. There is a pool and a recreation centre "somewhere close by." There are four small rooms, a kitchen about the size of this one, and a slightly larger sitting room. Mikio slides the photographs across the surface of the tablet, and she leans in, pretending an interest she does not have, to conceal her dismay.

"The commute for Mikio will be longer but easier. Benjiro and I will take a different route but just about the same time. Keiijiro will be closer to the academy. We should find out in the next month if he has been accepted."

Mikio's hand is trembling. He is so tired. She wants him to have his dinner, watch some TV, and go to bed. All without the effort of responding to the presence of his mother-in-law. Tears are building in her eyes, and she feels the clench of grief in her throat. If she speaks, Cynthia will be furious.

One of these quarrels will kill this man.

She pats the tablet: the closest she will come to patting her son-in-law's handsome hand. She sits back and straightens her sweater, smoothing down the button band. She recalls with horrifying clarity her mother pulling on the button of her sweater and she hides the gasp of pain by bending to pick up her basket. This move signals to them all she is heading for bed. She has to speak before she does.

She hears in the roaring in her head her Jack's voice. He is cheering her on, urging her to be brave, to be bold, to be wise.

"Yes," she says, looking at her daughter, who for a moment looks about five years old. "Yes, it is a good idea. Your father would be proud to help you both into this new home. Yes. Sounds grand."

Cynthia and Mikio look at each other. Both too well schooled to show it, they are shocked. They have been rehearsing this conversation for days. She is sad about that. She steps carefully around them and gets to the hallway.

She turns.

"I will have to learn all new routes to get to my gardens and museums," she chirps, using all her inner fortitude to put a merry tone on her statement. "Benjiro can help me."

FIFTY-ONE

Ivy is sitting on a hard plastic chair at the medical clinic. She has found her way there partly by reading the subway map and partly by asking the woman at the station for the extra instructions that are so crucial for arriving anywhere. With these extra instructions, she has found her way to the clinic where Cynthia and the boys go for medical attention. Even though she shouldn't be, she is startled to open the door and find a room filled with Japanese people. Several bow slightly, still seated, and everyone studiously looks away as she finds a seat. This must be what it's like to come to Vancouver as a foreigner, she considers, as she inspects the room for the ticket dispenser that will tell her when she can expect to be seen next. The room is fastidiously tidy; no decades-old magazines are strewn about old coffee tables. Indeed, there are no coffee tables or any semblance of a place to put stuff down.

A door opens, a young man appears and speaks in Japanese. Apparently, he has called a name, because one of the people seated in the room rises and disappears into the hallway. She detects a veritable buzz of activity beyond that now-closed door. She feels the clench in her belly,

303

the too-familiar clench of anxiety. Oh, shit, she mutters to herself. She looks around again and meets the gaze of a woman about her age. This woman extends a folder, and points to the words on the label of the folder. She does not possess such a folder, and she has no idea how to get one. She smiles helplessly, so that the woman bends toward her to whisper instructions.

Ivy goes to a small bubble-glass window and taps on it. Nothing happens. I feel like Alice with the Rabbit, she reflects, then smiles at her own foolishness. The Rabbit will hand her a concoction, which she will drink *before* she reads the label, she will fall into a hole, she will encounter guards dressed like playing cards, a gigantic Cheshire cat, a perpetually angry queen . . . oh, wait. She's already done that. Now she is smiling for real, just as the glass panel slides aside and she is confronted by a woman who, after several failed efforts, does not understand English at all. Ivy perseveres, however, and secures the valuable folder with, indeed, her name on it: Ibee Birch. Subsiding onto her chair, she considers this folder with nothing in it but a page of what look like questions. Panic sets in. How will she complete this questionnaire?

"May I assist?" sounds a pleasant female voice at her shoulder, a woman about Cynthia's age holding a toddler on her lap. Between them, in that lovely allusive manner of Japanese strangers, they work through the New Patient Questionnaire. The woman translates a question and then pointedly looks away while Ivy answers it. Still grey haired, stooped, and over weight, she peers through her plastic-framed reading glasses at the sheet. Considering all that has happened to her, she finds herself checking Widowed as effortlessly as she writes her full name and birthdate. Widowed. Widowed. She writes down the pills she takes every day: Synthyroid; an unpronounceable one for cholesterol, high blood pressure medication bought online by Cynthia from who knows where, iron, calcium, vitamins. She wonders if she should also record the tea Mikio makes for her every night — a tonic, he tells her — and the drink made for all of them each morning — vitamins, Cynthia tells her boys, as they all stand in the kitchen gagging down the concoction. The length of this list is no longer alarming. At fifty-eight she took no pills, and twenty years later she takes not so many. Perhaps this new doctor will also express surprise, as her family doctor did so many years ago.

She can find nowhere on the form for her height and weight. Maybe in this enlightened country no one cares about such things. Wouldn't that be a treat? At seventy-nine, maybe she's shrunk even more and is no longer five foot three? She still tries to see in the mirror her side view, to see if she is beginning to develop a dowager's hump, the signal of old age and fragile bones.

The questionnaire asks about health problems, and the list is long. The two women go through, and by about halfway, her helper is no longer looking away to protect her privacy. She says the ailment, Ivy shakes her head and on they go. The list is so long and so alarming that before they reach the end they are giggling, having turned the list into a chant like a nursery rhyme. By now, others in the waiting room are engaged, smiling slightly and congratulating her on the series of Nos she has recorded.

"Reason for attending today?" her helper asks, and just then the door opens and she is called. She rises, still holding her toddler in a seated position, turns, smiles, and bows.

Ivy subsides, the sheet nearly completed, wondering where to write "persistent stitch in left side about three inches to the left of the navel, if you're standing inside my skin looking out." This detail makes her laugh to herself, shaking her wobbly head. She tucks her pen away and closes her folder. She is ready.

The waiting room really is pristine. She no longer asks herself, almost out loud, "How did I get here?" because she knows how she got here. She knows which turns, which streets, which subway line, which block will lead her safely back to Cynthia's apartment — home. That she no longer asks herself, "How *did* I get here?" saddens her. She no longer looks for the answer to guide her out and back to her earlier self. Jack is gone, she has been so long in Tokyo she is seeking a family doctor. This, my friends, is it.

She wonders if this clinic doctor will be hurried, will read her chart while greeting her, and tell her she has to lose weight.

Her name is pronounced the way Japanese people pronounce it and she follows the young man into the hallway, and he shows her to a small room and gestures to a chair. She has barely sat down when the doctor arrives. He is perilously young, his smooth face barely shave-worthy. She remembers Japanese men do not need to shave often, and she feels herself blushing. He is wearing his hair in one of the styles Keiijiro emulates, and he even has a streak of neon purple visible in the hair above his ear. He takes her folder and then sits relaxed before her.

"Good afternoon. I am Dr. Nakagawa. It is my pleasure to meet you. I hope you did not wait too long?" He stops speaking and she realizes he is waiting for her to reply.

"No. No. I had just enough time to fill out the form — I hope I did it completely."

He opens the folder and then frowns. "I do apologize. You should have been given an English form. We have one. We also have Spanish, French, Russian and of course Arabic." He smiles, while she resists asking why "of course" Arabic. He looks, in this moment, in his pride, like Benjiro.

I wonder if he likes to play Monopoly?

"Let me measure you and weigh you. That is always a good detail."

Ack. The truth is going to come tumbling out in the numbers. She is escorted to the fancy electronic device, he tells her "not to bother" to remove her shoes and suddenly metric numbers are flashing at her.

"My shoes," she begins, wondering how much her shoes weigh. It is late afternoon, she swells like a melon in the late afternoon.

"You weigh 155, Mrs. Ibee. You are five foot three."

She gapes at him, although he is looking down. She has lost fifteen pounds. This is some kind of miracle. With her shoes on.

Dr. Nakagawa is polite and attentive. He helps her to remove her sweater and blouse, listens to her heart, thumps her back, looks in her mouth, her ear, her eye. All the while he is explaining why he is doing each check. He looks into her eye, explaining about blood vessels. He asks her to remove her shoes and socks, and discovers the pads she wears to protect her toes. After each check, he says, "This is good. I am content." He pats her arm as he helps her back into her blouse, then takes her blood pressure with a device like nothing she has ever seen before. He asks her what blood pressure medication she takes, and listens carefully as she explains the history of the medication.

"Your blood pressure is quite good for a woman of your age, Mrs. Ibee. You must get a good amount of exercise. Do you do Tai Chi?"

She thinks about all the walking she does and shakes her head no at the same time. Her head wobbles a bit, and Dr. Nakagawa notices.

"This tremor? Is it new?"

She answers. This young man then asks her about her widowhood. How long, when, how is she feeling? As she begins to answer, her eyes brim with tears, and he again pats her arm.

"It is not easy. A new life alone, a new life in a new country. I have been to Vancouver. It is beautiful. You must miss it very much."

She nods, afraid to open her mouth. Afraid she will begin to cry and never stop. This kind young man is a balm to her sorry soul. He reports her heart is sound, her lungs are clear, her eyes reflect good blood vessels; he advises she get her eyes checked for glaucoma and cataracts, and then he listens attentively as she explains about the stitch in her side. His hands, when he examines her belly, are warm and she feels as if, somehow, he can feel all the troubles her body has seen her through in the past months.

"I believe you may have a bit of diverticulitis. Nothing serious. A bit of a kink in your plumbing." He smiles at his own metaphor. "If you would like, I will order some tests. Some of them aren't very pleasant, such as the colonoscopy, but if you would like to ease your mind . . . I think it is nothing serious. I suggest avoiding nuts and such, and I recommend a session with our nutritionist to rule out which foods may be causing you this pain. What would you like to do?"

She elects for the nutritionist and ruling things out over a colonoscopy. She has heard far too many horror stories about this procedure to wish it on anyone, most of all herself.

"I do want to have a few tests done to see what this tremor is about. Are you willing to do that?

She is so unused to being asked these sorts of questions, she agrees, and when she leaves she has a sheaf of papers with places and dates for further tests. On the way out of his office, he leads her to the foot care nurse, who takes care of the jagged toenails in minutes. She is advised to make a recurring appointment for foot care.

She leaves the clinic, feeling — well, lighter for one thing — but also as if she has actually been seen by a doctor.

Who would have thought? she muses as she makes her way through the chaos and crush of I-line at four thirty in the afternoon. Who would have thought?

Standing on the platform, she plans her next trip to Nature Study Institute to visit the Do Not Climb Pine. It is spring and the cherry blossoms are everywhere. A year. She has been in this city for a year almost to the day. She remembers the moonlight tracing a path across the Fraser River to her window on her last morning in Vancouver. Her home. The willow trees at Second Beach would be leafing; the fir and cedar in the parks greening up. She imagines Jack alive and well, waiting for her to finish her shopping for dinner at Lonsdale Quay. Ever patient, he would sit at one of the window seats so he could watch the gulls on the patio shrieking at passersby who have no food to offer. He is there.

She sees him, waiting.